MW00774431

Suspended Game

Roz Lee

Print ISBN-13: 978-0-9863999-6-1
Published in the United States of America

DEDICATION

For Terrell and the two Margaritas that made this story possible.

CHAPTER ONE

Jimmy Doyle Walker unfolded from Harvey's 1936 Ford Roadster and eyed the open-sided tent bearing a hand-painted sign that read, REVIVAL OF THE SPIRIT. Music couldn't possibly float on the humid air, but a familiar hymn hung in the atmosphere like a boom ready to drop. "You've got to be kidding me."

His buddy, Diplomats second baseman, Harvey Timmons shrugged. "A little religion never hurt anybody."

Jimmy Doyle adjusted his suspenders and slipped on the suit coat he'd abandoned for the drive. He was used to people trying to reform him. During the five years of exile from the game he loved, better people than Harvey had hinted that he could do with a bit of salvation. What they didn't know was, clearing his name and getting back in the game was all the salvation he'd wanted.

Following his friend across the ankle-high grass trampled by the hundred or so people congregated in the shade of the white canvas, he silently cursed the summer heat. "You're going to owe me big-time for this."

"Shut your yap and come on."

Jimmy Doyle smiled at his friend's back. It was difficult to hold a grudge against Harvey. The man seemed to smile all the time and never had a harsh word for anyone. That made his sharp command all that much more amusing.

Removing his hat, he ducked beneath the ruffled edge of the canopy. What little air that stirred outside hadn't found its way inside. Spying two empty folding chairs on the back row, he grabbed Harvey's sleeve before his friend could drag them to vacant seats in the front. The last row was perfectly fine. With a little luck, an errant breeze would find them there.

The stout woman next to him elbowed him in the ribs to hand him a hymnal. Even though he knew the hymn they were singing by heart, he took the book anyway, smiling his thanks as he added his voice to the song. Nothing said *sinner in need of reform* like nonparticipation. He'd play along until he could get the hell out of there.

This was the first Sunday they'd had off in ages, and the last place he wanted to be was at some holier-than-thou tent revival meeting. He'd grown up attending church services, but once he'd left home, he'd never felt the call to attend regularly. Harvey was one of the few teammates who didn't go out of his way to avoid him, as if the stain on his career that would never fully go away might somehow rub off on them if they got too close. So when he'd extended the invitation for a drive in the country today, Jimmy Doyle hadn't thought twice about accepting.

He was rethinking his decision now. The afternoon heat ramped up right along with the preacher's rhetoric. Beyond the small stage, the breeze, no doubt held back by the hand of Satan, stirred the grass but never made it inside. Sweat trickled down his spine, dampening the back of his shirt. He pulled his handkerchief out to wipe his brow while fighting the urge to vault over the back of his chair and escape. He'd never been a fan of browbeating sinners to repent, preferring a subtler approach to sway people to do the right thing. If his brush with ignominy had taught him anything, it was not to trust those who protested loudly. He wouldn't trust this preacher as far as he could throw him.

Since he couldn't bolt without calling unwanted attention to himself and Harvey, he let his gaze wander over the crowd of worshippers. It always amazed him how many people came to these things, and this one, on the outskirts of the nation's capitol, was no different. Everyone wore his or her Sunday best, from the housewives in their lace-collared frocks to businessmen in suits. A few rows up, the young woman occupying the aisle seat caught his attention, and once he noticed her, he couldn't look away.

He'd guess her to be in her early twenties. No family surrounded her—no husband, no children, no parents. That, in itself, set her apart. A woman her age shouldn't be alone.

She wore her auburn hair in a tight bun at her nape, indicating she kept it long when most women her age were cutting theirs short. A nondescript hat crowned her head. Her dress was plain, no fancy trim for her, and her white-gloved fingers clutched a small purse in her lap. They'd reached the portion of the service where they passed the donation basket. Something inside him shifted as he watched her open her purse and select a single coin. He could almost see the way it ripped at her heart to drop the coin in the basket. Maybe it was the straight line of her back, something she'd maintained throughout the interminable service. Or perhaps it was the way her fingers curled into a fist the second the coin hit the basket, as if she was tempted to fetch it back before passing the collection on to the person on her left, but he'd bet his bottom dollar that parting with the money had nothing to do with her financial situation.

When she bowed her head for the prayer, he cut his eyes to her. Sweat glistened on her nape. He licked his lips. He could almost taste her salty sweetness on his tongue.

He nudged Harvey in the ribs. "Who's that?" he asked behind the paper program someone handed him when he arrived.

His friend followed his gaze. "Never seen her before," Harvey whispered before returning his attention to the final hymn.

Jimmy Doyle sang the lyrics from memory. There was something about the woman that drew him to her. She wasn't beautiful, but he'd never cared much for outward beauty. It was what was on the inside that mattered most to him. Her posture screamed of tight control. He'd seen that look before, knew the challenge of breaking through barriers to get to the heart of a woman. She'd never find the answers she was looking for until she let another carry her burdens for her.

EVELYN SQUEEZED HER eyes shut and let the nickel fall into the collection basket, passing it on before she changed her mind and snatched the money back. Only a sinner like her would begrudge God a meager coin. She stood to sing the final hymn, anxious now to escape the stifling heat and the reminders of how far she fell short of the glory of God.

The preacher called sinners to repent. He promised salvation for those who laid their burdens at the Lord's feet. "Cast the yoke of sin off your shoulders," he cried, "and the grace of God will be yours."

Several people made their way forward to kneel and accept God's forgiveness, but Evelyn's feet remained rooted in the soft earth of the hay field. Forgiveness was for those who renounced their sin, who put it from their hearts and minds—things she had tried to do and failed. No matter how hard she prayed, or how righteous a life she lived, her sins remained written on her soul, visiting her in the dark of her lonely nights, condemning her to eternal damnation.

A demon lived inside her—her father and her ex-husband had said so—and she believed them. Why else would her mind and her body crave the things it did? She'd tried repenting. Had prayed for the longings to go away. Had let an entire congregation lay healing hands on her, and still, wicked desires stirred her body and disturbed her dreams. Satan dwelled inside her as surely as the sun rose in the East every morning.

Hope had drawn her to this tent today, but as the preacher laid hands on the repenting sinners, she knew in her heart his sermon had changed nothing. His words were as hollow as the ones she heard every Sunday morning at the church down the street from where she lived. Salvation was not to be hers, not in this lifetime.

Preacher Nathan placed his hands on the head of a woman kneeling at his feet. After commanding the demons to leave the woman, he offered a blessing no different from the ones Evelyn had heard a million times over, then helped the new child of God to her feet. The woman's face glowed with life and love, her expression one of wonder as tears of joy streamed down her cheeks.

Evelyn couldn't bear to remain there another minute. While the congregation raised their voices in celebration at the salvation of another soul, she stepped into the aisle and, head down, fled as fast as her feet would carry her.

It was a long walk back to town, but she'd rather walk than share a car with strangers the way she'd gotten there. Her emotions were too raw, her disappointment too fresh for her to listen to the inevitable recounting of Preacher Nathan's success. How many souls had he added to his saved tally today? How eloquent were his words? How fortunate they all were that he had answered God's calling and brought the Word of God to their neck of the woods today.

"Bullshit," she mumbled to herself. It was all bullshit. Only one who knew a demon's grip firsthand could understand that Preacher Nathan was all show. God had not been present in that hell of a tent, and he most certainly had not cast any demons out of bodies. If he had, he would have recognized the one dwelling inside her and cast it out above all others.

She drew the cooler air into her lungs and focused on the horizon, putting one foot in front of the other. "Nothing but bullshit." The breeze carried the softly spoken words from her lips.

"What's bullshit?" Evelyn started at the masculine voice close behind her. A second later, the owner of the voice joined her, matching his longer gait to her shorter one.

"Nothing." She continued walking, resisting the urge to look at the man beside her. What was he doing here, anyway? "I'm not going back, if that's why you came out here."

"Nope. Not why I'm here."

They continued walking in silence until she stopped on the edge of the gravel road. The man was a full head taller than her five feet three inches. He was one of the most handsome men she'd ever seen, with sandy hair and eyes as green as winter wheat that seemed more amused than angry at her assumption that he'd been sent to drag a stray sheep back to the fold.

"Then why are you following me?" The last thing she needed was a Goody Two-shoes meddling in her life. Her demons were hers to battle. She'd been doing it alone, and she would continue to do it without any help from a stranger.

He shrugged his wide shoulders. "Don't know, exactly." He looked back the way they'd come as if he wasn't sure why he was standing on the side of the road instead of back there, watching the spectacle. When he turned back to her, the amusement was gone, replaced by an expression that sent a shiver along her spine. She took a step back toward the safety of the tent.

"Please, don't go." The plea in his voice stopped her. "I saw you in there, and I knew I needed to get to know you, so I followed you out."

HER EXPRESSION CHANGED from alarm to curiosity. He hadn't imagined the interest in her eyes when she'd first checked him out either. And now that he saw her up close, he didn't know why he hadn't seen her beauty before. Her skin was flawless, like the finest porcelain. Sunlight glinted off the streaks of gold in her hair, making her look like an angel. An annoyed angel, but he could work with that. The revival would be breaking up soon; he didn't have much time to convince her to give him a chance. He was taking a calculated risk, but some things in life were worth it. "I don't know about you, but I couldn't take another minute of that."

He considered her silence a good thing and continued. "I'm glad you left."

She glanced back at the tent where people were beginning to meander out, and then back to him. Without another word, she moved past him down the road toward town. He fell into step beside her.

"I don't know what you want, but you aren't going to find it here." He'd heard subtler turndowns, but she wasn't going to get rid of him that easily. It had been a long time since he'd seen a woman who intrigued him the way this one did, and he wasn't going to let a few barbs deter him.

"The only thing I want is to get to know you. I'm Jimmy Doyle, by the way."

"Like I said, Mr. Doyle, I'm not interested."

He chuckled at her mistake. "Walker. Jimmy Doyle Walker. I'm thirty years old, never been married, and I play baseball for the Washington Diplomats. I'm originally from Texas—grew up on a dirt farm there before I left to play ball."

He hoped opening up some would encourage her to do the same. That had been his error. Shoulders back, she continued to walk as if he didn't exist. A few cars passed them, kicking up a cloud of dust thick enough to choke a horse, but she continued on like a soldier marching to war. Another car passed, this one too close. He grabbed her arm, pulling her off the road and into the shade of an old oak tree.

"What are you doing? Let go of me!" She wrenched her arm out of his grasp. Her chest heaved with indignation and exertion. He had to force his gaze up to her face. The minute he'd touched her, his dick went hard. Seeing her breasts press tight against the thin fabric of her dress only made his situation worse. He'd have her, but not until she gave herself to him. Convincing her to surrender her control was going to take time and patience. He had plenty of the former and not so much of the latter.

"Those people are drunk on believin', sugar. You think they didn't see you leave before the show was over?" He pointed at the car disappearing down the road. His heart was beating with a combination of fear and lust; he didn't know which one fueled his outburst, and he didn't care. Keeping her safe had suddenly become a top priority for him. "That one only wanted to scare you.

The next one might not miss. Unless you're prepared to plead your case at the pearly gates today, best you wait awhile."

He hated the look of fear on her face, hated that he'd put it there. He reached for her, pulling her into his embrace. "You're okay, sugar. No one is ever going to hurt you again."

EVELYN'S MIND REELED. Pressed up against his solid chest, his strong arms enveloping her in a gentle yet unbreakable hold, she felt safe. The feeling was absolutely absurd considering she didn't know him from Adam, but there it was. If she let him, this man would take care of her.

She'd thought that about another man once, but he'd seen into the darkness of her soul and cast her out. This one would too, but for a moment she wanted to believe his words, wanted to revel in the illusion of safety he'd built in the span of a few minutes.

His big hands stroked her back, and she could feel his cheek pressed to the top of her head. He smelled of starch and fresh, clean man. She allowed herself the luxury of wrapping her arms around his trim waist. The muscles of his back were as hard as the rest of him. Just as the thought entered her mind, one hand dipped low on her back, holding her firm while he stepped into her. The unmistakable ridge of his desire pressed into her belly.

The demon inside her roared to life, flooding her body with heat and desire. The flesh between her legs swelled, and her womanhood melted for him. She used to pray for this heathen need to go away, but that had proved useless. There were only two things that could make it go away, and since she wouldn't debase herself with this man or any other, tonight she'd feed the demon herself. She had become adept at bringing on the forbidden pleasure. Afterward, she'd find a measure of peace. But it never lasted for long.

"My buddy is here. He'll give us a ride home."

Dazed by the need clawing at her insides, she was barely aware of him helping her into the backseat of a car and joining her there. She gave him her address, which he conveyed to the driver, and then he wrapped his arms around her and held her close until they pulled to the curb in front of the boardinghouse she'd called home for the past five years.

With his arm still around her waist, he leaned down to speak to the other man. "Thanks, man. I'll see you tomorrow at the game."

They were alone on the sidewalk. She didn't know what to do. Men weren't allowed inside, not that she had any intention of inviting him in. His stomach rumbled. He squeezed her hip against his and chuckled. "I'm starving. Have dinner with me?"

Evelyn eyed the clapboard building. Lace curtains hung limp in the open windows. A record played on the Victrola in the downstairs parlor. The murmur of female voices fell in the early-evening heat. There was nothing for her inside. It would be hours before the house was quiet enough for her to assuage the need inside her without fear of anyone hearing her muffled cries of ecstasy. She looked to the man beside her. Fool that she was, she trusted him.

"There's a diner on the next block."

CHAPTER TWO

Jimmy Doyle requested the empty booth in the back so they could have a modicum of privacy. For a moment, he was afraid she would balk, but she surprised him by squaring her shoulders and following the waitress as if his request didn't have *scandal* written all over it. She took the seat with her back to the restaurant, which suited him just fine. She'd be less guarded with her facial expressions if she knew only he could see them. He had every intention of learning all he could about her in the time he'd been given. Starting with her name.

As soon as the waitress left to fill their beverage orders, he said, "I don't even know your name."

He saw the lie in her eyes. There would be honesty between them, if nothing more. "Don't even think of lying to me." He tempered the authority in his voice, knowing somehow that unleashing his full dominant nature on her at this point would send her running, and he wasn't going to lose her.

She opened her mouth, then closed it. Finally, she said, "Evelyn."

He raised an eyebrow, silently demanding more.

"Evelyn Gardner."

"And where are you from, Evelyn Gardner?" He'd drag every scrap of information out of her if he had to, but he hoped by the time he said good-bye to her this evening, she'd feel comfortable enough to answer anything without hesitation. Gaining her trust would be the first step to owning her.

The waitress set two sweating glasses of iced tea on the table, then pulled an order pad and pencil from the pocket of her apron. "What'll it be?"

He nodded at Evelyn. "Anything you want, sugar. My treat."

"I—"

"You can. Let me buy you dinner." He hoped his tone conveyed that there were no other expectations connected to the offer. He simply wanted to feed her. Letting him take care of her basic needs was something she would have to get used to.

She raised the menu, looked it over quickly, then placed her order. It wasn't much, but he'd see that she ate it all. He ordered, handed the waitress both menus, and turned his attention back to the fascinating woman across from him. He couldn't remember wanting to know every little thing about a person the way he did her. She was going to be a challenge. Once he could restrain her, he'd devise ways to make her talk. Ways they'd both enjoy. His dick stood at attention, ready to heed its master's call.

He lifted his glass to his lips. "You were saying?"

Evelyn's lips caressed her glass. He watched the muscles in her throat work as she swallowed. Christ, he couldn't wait to wrap his hand around her throat and feel those same muscles contract as she swallowed his cum.

"I grew up in central Virginia."

Patience. Her answer was vague, but he sensed that she was telling the truth. He prodded for more. "Family?"

Her gaze flitted away; then her eyelids closed, and she shook her head. He recognized shame when he saw it. He'd seen it often enough. "I won't think less of you, no matter what you tell me."

She pressed her lips into a thin line. So, she wasn't ready to tell him her story. He couldn't blame her. He wasn't ready to tell her everything yet either. He backed toward safer ground. "What do you do for a living?"

11

"I'm a switchboard operator."

There were few jobs a respectable woman could hold, and that was one of them. He laid his hand on the table, palm up. "Let me see your hand." He was a perverted fuck, and he knew it. Wanting to see the hands that shoved things in and out of tiny holes all day amused him.

She rested her gloved hand on his palm. There was a tiny stain on the tip of her index finger—a small imperfection on an otherwise perfect canvas.

His eyes met hers, held her gaze. "I want to see your hands." He tugged on the fingers, one at a time until the worn glove slid free, leaving her bare fingertips resting on his skin. *Fuck.* He was going to lose it right there, and that was not acceptable.

Sliding his hand beneath hers, he clasped his fingers around her wrist. Her pulse raced as fast as his, another reason he shouldn't be doing what he was. Neither one of them was ready for what he wanted to do with her, but it was only her hand, he reasoned. Touching her this way was inappropriate as hell, but he couldn't stop. He needed to feel her skin, and it was imperative that she get used to him touching her. It was never too soon to begin teaching her to accept him.

"Keep your eyes on mine, sugar. Don't look away, no matter what." He explored her fingers with his thumb, rubbing it along the length of each one before repeating the process, this time gently nudging into the soft flesh between each digit as he went from one to the next. When her eyes dilated and her breath grew shallow, he almost came in his pants. Shit, she was a natural submissive, and he couldn't wait to have her completely under his spell. The things he'd do to her body. The pleasure he'd wring from both of them.

"Your hand is incredible, sugar. I can imagine these fingers shoving in, pulling out. All. Day. Long." He turned her hand over and began massaging her palm with his thumb. "Does your hand cramp at the end of the day?"

"Sometimes." Her lips barely moved as she formed the word.

He pressed his thumb hard into the center of her hand. Her fingers instinctively curled inward, encasing his thumb in the sweetness of her embrace. He returned to stroking her skin. "And do you massage the ache away? Alone? In your bed?"

Heat crept from the prim lace collar of her dress to her neckline, yet she held tight to his thumb. God, he could do this all night, tease her, stoke her need. One day soon he'd take care of her himself, but tonight, it would be enough to know that the hand he held in his now would be between her legs tonight, massaging away the ache he'd put there.

The clatter of plates and squeak of rubber soles on linoleum alerted him that they were soon to be interrupted. He glanced up and noted the waitress headed their way. With a gentle smile, he tugged his thumb from her grasp and pulled his hand to his side of the table. Turning her face to the wall, Evelyn tucked her hands into her lap.

Once the waitress left, he reached for her again. "Give me your other hand." She hesitated for only a second before presenting her gloved hand to him. He stripped the garment from her fingers, set it atop the other one. "Eat."

EVELYN RUBBED HER palm where he'd touched her. It wasn't much more than two people holding hands, but it had felt much more intimate. The demon inside her had come to life, humming, heating her core, planting an unholy need between her legs every time his thumb pressed into the soft webbing between her fingers. The demon inside her had begged for another part of *him* to press deep into her core. The wicked flesh between her legs pulsed with need. Her breasts strained against the confines of her new brassiere. She'd never owned one before, but now she was grateful for the concealing fabric, even if the stitching rubbed painfully against her nipples. At least *he* couldn't see what his touch had done to her, and she'd never tell.

She picked up her fork and speared into the meatloaf. The man across from her made her body hunger for more than food.

She'd be wise to never see him again.

"When's your next day off?"

His question startled her from her sinful thoughts. This was her opportunity to tell him that she didn't want to see him again, but when she opened her mouth, she said, "Next Sunday."

A frown marred his handsome face. "I'll be in Chicago next weekend."

Relief quickly gave way to disappointment. She could never let this man get too close, but at the same time, she didn't want to let him go. "I get two days off the following week. Friday and Saturday."

He consulted a worn scrap of paper he pulled from his wallet. "I'll be in New York." He refolded the paper, then put it away. "Do you have a telephone?"

She shook her head. "There's one in the parlor. It costs a nickel a call, and there's a five-minute time limit. I rarely use it. There's no…privacy."

He looked up from his meal and nodded. "I'll write to you, then. You'll read my letters, won't you?"

Her heart skipped a beat. "Yes. I'll read your letters."

He didn't touch her again, not even when he walked her back to the boardinghouse and bade her good night on the sidewalk. Alone in her room, she stripped, then pulled a thin cotton knee-length gown on. At the front of the house, her room absorbed the afternoon heat and held on to it like a skinflint. In the winter, that worked to her advantage, but not so much the rest of the year. Fortunately, she had two windows, one overlooking the front yard and the other a little-used side yard. Tonight, she opened both, hoping a crosswind would blow across her bed, situated between the two portals.

Evelyn turned out the lights and stretched out on top of the covers. Minutes seemed to drag into hours as she waited. Eventually, the household sounds gave way to crickets chirping and the rattle of the occasional passing car. Only then did she lift her gown to her waist and touch the aching flesh between her legs.

Behind closed eyes, she saw the man she'd met at the revival. He'd held her tight against him, tight enough to prove his desire for her. Evelyn stroked her swollen tissues, imagining her fingers were the steel rod she'd felt pressing into her belly. A sigh escaped her lips as she felt the weight of his body bearing down on her, opening her, filling her.

How wonderful that would feel. She spread her legs wider to accommodate his hips—scraped the heel of one foot along the calf of the other leg, imagining hairy legs scraping alongside hers. Everything hard about him rubbing against everything soft about her.

With her free hand, she shrugged the thin strap off her shoulder and pushed the fabric aside to expose her breast. A gentle breeze teased the filmy curtains and brushed across her heated flesh, causing her nipple to pebble. Evelyn pinched the hard tip, imagining his hand there, massaging, testing the weight. She wet her fingertips with her tongue, then dampened the tight peak. Cupping the soft mound, she offered her breast to her imaginary lover's mouth at the same time slipping the fingers of her other hand lower, into the damp, recesses of her sex.

Stifling a groan, she rolled to her stomach. Careful not to rock too wildly and set the bedsprings to squeaking any more than they normally would, she rolled her hips against the heel of her hand while moving her fingers inside her, feeding the demon with slow thrusts.

Another welcome breeze unfurled the curtains, then danced like a lover's caress across her backside. Evelyn clenched and released the twin globes. The tight bud hidden there pouted, wanting attention too. She ignored the sullen hole. Tonight the beast would have to be satisfied with what she was willing to give.

Thrusting her fingers deeper, she ground her pelvis against her hand. She repeated the movement again and again until the demon finally had enough and released its grip on her insides. Evelyn buried her face in her pillow, silently screaming at the deity that had cursed her to a life of carnal need and sin.

❦

Jimmy Doyle strolled away from the old house in the residential district where Evelyn lived. He could catch the streetcar a few blocks over to take him across town to the small apartment he'd rented when the Diplomats offered him a contract. It wasn't anywhere near as nice as the one he'd had six years ago, but it was quiet and clean, and close to the ballpark. He didn't need to use his car often these days, but he kept it anyway. No doubt, he could find a car to borrow when he wanted to go out to the farm, but the fewer questions asked about where he was going, the better.

An image of Evelyn popped into his brain and stirred his blood. She was a temptation he knew he should resist, but as soon as he'd touched her, there was no going back. Looking into her eyes across the table while he made love to her hand told him a lot about the woman. She was all prim and proper on the outside, but he'd seen the banked heat in her eyes. She was trying hard to deny what her body wanted, but anyone who took the time to look could see the prize waiting for the man who broke through the walls she'd put up.

As the trolley carried him away from her, he wondered what had transpired in her life that she was alone in the big city instead of some farmer's wife with a passel of kids and one on the way. Behind the passion, he'd seen fear. She'd been cautious with the information she shared. A woman alone couldn't be too careful, he supposed, but that hadn't stopped him from trying. He wanted to know everything there was to know about her. He'd have his answers, eventually, but he'd have to take his time. Slow was the only way to go, or he'd scare her away. And that wouldn't do.

She was still on his mind the next day when he arrived at the ballpark. The Diplomats' season was going well. If they continued to rack up wins, they had a real chance of winning the pennant this year and going to the World Series. For as long as he could remember, he'd wanted to play baseball. For most of the kids he'd grown up with, the game had been a way to pass the time in the summer when there was nothing to do on the farm but watch the crops grow. Later, the ones who had stayed in school found that girls liked a guy in uniform, even if it did have a number on the back.

While they'd dreamed of ways to ask a girl out, he'd dreamed of playing for a real team, in a real city. He couldn't see settling down with any of the girls he knew. They wanted a man with simple needs. They wanted kids and someone on their arm at church every Sunday. Ever since that night when he was sixteen and witnessed the darker side of love, he knew he would never be the man they wanted, but as certain as he was of that, he was also certain there was a woman out there for him. One who would see the darkness inside him and not be afraid.

After years of looking, he thought he'd found her—in, of all places, a holy-rolling tent revival meeting.

Evelyn had looked in his eyes, and though she'd been wary, she hadn't run. When he'd made love to her hand, she'd looked as if she might melt into a puddle right there in the diner.

The first few innings went as expected. A shortstop in his former life, since returning to the game, he'd been assigned to play first base. He supposed it suited him now. He'd worked hard during his time off, and his body reflected the manual labor with strong muscles and power at bat, but the years away had stolen some of his agility along with his good name. Not much had been said of his return other than that all charges against him had been dropped. Legally, he was out of trouble, and his suspension had been lifted, but trust and friendships couldn't be restored with the stroke of a pen. He'd come to expect the animosity from the other players in the league, so in the sixth inning, when there was little hope of the opposing team winning the game, he wasn't surprised when the first pitch came right at him, instead of over the plate. He dodged, but his efforts proved to be too late. The ball glanced off his forearm, sending him spinning to one knee in the dirt.

The umpire inquired of his ability to continue, then sent him to first base. Before his slide into infamy, a beaning like that would have brought his team manager out to protest, but not now. As he made his way to first base, the Diplomats' dugout was eerily quiet. Most of his teammates grudgingly accepted him on the team, but few actually thought he belonged there. He'd earned the trust of some, like Harvey, but not even they raised a voice in his defense.

He couldn't get the girl from the previous day out of his mind. When he should have been following the game from the bench, he was reliving every minute he'd spent with Evelyn Gardner. He loved her hands. Delicate yet strong, they said a lot about the woman she was. As a switchboard operator, she probably barely got by, which explained the stain on her glove. His mother certainly never would have worn a glove with a stain on it unless she'd had no other choice. When a person had to choose either room and board or frivolous things, the former would win every time.

Her responsibility should be rewarded.

CHAPTER THREE

Evelyn rarely received mail, but every day when she arrived home, she stopped at the long table in the entryway to scan the letters and packages there. Nearly a week had passed since Jimmy Doyle had promised to write, and each day there was no letter, her disappointment grew. When her gaze landed on the envelope addressed to her, her breath caught. She picked it up gingerly. A small box lay beneath, also addressed to her. She glanced around. No one would see her open her pocketbook and place the items inside, away from prying eyes. She considered some of the other boarders to be friends, but she wasn't ready to explain to anyone about the man she'd met. For as long as she could, she wanted to keep him all to herself.

Two meals a day were included in her monthly rent, breakfast and supper. Most days she ate both, but tonight she breezed through the kitchen for some fruit and a glass of milk to take to her room. For reasons she couldn't explain, she wanted to be alone with her thoughts.

She took the stairs to her room and shut the door, turning the key in the lock for good measure. Most of the time she didn't bother with the lock. No one would dare enter without knocking first, but it seemed the right thing to do on this occasion. Leaning back on the door, she clutched her handbag to her chest and closed her eyes. A smile broke across her face as she recalled the time she'd spent with the baseball player. To anyone observing them, he'd been a perfect gentleman, but when he held her, when he touched her, there had been an undercurrent of desire she couldn't have mistaken. Her body had responded to his in a way she hadn't felt in years.

She dreamed of a man wanting her the way the men did in the trashy novels all the women in the house were reading. The men always arrived and swept the women off their feet. And that was just the way she'd felt from the first moment she'd seen Jimmy Doyle, like the ground was shifting under her feet. His touch had awakened the demon inside she'd tried so hard to cast out.

But somehow, the feelings that had felt so wrong when she was married didn't feel wrong at all when she was with Jimmy Doyle. There was something about the way he looked at her that made her think he saw her deepest, darkest secrets and, instead of denouncing her for them, encouraged her to open the windows of her soul.

She pushed away from the door and undressed, hanging her work frock on the hook next to her Sunday dress—the one she'd been wearing when she met Jimmy Doyle. She let her hand drift over the crepe fabric, reliving that day as she had a hundred times since he'd walked her home after buying her dinner. When she closed her eyes, she could still feel the way his fingers stroked her hand, like he held precious china instead of a workingwoman's hand. Just remembering how he'd pressed his finger to the sensitive skin between her fingers, nudging in a manner reminiscent of another act—one she ached to experience again—made her wish there could be more between them than letters and souvenirs sent from his trips.

She shouldn't have let him touch her that way, but it had been years since she'd felt the caress of another human being, and oh, how good it had felt. His skin was warm, and the strength in his calloused fingers had made her feel feminine. There was nothing feminine in her day-to-day routine. She worked long hours that left little time for anything else, and though she worked with other women, there was never a minute for them to converse on topics of interest to them as females. Exhausted at the end of each day, they parted ways without fanfare. So, having Jimmy Doyle treat her like a lady—buying her dinner, holding her hand, walking her home—reminded her of the days before she married when young men her age came courting.

She'd thought she would marry one of them, but her father had other ideas. The man he'd chosen for her had been nearly old enough to be her father, and there had been no courting. Curtis had shown up to dinner one night, and her father had told her they were to be married. Seven days later she became a bride, then a wife in a matter of hours. A year and a half later, her husband denounced her as a sinner, and her father took up the cry, casting her out of the family without ever hearing her side of the story.

She'd been a month shy of her twentieth birthday when she landed in Washington, DC with two dresses, no skills, and a dollar in her pocketbook. She'd been fortunate to find employment and a place to stay within the first week. Ever since, she'd maintained a low profile, not letting anyone get too close. Shame and guilt were constant companions along with fear. She doubted her father would come looking for her, but she had no intention of making it easy for him to find her if he did. That part of her life was over, and until she'd met Jimmy Doyle Walker, she thought the chapters of her life would be reduced to those two—before and after. One afternoon spent with the baseball player and she felt more alive than ever before. He'd held her hand and, in that simple gesture, renewed her hope.

She ate the snack she'd brought and drank the milk before it got warm. She placed the empty glass on the dresser next to the door so she wouldn't forget to return it to the kitchen then opened her purse and removed the letter and parcel. Which one to open first? Unable to decide, she placed them both on the bed, then sat staring at them. Her hand hovered over the letter. Jimmy Doyle's handwriting was strong and surprisingly neat. The return address was a downtown apartment, near the stadium and not far from where she worked.

Had she seen him in the area and not known who he was? She thought of all the anonymous people she encountered walking from the trolley stop to her job. He might have been one of them, or perhaps he was one of the men who ate at the diner around the corner where she bought her lunch most days. Her heart sped up imagining the two of them crossing paths and not knowing.

She smoothed the rumpled envelope with her fingertips, then moved to the package. The course brown paper gave no clues as to the contents. Like a Christmas present, the mystery called to her. Without giving her decision another thought, she picked up the package. The twine binding came away easily. Evelyn peeled the wrapping away.

She stifled a gasp with her fingertips to her lips. She'd never seen a more beautiful box. The glossy black, embossed cardboard with gold lettering indicating an exclusive ladies-wear shop downtown took her breath away. The displays in their window drew women like flies, but few ventured inside, and fewer still made a purchase. Whatever was inside this box had to be dearer than angel wings.

With trembling hands, she pried the top off.

"Oh!" Inside, wrapped in the thinnest tissue possible, printed with the store's name in gold, lay the most exquisite gloves she'd ever seen. Without touching, she noted the quality in the simple, graceful lines. Daring, she reached out. The tip of one finger skimmed the impossibly soft leather. Never in a million years could she afford something like this for herself. Sadness washed over her. As lovely as they were, she couldn't wear them. Doing so would invite questions she couldn't answer.

Sighing, she left the box open and picked up the letter. The seal slipped open easily enough with just a fingernail beneath it. Evelyn pulled out the folded sheets of paper and sat back against the headboard to read.

Dearest Evelyn,

I hope this finds you in good health. I wanted to thank you for the other day. I can't remember a time I enjoyed more. I wish I could be there with you when you open my gift, but by the time you receive this, I'll be on a train with the team. Our first stop is Chicago, then on to Detroit and Cleveland before returning home. Wish me luck.

I miss you already. I hope I'm not too forward saying that, but it's true. You captivated me from the moment I saw you in that godforsaken tent.

I feel confident in calling it that since you seemed to have felt the same about the place as I did. Despite my skepticism about a holy presence there, I will forever be grateful I went, because I met you there.

Lovely Evelyn. I can't get you out of my mind. When I close my eyes, you are there. Your eyes seem sad, but when you smile, they light from within. Your lips tempt me to taste you. Even now, alone in my room, I long to make you smile. I hope you smiled when you opened my gift. Please accept it, my wonderful girl. They are the finest I could find, because a woman such as you should have fine things. The clerk assured me you would love the way they feel against your skin.

I want to think about you wearing them, even if you only wear them for yourself. Please, if you haven't already, put them on. If I close my eyes, I can see them on your slender fingers, holding my letter. Thinking of you doing so makes me breathless.

I hope they fit. When I held them, I envisioned your hand in mine and thought they were a perfect match.

Are you wearing them, sweet Evelyn?

She glanced at the gloves, wishing with all her heart she could keep them but knowing she couldn't. Accepting an expensive gift from a gentleman, especially one she'd met once, just wasn't done. Returning her attention to the letter, she read the first page twice over, hardly believing his words. He missed her? He couldn't stop thinking about her? And the things he said. *A woman such as you should have fine things.* Why, that was positively scandalous! And talking about the way the gloves would feel against her skin!

As she committed the words to memory, her body heated

from within. Even in her dreams she'd never hoped a man would say such things to her, but Jimmy Doyle had. She held the proof in her trembling hands.

Eyeing the gloves, she fought the urge to see if they felt as wonderful as the clerk said they would. She could still return them. What would it hurt to try them, just once? Giving in to her curiosity, she set the letter aside and pulled the gloves from the box.

The soft leather felt like a second skin, softer even than her own. She never wanted to take them off, but she would, of course. Yet for a few minutes, she would indulge herself with the fantasy.

Are you wearing them, sweet Evelyn?

"Yes, I am."

I would love nothing more than to feel the heat of your hand through the leather, but since I can't be there to touch you, will you do something for me? Will you touch yourself? I want to imagine your hands stroking your beautiful body. Will you do that for me, sweet Evelyn? Remove your clothes and lie on your bed. I'll wait, breathless, for you to do as I ask.

She dropped the letter as if the paper had suddenly caught on fire, then stripped the gloves from her hands and tossed them carelessly beside the box they'd come in. The warmth of the afternoon had become oppressive. She moved to the west-facing window, opening it wider and pulling the shade down, casting half the room in a purplish gloom. Glancing at the scandalous items on her bed, she blew out a frustrated breath.

What was her problem? No one could see her. No one would know, not even him, if she followed his instructions. What harm would there be in touching herself if no one was there to witness it? A nervous laugh escaped her lips. The preacher they'd heard on Sunday would probably say it was a sin to engage in such activities, but she'd never understood that type of reasoning. Why would

God have given people the ability to enjoy corporal pleasure if he didn't mean for them to experience it?

She stared at the letter. It would be hours before the sun went down, and in this sweltering heat, who could fault her for wanting to cool off?

Before she could change her mind, she went to the other window and pulled the shade low, deepening the gloom to twilight. Once she'd discarded her slip and panties, she crossed to the bed and flicked on the lamp on the nightstand. She picked up the gloves, then set the box carefully aside before pulling the covers back and lying down. It felt positively wicked to lie naked in the waning daylight.

Evelyn pulled the gloves on, then picked up the letter.

I can see you in my mind, beautiful woman. Your creamy skin is like silk, and your breasts are topped with dusky pink rosettes. Am I right, my darling? If so, touch yourself there. Draw your fingers over those peaks. Tease them with your fingertips until they stand tall and proud. If I were there, I'd take them in my mouth and worship them. I'd cup them in my palms like the precious globes they are. Can you imagine my touch, sweet girl? Does it feel good when I touch you? Do you want more?

Move your hand lower, darling. Stroke your palms over your stomach to the swell of your womanhood. God, you are so lovely. It's hard to write this with my eyes closed, but I must see you as you are now. Do the gloves feel good on your skin? Do they add to your excitement?

Breathe deep, my lovely. Can you smell your arousal as I can?

Evelyn inhaled, filling her lungs. Indeed, the musk of her arousal hung heavy in the air. She let the breath out on a groan.

I wish I had something of yours, a handkerchief or a pair of panties, to carry with me. Maybe it is best that I do not. I don't think I could bear to breathe you in and not touch you. That's why I held your hand the other night. I had to feel your skin against mine, darling. It was as necessary to me as breathing air.

Did you feel the same way? I think you did. You could have pulled your hand away, but you did not. Could you feel my need as I could feel yours?

Move your hand lower, dear girl. You must be aching for release by now. If I were there, your waiting would be over, but since I am not, you will need to ease the pain yourself. Do not be shy. There is no one but you and I here, and I want there to be no secrets between us.

Find your clitoris, Evelyn. That little nub of desire needs your attention. Rub it lightly. Doesn't the leather feel wonderful, as if someone else's hand is there between your legs? Can you see me there, sweet woman, my body alongside yours, my hand cupping your mound of Venus?

You need more, don't you, darling? I'm going to give you everything you need. Open your legs wider. Let your middle finger find the wellspring of your honey. That's it, sweet girl. Dip your finger inside for me. Flex your wrist so the heel of your hand is flat against your clitoris.

Ah, yes, that feels so good, doesn't it, sweet thing? Rock your hand. Do you see me, Evelyn? Am I there with you, giving you pleasure? You are near to coming, I can feel your body tensing, preparing to fly. Work your finger in and out. Faster. Harder. So near to the edge you can taste the air of freedom. Just one more thing, and I'll let you come, my darling. Arch your back, baby. Show me your beautiful breasts.

Yes, that's the way. Thank you, darling. You are so perfect. I knew you would be. Force that finger deep and hard. Yes! Come for me, sweet Evelyn. Let go. I'm there to catch you.

Evelyn rolled to her side, clamping her hand between her thighs and burying her face in the pillow to muffle her scream. Her vagina clenched and released over and over again, rocking her body with hard jolts that felt like cramps but were too wonderful to be anything so vile. She'd made herself come before, but those had been nothing like this. This was cataclysmic. She was weak and soaring all at the same time.

When her body calmed, she extricated her hand from between her legs. "Oh, no!" She sat up, staring at the soiled glove. *What have I done?* Her heart ached, but there was nothing to do for it now. The damage couldn't be undone. She picked up the letter she'd dropped in the throes of the most powerful release she'd ever experienced, and began to read.

You are magnificent, my darling. I feel as if I were there, but ache because I was not. I can almost see the frown on your face. Are you worried about the gloves? Don't be. Wipe away the dampness with a cloth, then lay the gloves on the dresser to dry. They'll be as good as new in the morning.

Did I please you, Evelyn? I should not tell you this. No gentleman would, but I am so hard for you I cannot walk. I must end this letter now and take matters into my own hand while imagining I am with you.

Until I see you again,
Jimmy Doyle Walker

CHAPTER FOUR

He couldn't stop thinking about her. Worst of all was the uncertainty. Sending the gloves had been inappropriate and the accompanying letter downright scandalous. But she made him forget propriety. Up until he'd met Evelyn, he'd thought of little else but clearing his name and getting back on the field.

As he stepped up to bat against the White Sox, his tension had nothing to do with the scorn pouring from the opposing team and everything to do with worry over what, if anything, he should do next in regards to Evelyn. He had no idea if she had done the things he'd asked in the letter. For all he knew, she might have burned the scandalous letter and returned the gloves to the store and taken the cash instead. The amount he'd paid for them was ridiculous, but as soon as he'd touched them and felt the soft doeskin, he knew he wanted her to have them.

No woman of his should have to wear yellowed gloves with stains on the fingertips.

Mine.

As that thought settled in his brain, he dug his right foot into the batter's box. For the first time since his return to the game, the derisive comments coming from the stands barely registered. The commissioner had declared him innocent of all charges, and whether anyone else agreed with the decision or not, he was back in the game to stay.

The first pitch came in low and too far outside for his taste. He checked his swing. The umpire yelled, "Strike."

Jimmy Doyle turned an incredulous look in the man's direction. With a wry smile, the official shrugged, adjusted the thick pad protecting his chest, then stepped back in position behind the catcher.

This umpire wasn't the first one to make his opinion of Jimmy Doyle's return clear via his calls, and he wouldn't be the last. Shrugging the animosity off, Jimmy Doyle focused on the pitcher. The next pitch broke inside. He twisted his upper body, but he didn't move fast enough. The ball hit him square in the ribs, knocking him off balance. His ass hit the dirt with a thud that rattled his teeth. *Goddamn, that hurt.* The catcher hovered over him, a satisfied smirk on his face. *Bastard.*

Refusing to show any weakness by cradling his bruised ribs, he rolled to his knees and stood. He waved off the team manager, who was taking his own sweet time coming out to check on his player, and trotted to first base. He was a target for every pitcher in the league. Even though he had been cleared of the charges leveled against him, they all felt compelled to add their own brand of punishment to the five years of exile he'd already suffered.

The first-base coach met him with a questioning look. "I'm fine," he assured. "Just another bruise." Nothing some liniment wouldn't cure. He smiled at the vision that popped into his mind of soft, feminine fingers applying the healing liquid to his skin. It would almost be worth getting nailed by a pitch to have Evelyn's hands on him.

"What are you smiling at, asshole?"

Jimmy Doyle turned to see the White Sox's first baseman glaring at him. "Maybe I like pain," he countered. He knew plenty of people who did, but he wasn't one of them. The liniment responsible for his good mood had been a gift from a friend who knew more than most about the giving and receiving of pain. He'd even offered to strap a few people on Jimmy Doyle's behalf. He had laughed the offer off, knowing his friend would get way too much enjoyment out of evening the score for him.

"What's that supposed to mean?"

"Nothing. Absolutely nothing." Jimmy Doyle tagged the base, waited for the pitcher to get set on the mound before taking a leadoff step toward second base. He'd said more than he should have already. Engaging the enemy in conversation wasn't going to change public opinion. The only way he was going to earn back the respect he'd had before his exile was to play the best game he could, and that meant focusing on each play instead of letting a woman dominate his thoughts. Pushing Evelyn from his thoughts proved more painful than the bruise on his ribs.

After the game, Jimmy Doyle spent another near-sleepless night thinking of Evelyn, imagining her doing all the things to her body he'd encouraged her to do in his letter. Walking purposely along the downtown sidewalks, looking for another gift for her, he hoped the fresh air and exercise would clear his head. Perhaps he was crazy to spend his money on gifts for a woman he had just met, especially since he wasn't sure if she had even kept the first one he'd sent, but something deep inside him told him Evelyn would have followed his instructions down to the very last one.

The idea of pleasuring her, even when he wasn't there, made his dick hard. He hoped one day to personally take her to the highest peaks of sexual pleasure, but until then, he'd encourage her to find gratification through his letters and the gifts he felt compelled to send her.

He found the shop he was looking for, a small establishment with fancy lettering on the window and an array of women's fripperies on display. The bell on the door jangled, and all eyes turned to him. A customer at the counter blushed brightly, but the two salesclerks only smiled. He supposed they were accustomed to men buying gifts for their wives or more likely their mistresses. The one nearest the door excused herself from the group and approached.

"May I help you?"

Jimmy Doyle removed his hat, glancing around the shop before letting his gaze rest on the clerk. "I'm looking for handkerchiefs. Something tasteful, but of good quality."

The woman took in his suit, and finding his grooming to be acceptable, he supposed, she motioned for him to follow her. He stood at the counter while she selected several boxes from the shelves behind. After spreading the selections in front of him, she lifted the lid on the first one. "This one comes from France. The lace edging is handmade by nuns in a convent."

He shook his head. "I was thinking of something more subtle."

She tapped the third box. "This one, I believe." She opened the box to reveal a square piece of cloth with rows of tiny holes along the edges. "The same nuns did the cutwork on these. The fabric is the finest linen, durable yet lightweight."

"Can I touch it?" The design was just what he'd had in mind, practical yet elegant, like Evelyn. More important was knowing how the fabric would feel against her skin.

"Of course." The salesclerk handed him the one on top. He let the fabric drape over his palm, then rubbed one corner between his thumb and forefinger. "The nuns claim to have a secret process for making their linens this fine. We've been fortunate to obtain a few sets of bed linens made from the same fabric. If you'd be interested."

He handed over the handkerchief. The image of Evelyn naked and sprawled out on luxurious sheets heated his blood. "I'd like two of these, please. Can you send them to an address in Washington, DC?"

After scrawling Evelyn's address on a card, he paid the exorbitant price named and left without inquiring about the bed linens. As much as he would love to make his fantasy come true, buying the sheets would be putting the cart before the horse. One day, he hoped to swaddle Evelyn in luxury, if she would let him.

Walking away, lighter in pocket but heavy in heart, he wondered again if he had just thrown good money away.

❧❧

Evelyn's heartbeat accelerated the moment she saw the small package waiting for her on the table in the entryway. For the past few days, she'd rushed home after work, hoping against hope for another letter from Jimmy Doyle and praying she saw it before anyone else in the house did. In all the years she'd lived here, she'd only ever received official mail—tax bills and the occasional advertisement. If anyone noticed an envelope addressed to her in a strong, masculine hand, no doubt, they'd ask questions.

Beneath the package was indeed another missive from the baseball player. Evelyn stuffed the envelope into her handbag and took the stairs to her room as if nothing had changed in her world—which was as far from the truth as possible. Everything had changed.

In the week since receiving his first letter and the extravagant gloves, she couldn't deny that the world was a brighter place. As he had said, the gloves were no worse for the wear if properly cared for.

Closing and locking the door to her room behind her, she eyed the gloves lying atop her dresser. Last night, like every night the past week, after reading his letter, she'd carefully tended to the gloves and spread them out to dry.

She was the wickedest of women for touching herself in that way night after night, but the physical pleasure made her feel more alive than she had in years. His words would have scandalized most women, but for her, they were a balm to her soul. For the first time in her life, she had begun to believe there could be someone out there whom she could confide her deepest, darkest desires to and not have him condemn her as a whore.

As was her daily routine, she opened her windows wide to let in what little breeze might be stirring. After pulling the shades down just enough to block the worst of the sunlight, she closed the sheer curtains before removing her work frock and hanging it on a hook. Then, because the late-spring heat had risen to unbearable levels, she undressed down to her drawers. A few pats to the back of her neck with a washcloth she'd dampened helped lower her core temperature.

While she went through her customary after-work routine, her gaze kept straying to her pocketbook. Inside was another letter from Jimmy Doyle and a package too. He'd already spent a small fortune on the gloves, but she supposed the cost wasn't much to a man like him. She'd heard baseball players made good money. They certainly made more than a switchboard operator. Every extra penny she could save went into a sock she kept beneath her mattress. The meager collection was all that stood between her and life on the street. All the more reason she should have returned the gloves. And the reason she shouldn't even open the package she'd received today. Nothing good could come of accepting gifts she could never afford to purchase on her own.

She stared at the package, her thoughts going back and forth between what she should do and what she wanted. In the end, want won out. The moment the outer wrapping fell away and she saw the beautiful packaging, all thoughts about returning the gift vanished. The glossy box with the understated design embossed on the top screamed elegance. She'd never wished for expensive things, had always been content with purchases within her means, but Jimmy Doyle's presents made her feel special. And didn't every woman long to feel special?

She opened the box with care then pushed the tissue lining aside to reveal two ladies' handkerchiefs. The simple embroidery and cutwork design on them were beyond lovely. Workmanship of this caliber didn't come cheap. She brushed away a tear before it could drop from her cheek to the fine linen squares. It would be a shame to soil something so beautiful.

Forcing her gaze from them, she picked up the letter. The postmark, like the one on the package, was from Chicago. A pang of envy stabbed at her heart. She'd never been anywhere but her home in central Virginia, and the place she'd ended up, Washington, DC. How many times had she stopped on her walk to work to daydream over the posters in the travel office depicting train trips across the country or giant ships carrying people across the sea? Oh, and the adventure of flying! She didn't think she was brave enough to try air travel, but it was fun to dream.

With a sigh for dreams beyond her reach, she slipped a fingernail beneath the flap of the envelope and retrieved the folded papers inside. She'd read his first letter so many times, seeing his bold handwriting made her heart flutter in anticipation.

My dearest Evelyn,

I can only hope my last letter did not offend. I think of you almost every minute of every day, even when it isn't wise. Baseball can be a dangerous game if a player allows his mind to wander. Do not worry, I do my best to put you from my thoughts while I am on the field, but when I am not, you are my first and only thought.

When I think of you, I see a woman of depth and integrity, who, for reasons that escape my understanding, seeks to cleanse her soul. Sweet Evelyn, I hope one day you will honor me with your trust so I might help you see with clarity the truth I see in you. There is no stain on your soul. You are purity itself, my darling.

Do you like the gloves I sent? It's difficult for me to sleep at night, imagining you wearing them, and only them. When I am particularly lonely, I let myself imagine your gloved hands touching me. I believe the stimulation would be too much to endure, and I am a person known for maintaining control. For now, I will content myself with the fantasy, but I would very much like for you to test my mastery one day soon.

Today, I have sent you two handkerchiefs. One for you to keep, and one for you to give to me when we meet again so I might carry a part of you with me wherever I go. I can see the crease between your eyebrows now, love, and the image makes me laugh. You are wondering how a handkerchief I picked out for you will remind me of you. Am I correct?

Evelyn dropped the letter to her lap. He knew her so well, and they'd only spent a few hours in each other's company. Yet in their short acquaintance, he had discerned much about her personality and mannerisms. As with the gloves, if she had the coin to make such extravagant purchases, she would have chosen exactly as he had. Both were understated in their elegance, yet the craftsmanship was beyond exceptional. No doubt they were worth every cent he'd paid for them.

She closed her eyes and brought his image to mind. She'd learned a thing or two about him in the short time she'd known him. If she were a betting woman, which she most certainly was not, she would wager there were hidden depths to Jimmy Doyle too. Behind his laughing eyes were shadows he concealed with a devil-may-care facade. He'd been at the revival meeting too, she reminded herself.

Using the envelope his letter came in as a fan, Evelyn stirred the air in front of her face. She licked her dry lips, then rose to fill a glass from the bathroom sink. After downing the tepid water, she picked up the letter and resumed her position on the bed. There was no denying he'd piqued her curiosity. She read on.

I remember your scent like it was yesterday. You smell of summer roses, which is very appropriate for you, my sweet girl. They begin as buds, their beauty cocooned from the wind and the rain, the storms of life. Eventually, they grow strong enough to let the world see the beauty they've held inside. They risk much in doing so, but not even the threat of a storm can hold them back, once they realize how strong they are.

Unfurl for me, dear Evelyn. Let me see your beauty. Let me drink in your unique scent. With me, you will always be safe.

You will be reading this after work, which means your room must be uncomfortably warm. There is no hope for it, darling. Remove your clothes and lie on the bed with nothing but this letter and one of the handkerchiefs I sent you.

Oh! Her fingers tightened on the thin paper, wrinkling it terribly. She took a deep breath and let it out, suddenly aware that her breathing had grown shallow as she read his provocative words. No one had ever likened her to a rose, and if they had, she would have scoffed at the comparison. But again, Jimmy Doyle's

35

vision made her think differently. She did hold herself tight against the storms of life. She had to. There was no one to do it for her, but oh, how she was tempted to open for him, if only in the privacy of her room.

Who would know? No one but her, and God, if the devout were to be believed. She'd long since quit believing that God watched over her. If he was there, surely she wouldn't be the sinner she was. Using the papers clutched in her fist, she fanned herself again. He was right. Her room was beyond stifling.

Decision made, she removed the last of her clothes, then pulled back the covers and stretched out on the bed. She breathed a sigh of relief as her back met the cool sheet. Letter and handkerchief in hand, she read.

My, God, you must be lovely, my dear one. If I were there, I would learn every inch of your body with my fingertips; then when I was through, I'd begin again, studying with my lips until there was no part of you I did not know. But as I am not there, I will have to rely on my imagination, though I am sure it does not do you justice.

Please excuse my shaky penmanship. My fingers ache to touch you, so much so I find it difficult to hold my pen firmly. My infirmity will not keep me from seeing to your pleasure, my darling. You will always come before all else in my life. I hope you believe me. I sense others have let you down in that regard. Perhaps you will confide in me one day, and I will take those persons to task for hurting you.

I'm sorry if I have brought unpleasant thoughts to your mind. Please forgive me, sweetheart, and let me do what I can to replace those memories with more pleasant ones.

Are you lying down, sweet Evelyn? I know you are, because I asked you to, and you want to please me, don't you, darling? I can't tell you how happy it makes me to know you trust me with your body. I would never misuse something so precious.

Fix the handkerchief in your right hand so all four corners make a fan. Now brush the fabric lightly over your breasts like angel wings fluttering against your skin. That feels wonderful, doesn't it, darling? I can see your back arching, offering your creamy mounds up for me to taste. Wet the tip of your left index finger with your tongue, then apply the dampness to your nipples. Ah, yes. I'm smiling, sweetheart, imagining how your nipples are tightening, becoming hard little buds, aching for my mouth to suckle them.

God, how I long to taste you. You have captivated me, sweet Evelyn. Once I have you in my arms, I don't know if I will be able to let you go.

I won't rush you, darling. I would never take more than you are willing to give, but know that I want all of you—your past, your present, your future. I want your mind, your heart, your body, and your soul, if I could possess it.

Do you want me too, darling? Drape the handkerchief over your stomach and spread your legs. Touch your secret place. Yes, you are wet and swollen, aren't you, babe? It is perfectly natural for your body to prepare to welcome me inside. My cock has hardened, painfully so, in anticipation. I want nothing more than to bury myself inside your heat, to make love to you so you know that my mind and body, and yes, my heart, are yours.

Stroke your flower for me, sweet Evelyn. Part your petals and dip into the core. Make yourself slick, my darling. I'm a horny bee, buzzing around you, wanting to thrust inside you, to taste your sweet nectar. Open wide for me. God, yes. That's it. Welcome me in.

Use your fingers, sweet girl. Feel me inside you, stroking, sliding in your wetness, cocooned in your heat. Let your thumb work your clitoris, babe. Let the pleasure overtake you, my darling. Fly into the universe, knowing I will be there to catch you when you come back to earth.

Evelyn stroked between her legs, mortified at how wet she had become. No matter how much she'd prayed her body wouldn't react this way to thoughts of a man entering her, she'd never been able to control the moisture pouring from her. Her ex-husband had been disgusted by her physical reaction to intercourse, but Jimmy Doyle seemed anything but disgusted. He *wanted* to feel her slick juices on his member. Oh, and how she wanted to feel him filling her, sliding in and out of her sheath.

Wet, sucking sounds filled the small room as she worked her fingers in and out. Jimmy Doyle knew a woman's body well. Paying attention to the crux of her womanhood increased her pleasure until the muscles deep inside coiled tight.

She fought the urge to clamp her thighs together, wanting to imagine him nestled between her legs, his body plunging deep inside hers.

When her body finally broke free, she held her thighs apart, letting the inner contractions roll through her like ocean waves, pulling her under, then tossing her up for air. The orgasm seemed to go on forever, leaving her brow covered in sweat and moisture gushing from her core.

Gasping, she relaxed her arms, letting her legs fall limp to the mattress. A faint breeze, the first of the evening, ruffled the curtains and rattled the crumpled letter resting on the bed beside her.

How lovely you must be, your body flushed from the force of your climax, your muscles sated and pliant. I wish I had been there to see you go weak beneath me. I'd kiss you to let you know how much you please me; then I would thrust into you hard until I gained my own release.

I can't convey to you how difficult it is to give you this pleasure and not find any for myself. But your pleasure is my pleasure, sweet Evelyn.

Have you forgotten about the handkerchief, my love? I have not. Use it to clean yourself, sweetheart. Coat it with your desire so when I bring it to my face, your scent will fill my lungs and I will never be without you, no matter where I am in the world.

If I may be so bold, I will pay you a visit upon my return later this week. Perhaps we can talk over dinner?

Until we meet again,
Yours,
Jimmy Doyle

Evelyn smoothed out the wrinkled papers. Then, after folding them, she carefully stuffed them back into the envelope and held the square to her chest. She should be horrified by the things he had written, but she wasn't. Oh, the things he asked her to do were beyond scandalous, but who was to know besides her? For all he knew, she might have burned his letters and gifts.

She should burn them. If anyone were to see them, the good name she'd taken such care to build for herself in her adopted city would vanish.

Still clutching the missive over her heart, she crossed to the dresser, where she placed it atop the first letter hidden beneath her winter stockings along with the gloves he'd sent. Just for tonight, she'd keep the handkerchiefs out. Then they too would be consigned to the bottom drawer for safekeeping.

CHAPTER FIVE

Jimmy Doyle grabbed his glove before trotting out to his position at first base. The team had arrived back in Washington late the previous evening—too late to decently call upon a single woman. He'd lain awake most of the night, wondering if Evelyn would even see him when he asked for her. When he'd written the letters, he had been so sure he'd read her correctly, but as time passed, his confidence waned. It wasn't like him to question his instincts, but things were different with Evelyn. She was different.

He prayed he hadn't lost her before he'd ever really had her.

"Hey, Jimmy Doyle!" He looked up in time to get his glove in front of his face and catch the ball the second baseman threw his way. "You awake?"

"I'm awake." He returned the throw, silently cursing himself for letting his focus wander. He had a game to play this afternoon. Then he would see if he'd misjudged Evelyn Gardner or not.

❧

Sweat trickled down his spine as he made the short walk from the trolley stop to Evelyn's boardinghouse. Part of it was due to the record heat, and part of it was worry over the reception awaiting him.

He hadn't misread her, had he? He could still see the interest

40

in her eyes when he'd clasped her hand across the table. The pulse in her throat had raced like a filly down the backstretch. She held the reins tight on her passion, but with a little luck, she'd let herself go with his letters. He'd find out soon enough. He turned the corner onto the tree-lined street where she lived.

Every window in the three-story red brick house was open to catch whatever breeze might blow. Even though the front porch sat in shadow, no one took advantage of the rockers or swing. As he approached, the sound of women's chatter and the clink of utensils on plates met his ears. He'd managed to arrive at suppertime. For a moment, he stood frozen on the top step, wondering if he should come back later or not at all.

Before he could decide, footsteps bounded down the interior stairs, and a woman appeared on the other side of the screened door. Evelyn.

"Jimmy Doyle." She sounded breathless—most likely from sprinting down the staircase—but it sounded like music to his ears.

He removed his hat and held it in front of him to shield his growing erection as he stepped fully onto the porch. "I hope I haven't come at a bad time."

She glanced over her shoulder, then back at him. "Wait there. I-I need to get my things. I'll be right down."

Turning to face the street, he rolled his shoulders, releasing the tension tying him in knots. She hadn't sounded angry, but then again, she'd obviously been hoping no one else saw them together. He moved down the steps, and stopped halfway between the porch and the sidewalk. If anyone came along, he could say he'd stopped to enjoy the shade of the old oak tree gracing the front lawn. In this sweltering heat, no one would question him on that score.

God, he wanted to believe she'd gone to retrieve the handkerchief as he'd instructed in his last letter. But there was a real possibility she had gone to get both gifts with the intention of throwing them in his face.

When she walked out of the door with nothing but her pocketbook, he breathed a silent sigh of relief. He smiled, moving forward to fall into step beside her. She seemed to be in a hurry, either to put distance between them and the boardinghouse, or she had a destination in mind. It was too damn hot to proceed at that pace. At the corner, he touched her elbow, bringing them to a stop.

"What's the rush?" She glanced back in the direction they'd come. Then, instead of meeting his gaze, she looked down at her feet. Her cheeks were flushed, but he had no idea how much of her color to attribute to the heat and how much to chalk up to embarrassment. "If you don't want to be seen with me, I understand."

Her gaze snapped to his long enough for him to see the uncertainty in her eyes. Then she turned her face away, focusing on something…or nothing. He didn't know which. What he did know was, he needed to get her to someplace where they could talk. The high hopes he'd had when she met him at the door were melting in the sun. It was time to take charge of the situation.

"If you want to go home, I won't stop you. However, if you walk away, you won't see me again. No more gifts. No more letters." He paused to let her absorb his meaning. For his sake as much as hers, she needed to decide if she wanted to continue. "Or you come with me. There's a park a few blocks away. We'll find a place to discuss what's bothering you."

He took heart in that she didn't look toward the boardinghouse again, though she wouldn't or couldn't look him in the eye. She turned her head, gazing at a point beyond his shoulder. He couldn't read a thing on her face, and that concerned him more than the fact that they were risking heatstroke standing on the street corner without benefit of shade. If they were to continue, the ability to read her expressions was imperative.

With a faint nod, she headed off in the direction of the park. He followed a few steps behind, admiring the way her hips swayed and the delicate line of her shoulders. The thin cotton dress she wore did nothing to hide her womanly curves. Her calves were slim and toned, no doubt from her daily walks to and from the trolley stop. Undressing her was going to be pure pleasure.

The park was mostly deserted, surprising, given the heat sucking the life out of the city. Evelyn selected a bench beneath a shade tree and sat, clutching her pocketbook in her lap as if afraid it was going to jump up and run off on its own. He studied her for a second, then joined her on the bench. Silence enveloped them. It seemed even the birds and insects were conserving their energy.

"How have you been?"

"Fine." She looked his way, gracing him with the tiniest of smiles before looking away again. "Hot."

He didn't know how much he had wanted to see her smile until she did. His core temperature rose to match the sun's. Hot didn't come close.

"You received the gifts I sent? The letters?"

"Yes." She adjusted her purse. "I— You—"

"You can say anything to me," he said, giving her time to find the words she searched for. "No one will hear you, and I promise you, no matter what it is, I will never be angry with you."

BEFORE THINGS WENT any further, she had to tell him, give him the opportunity to walk away from whatever it was between them. "I have to tell you something."

"I'm listening."

"I'll understand if you change your mind about me."

"I won't."

He sounded so sincere she almost believed him. But even the local church had denied her membership because of her secret, so she held little hope a public figure like Jimmy Doyle would want to be associated with a woman like her. Still, she had to tell him. It was the only honorable thing to do. "I'm divorced."

"That changes nothing for me, Evelyn. Someday you'll tell me all about it, but for now, can we get back to what we're here for?"

A couple of boys on bicycles circled the park, then rode off down a side street in a cloud of dust. Evelyn watched them go, then turned to face the man she'd been dreaming about for the past three weeks. He was more handsome than she remembered.

There was an air of confidence about him that made her believe him when he said her past didn't matter and she couldn't anger him. The words he'd written to her conveyed the same self-assured, calm manner. It had coaxed her to do things that, in the light of day, she could hardly believe she'd done. How could she find the words to tell this man how much his letters and gifts meant to her? The only other person she'd allowed to see her carnal desires had condemned her for them, but Jimmy Doyle encouraged them.

She squirmed on the hard seat. Just thinking about touching herself made her ache with need. Yet…he understood. He'd sent the gifts for the express purpose of having her stroke her inner demons to life. As if her desires were normal. Could they be?

She had no idea. After the things her ex-husband had said to her, she didn't dare discuss her physical needs with anyone else. But for some reason, she sensed Jimmy Doyle would be proud of what she'd done, not disgusted.

Hands shaking, she opened her pocketbook, took out the handkerchief she'd cleaned herself with the previous week, and clutched it tight. Handing it to him would say more than any words she might come up with. Handing it over would be tantamount to admitting to doing everything he'd told her to do in his letters. And what other conclusion could he draw from that, except she invited more of the same? Perhaps he'd even think she wanted…him.

Would that be so bad? He was a good man—a solid man. Still, the handkerchief was a test. She'd recognized that from the beginning. The only thing left to discover was if by handing it over she passed or failed. If she failed, would she be any worse off than she had been before she met the baseball player? She'd been alone and afraid to let any man get close. But if she passed his test, what kind of sensual delights might he show her next?

Understanding she had nothing to lose, she looked straight ahead and held the scrap of expensive soiled cloth out to him. Both of his hands closed over hers, encapsulating them in his heat. She bit her bottom lip to stop it from quivering. He was holding her hand. Nothing more, but the gesture meant so much more.

"Look at me, Evelyn."

Why was he making this so difficult? Why couldn't he just take the cloth and go away? The letters were enough, weren't they?

She was being unfair to him. He had his needs too. He'd said as much in his letters. It made sense that he'd want more from her. She wanted to give him more, but she wasn't sure she could.

He repeated the command. This time his tone implied he wouldn't take no for an answer. Evelyn forced a breath in, out, and turned to face him.

His smile held a bank vault of understanding, as if he knew how much it had cost her to face him. His hands, wrapped around hers, held her in a gentle but firm embrace, yet she felt certain she could pull away at any time and he'd let her go.

"The choice is always yours, sweetheart. We'll always proceed at your pace, not mine. I know you feel you have made a decision, but I want you to think on what I'm about to say. If your decision is still the same afterward, then, and only then, will I accept your gift."

"But—"

He shook his head. "Yes, what you are giving me is a gift. I'm not talking about the handkerchief, Evelyn. It's only a symbol of what I want from you. I will take nothing you do not freely offer. I will put your pleasure, your needs, before my own. I want and need things from you that will shock you, but I believe you possess the kind of passion that needs expression beyond what society labels appropriate. I will never cause you harm. There are many ways to achieve pleasure, and I want to show them all to you. Let me say it again—I will not take anything you do not freely offer. In return, I pledge you everything I am. I will command your body, but the power to stop what is happening or to end our relationship altogether will always be yours."

He moved closer, resting their hands on his thigh. "Think about it as long as you want. I'll answer any questions you have. Then, when you have made your decision, either remove your hand or entrust the handkerchief into my care."

Her heart threatened to beat right out of her chest. She was sure she looked a mess, having run out of the house without a care for her appearance. Jimmy Doyle, however, looked dapper in a white dress shirt and tan slacks held up with suspenders. In deference to the heat, he'd loosened his tie and rolled his sleeves up to expose muscled forearms. Just looking on such a blatant display of masculinity made her tingle inside. Imagining his hands on her, touching her the way she'd touched herself, and more, made her knees weak.

She was grateful he'd given her time to think about what he'd said, even if all she could think about was him. What he was asking sounded ominous, considering she had very little experience with men. Telling her he wanted things that would shock her wasn't news, and she knew all too well the limits to what society deemed appropriate. She'd tried to live within those parameters, and she'd succeeded until she met Jimmy Doyle. Denying her attraction to the man was useless. Her body betrayed her in wicked ways, craving things she had no words to describe. But she sensed the man sitting beside her not only knew the words, but he knew how to fulfill her needs—and he'd do it without censure.

She had no choice. Going back to living the way she had been before she met him wasn't possible. As far as she was concerned, she'd served her time for something she didn't consider a crime. He was offering her a chance to live again, and she was going to take it, even if she didn't have a clue what his words meant. One thing she understood—and she was going to cling to it—was his promise not to harm her. Maybe it was the way his voice hadn't wavered when he made the promise. Or perhaps it was the way he held her hand protectively in both of his, but she believed him.

"You won't do anything I don't want to do?" She wanted to hear him make the promise one more time.

"You can say no at any time, and I'll stop. We can discuss what's happening, if you want to. The decision to go forward is always yours, just as it is right now."

She closed her eyes against the setting sun. Despite the record heat, a chill raced down her spine when she considered what she was about to do. The only other time she'd dared to follow her instincts had ended in disaster. Years later, she understood denying her needs wasn't an option. Perhaps it was wrong to want the things she did, but it didn't feel wrong. Not with Jimmy Doyle.

Evelyn breathed deeply, then let it out. Opening her eyes, she turned to her companion. "I don't even know the questions I should ask."

"I don't expect you to, but the questions will come. When they do, we'll talk about them."

A few weeks ago her path had been mapped out for her. She knew every brick beneath her feet and where every turn would take her. Her future had been cloaked in gray, everything looking the same for as far as she could see. There was safety in knowing there were no surprises in store for her.

Ah, but life, it seemed, had more surprises in store than she'd thought. Since she'd met Jimmy Doyle, her life had taken on color. The signposts telling her which way to go had disappeared, leaving her confused and frightened. But if there was one thing she understood about life, it was that you couldn't go back. You could only go forward. There was no map for the path before her, but this man was offering to be her guide. All she had to do was trust him.

In the shelter of his hands, she released her grip on the handkerchief, entrusting her body, her life, her soul to him.

HE WAS ALMOST grateful for the heat. Anyone would assume the sweat trickling down his temples and spine was a result of the weather rather than the anxiety clawing at him while he waited for Evelyn to come to a decision. He'd asked a lot of her. She'd been married, but compared to him, she was innocent. If she handed over the handkerchief, he had every intention of initiating her to his sexual preferences. Ever since he'd held her against him on the side of the road the day they'd met, he'd imagined all the things he wanted to do to her. She had no idea the kinds of things awaiting her if she was brave enough to accept his offer.

He'd have to take it slow with her. Even though he sensed her passions ran deep and dark, her knowledge of his world was nil. Like he'd done with the gloves and handkerchiefs, he'd reveal his needs one at a time. Once she became comfortable, he'd introduce her to another delight. He'd gradually solicit her trust until she gave him everything. Then, and only then, would he take her in the way he so desperately wanted.

Until then, he had to give her every opportunity to walk away. Even if it killed him.

The sun hung over the treetops, a blazing orb that threatened to sear them both before it slipped low enough to cast them in shadow. Evelyn was as still beside him as the statue guarding the park entrance. He wanted her. He could still recall the sheen of perspiration on the back of her neck in that godforsaken tent, and how he'd wanted to lick it off. Not a day went by that he didn't think about all the ways he could use his tongue on her.

Sitting this close, her scent wrapped around him and made his mouth water. If she gave him the handkerchief, one of the first things he was going to do would be to taste her. She probably had no idea a man could want such a thing, but she'd learn soon enough. If she were his, he'd begin every day with his face buried between her thighs and end every day with his cock inside her. And in between, he'd taunt her until she begged to come.

But first, she had to give him the handkerchief.

Baseball had taught him many things, not the least of which was patience. Waiting for the right pitch had its own rewards, but waiting without vigilance did no good. It didn't matter how perfect the pitch; if the batter wasn't prepared to swing, nothing would come of it.

When her fingers unfurled, he was ready. He clamped his hands together, trapping her and the scrap of cloth between them, silently conveying a message of safety. Her gaze fell to their only point of contact and held steady. She'd taken an enormous step. It was time to lead her further down the path.

"I want to see you again. Alone. When is your next day off?"

He liked the way she didn't hesitate to tell him what he wanted to know. Teaching her was going to be a pleasure. Together, they decided on a mutually acceptable date and time to see each other again. With the handkerchief still secured between them, he walked her back to the boardinghouse. In the shaded yard he drew her around to face him, closing the distance between them so her nose almost brushed his chest. "Don't move, sweet Evelyn."

He counted the seconds in his mind until a minute had passed. She needed to become accustomed to being near him and, more importantly, heeding his instructions. Every cell in his body was attuned to hers, wanting more than the tentative contact of palms separated by linen. Soon, he told himself.

He pitched his voice low so there was no danger of anyone overhearing. "You aren't to touch yourself again until I tell you to. From now on, your body is mine. Do you have a dress that buttons down the front?"

"No."

"I'll give you money to buy one." She tensed, but he squeezed her hand, shutting down her protest before she voiced it. She'd been on her own for long enough. It was time she learned to let someone else take care of her. "Wear it the next time we meet."

Needing more physical connection with her, he rubbed his chin on the top of her head. Almost immediately he felt the tension leave her body. "Good girl. I should punish you for even thinking of defying me, but I realize how new it is for you to let me take care of you. You gave me the handkerchief, and when I walk away today with it in my hand, you become my responsibility. I will take care of your needs, sweetheart. All of them. In return, you will do as I say. I'll want you to dress in certain ways for me. It wouldn't be right to put that burden on you, so you will accept the money I provide for those items. It will please me to see you in a dress that buttons in the front from neck to hem. Do you understand?"

He smiled as she nodded. "That's my girl." She was a quick learner, though he knew this was one of the easiest things she would have to accept. Holding fast to her hand, he took a half step back and, with his free hand, reached into his pocket. He withdrew a five-dollar bill. Holding it up between them, he caught her gaze. "Buy something nice. Spend every bit of this if need be."

She wanted to protest; he could see it in her eyes and the color highlighting her cheekbones. It was a lot of money for a dress, but he didn't want her to skimp. He'd said he would take care of her, and he meant it. Seeing her in fine clothes would be worth every cent. "Take the money, sweetheart."

He lowered his hand to meet hers, shielding the transaction from prying eyes. Once she'd slipped the currency into a pocket on her dress, he asked, "Are you going to be all right?" Their talk today had to have been taxing on her, and this latest demand for her to dress to please him had to have shocked her.

"Yes. I think so."

"You're a very brave woman, Evelyn Gardner. You've given me a gift beyond measure, and I want you to know I value it more than my own life. You'll always be safe with me."

She studied his face for a moment. Then her gaze locked with his again. "I know."

He held her hand a bit longer, then pulled away, taking the handkerchief with him.

CHAPTER SIX

Evelyn usually grabbed a sandwich from the deli on the corner along with the other switchboard operators on her lunch shift, but today, she had something else in mind. She'd read in the newspaper about a place nearby where people gathered on the sidewalk to follow the baseball game taking place across town. Since meeting Jimmy Doyle, she'd developed an interest in the sport. The first time she'd picked up a discarded newspaper, she had to admit she'd been curious to see if he'd told her the truth. A single woman living alone couldn't be too cautious. He had sounded convincing when he talked about his baseball career, but seeing his name in the newspaper had eased her mind.

Ever since, she'd been on the lookout for discarded newspapers in order to keep up with the game. Reading about his success on the field made her feel closer to him. She felt as if she were leading a secret life, following the famous ballplayer by day while every night she read his letters in bed, pleasuring herself per his instructions.

It had only been four days since he'd told her not to touch herself without his permission, and though she'd routinely denied herself that feeling of abandon for years, the past few days seemed like an eternity.

Evelyn stopped short of the small crowd gathered around the

chalkboard mounted on the wall of the building. Other women skirted the group of men in business suits, but she appeared to be the only one interested in the score. She recognized the grid used to display the hits, runs, and errors per inning played. If not for the hours she'd spent studying the newspaper reports, she wouldn't have a clue what any of it meant. Trying to avoid drawing attention to herself, she crossed the street where a sorry excuse for a tree provided some shade. From there, she could see the board and eat the apple she'd picked up from a street vendor for lunch.

By the time she finished off the piece of fruit, the Diplomats were ahead by three runs. Unable to see the commentary below the score boxes, she had no way of knowing if Jimmy Doyle had contributed to the score or not. Heading back to work, she smiled to herself. Sneaking around to see a midgame score was silly, but in a way it made her feel more connected to him. As if checking on the progress of the game somehow created a link between them.

She made her way back to the switchboard, taking over her spot from the part-timer who rotated through the ranks, giving each of the regular operators a break. Feeling lighter for having ventured outside her comfortable environs, the rest of the afternoon seemed to fly by for her. When the evening shift arrived, Evelyn gathered her things and headed toward downtown. With a little luck, she could find a dress with buttons down the front before the shops closed for the day.

৵৵৵

"A package came for you today." Evelyn glanced at her landlady standing in the door leading to the dining room. "I put it in your room for you."

Evelyn swallowed hard and clutched the box from one of the best dress shops in Washington behind her pocketbook. It didn't take an accountant to figure out that she couldn't afford to purchase anything from such a shop. She'd hoped no one had taken note of the unusual amount of mail she'd received recently. It was too much to hope Jimmy Doyle's gifts wouldn't be noticed.

She plastered a smile on her face and turned toward the stairs. "Thank you, Mrs. Rubenstein. Sorry I'm late for supper. I'll be right down."

Without waiting for the older woman's reply, Evelyn raced up the stairs. Her landlady was nice enough, and a good cook, but Evelyn had learned at a young age to be wary of people who said they were doing her a favor. She dropped the items she'd carried up, the dress box and her pocketbook, next to the postmarked package sitting in the middle of her bed. She glanced around the room, looking for anything out of place. Everything appeared to be untouched. Knowing Mrs. Rubenstein would be counting the minutes until she came down to supper, she made a beeline for the one drawer she didn't want anyone nosing around.

Seeing everything appeared to be just as she'd left it, she smoothed a strand of hair back from her sweating temple and breathed a sigh of relief. She was dying to see what Jimmy Doyle had sent her, but the surprise would have to wait. She opened her windows wide before heading downstairs for the evening meal.

The disapproving look she received from Mrs. Rubenstein made Evelyn wish she'd stayed in her room. The woman had a strict policy regarding the behavior of the women she allowed to rent from her. No men were allowed in the house. Period. Dates could wait on the porch, but not a one was allowed to step over the threshold. A few renters had tried to sneak a man past the eagle-eyed landlady and had found themselves out on the sidewalk within hours of discovery.

Evelyn took a plate from the stack on the sideboard and filled it from the hot dishes arranged in precise order. Meat, vegetables, bread. Dessert was served once a week, on Sunday. As she helped herself to tonight's fare—roast beef, turnips, and biscuits—she tried to ignore the cold stare aimed at the center of her back. It didn't take a genius to figure out the old woman had taken note of the packages arriving for Evelyn, put their appearance together with the man coming to pick her up last weekend, and come to an unsavory conclusion regarding the chaste state of one of her longest tenants.

After downing her meal without tasting it, Evelyn returned to her room, locking the door behind her. She'd done nothing Mrs. Rubenstein could evict her for. Though she had no doubt the woman would have an apoplexy if she had any idea of the things Evelyn did alone in her room.

She went through her evening ritual, hanging her work frock before removing her undergarments. She wet a cloth and ran it over her body in hopes of cooling her skin to an acceptable, if not comfortable temperature. Not a breath of air stirred inside or outside. It was going to be another miserable night. Except she had another letter from Jimmy Doyle.

It didn't matter how hot the evening or what her landlady thought she knew. Jimmy Doyle's letters were like a gale-force wind sweeping through Evelyn's staid life. She'd lived by other people's rules her entire life—her father's, her ex-husband's, her landlady's. Others might think saying yes to Jimmy Doyle's rules wasn't any different, but it felt different. Instead of feeling boxed in, censured, she felt free for the first time in her life. If anyone had overhead their conversations, they wouldn't have found a thing to judge her on. Their words were carefully chosen to cloak a deeper meaning. It was as if they were talking in a code only the two of them could decipher.

Remembering his hand holding hers, the scrap of expensive linen trapped between them—so much more than a simple handkerchief—made a shiver, cold yet blazing, race along her skin. At odd times, she'd think about him and wonder if he carried the cloth square with him. Did he lift it to his face? After all these days, did it still smell of her arousal? Did he even think of her when they were apart?

She glanced at the parcel wrapped in brown paper and twine resting on her bed. Yes, he did think of her. Perhaps not as often as she thought of him, but the evidence of his steadfastness sat before her. She pulled his letter from her pocketbook, then sat on the bed, the crinkly envelope pressed to her chest. Her prudish landlady was correct—receiving gifts from a man wasn't proper. Every minute of her time in Washington, up until she'd met Jimmy Doyle, she'd been nothing but proper, and all she had to show for it was an endless stream of lonely nights.

She stared at the package, prolonging the thrill of discovering the contents, imagining what might be inside and the improper things he might ask her to do. When the suspense became too much to ignore, she worked the string loose and peeled the paper away. This box was pure white with gold lettering. The understated elegance of the script was designed to convey quality and exclusivity.

Evelyn closed her eyes and lifted the lid. When she opened her eyes and peeled away the thin tissue paper, she gasped. Inside lay a slip unlike any she had ever seen. The shoulder straps were bands of satin, so narrow they were almost nonexistent. She dared to slip her fingers inside the delicate bodice. The fabric felt like air, so sheer, to wear it would be like having nothing on at all.

Her hands trembled as she picked the garment up to examine the intricate and finely wrought details trimming the bosom and hem. She'd never seen anything so exquisite—so decadent. The garment was a pure luxury, nothing more. She could hardly wait to feel it against her skin. She quickly removed the last of her undergarments and pulled the slip over her head. It fell to her knees like a whisper against her skin. Never had she wished more for a dressing mirror than she did at that moment, though the fabric was so transparent she wasn't sure a mirror would reflect it. It must have cost a fortune.

Jimmy Doyle. Chagrined to have forgotten his letter, she found it beneath her discarded panties. Making herself comfortable on the bed, she pried the envelope open, being careful not to tear the flap. The sight of his bold scrawl sent a wave of heat coursing through her body. She shifted, lamenting the stifling summer heat turning her room into an oven.

My dearest Evelyn,

Even though we are of short acquaintance, I miss you more than I can say. I feel as if I've known you forever, but then I remember the few conversations we've had, and realize I know very little about you. Yet the things I do know are the only ones that truly matter. I know you are lovely, inside and out. I know your smile melts me, and that you do not do it often enough. I know bringing a smile to your lips more often is something I must strive to do.

I know when you look at me, I am captivated. I know I want to be the man you think you see when you look upon me. I know your passions run deep, and perhaps as dark as mine. I know you have entrusted me to guide you through the darkness and into the light.

I know I will do anything to be worthy of that trust.

I dwell in darkness, but you are like the brightest ray of sunlight, and I am drawn to your luminescence like a moth is drawn to a flame. You have the power to destroy me, but without you, I would be wrecked anyway.

You should see me, sweet Evelyn. I write this with your handkerchief pressed to my face. Inhaling your essence is as necessary to me as air itself. I long to hold you in my arms, to feel your skin against mine, to bury my face in the crook of your neck, to taste you, to drink you in, to possess you. I can hardly function without touching or smelling your handkerchief. If I did not share a room on the road with my friend Harvey, I would sleep with your scent on my pillow, as I do at home.

Does that shock you, dearest? Is it too much, too soon to tell you how I feel? It's not near enough for me to write these words. I must put thoughts into actions soon or die a slow death.

Did you get the package I sent? When I saw the slip, I knew it was for you. If I could, I would wrap you in nothing but the finest silk. Though it is torture not to be able to see and touch you, I want to think about that magnificent fabric caressing your body as I long to. Tell me, lovely girl, does it mold to the curves of your breasts? Does it brush across your mound when you walk? Does it feel as if I am touching you? Can you imagine, as I do, my hands memorizing every inch of your body?

Imagine me touching you, sweet Evelyn. No gloves this time. I know how much you like feeling them on your skin, but they will be there for you another time. Today, we will explore new sensations. You must learn all the ways of pleasure from the faintest of touches to the tiny bite of pain—to the darkest of desires. *There is a time and place for each. Trust me, darling, to guide you with a gentle hand through all of them.*

Cradle your breast in your palm. The weight is delicious, my sweet. I am painfully aroused just thinking about holding your tender flesh in my palms. Your skin burns hot beneath the cool fabric of your slip. Are your nipples standing hard and proud, aroused by the lightest of touches?

You must not neglect the sweet tips, darling. Pinch your nipples. Don't let the pain make you shy. It will only last a second, but the pleasure to follow will be worth the momentary discomfort.

Her breast felt heavy with arousal, and her nipples were tight beads, aching for attention. She gave them both a quick pinch, barely flinching at the brief stinging sensation.

Do it again, my Evelyn. My fingers are strong; they will not be so forgiving. Pinch until you want to scream.

Placing his letter on the bed beside her, she drew in a fortifying breath, then pinched both nipples as hard as she could. Pain nearly blinded her. She bit her lower lip so only a strangled scream escaped. She held strong as long as possible before releasing her tortured flesh.

Picking up his letter, she read.

That's it, my precious girl. I can see them now, looking like bruised rosebuds following a summer storm.

If I were there, I would soothe the pain away with my mouth, but since I am not, the task is yours. Lick your fingers, my passionate one, then wet the aching nubs. Do not have a care for your beautiful new slip. It will be that much lovelier for the evidence of your pleasure that will remain. I will walk around with a rod in my slacks, thinking of the stiff patches rubbing against your nipples all day long, as my tongue yearns to do.

When I close my eyes, I see your face bravely bearing the pain, only to light from within once the pleasure floods your system. Oh, what you do to me, Evelyn. I am a slave to your pleasure. My mouth waters thinking of suckling at your breast. My hands are jealous of yours, so much so it is difficult to pen this letter. I need to touch you, and I will. Soon.

Has the pain become something more, my darling? I know it has. I can almost smell the arousal dampening the soft folds between your legs. Oh, if only I were there to make the longing go away, but once again, it is up to you.

Put your hand on your stomach, precious girl. Feel the slide of silk across your skin, so cool, so light—a whisper. It feels good, doesn't it? If it were up to me, you would wear nothing but the finest silks and cottons against your skin—for your pleasure, and mine.

Are you wet for me, my precious Evelyn? As has become my habit, I've pressed your handkerchief to my face in order to savor your scent. Inhale deeply, my love.

Evelyn dropped the hand holding the letter to the bed and placed the other over her racing heart. Between the oppressive heat and Jimmy Doyle's words stealing the air from her lungs, breathing had become near impossible. She took a moment to let her heart rate settle; then she closed her eyes and drew in a deep breath. The musk of her arousal filled her lungs. Need, powerful and consuming, overtook her.

She longed for a lover's embrace. The need to touch herself, to put an end to the physical need, even if the spiritual need remained, shook her to the core.

When her limbs ceased trembling, she picked up the hopelessly crumpled letter and continued to read.

Does the smell of your own arousal increase your need? It does, doesn't it? You are so perfect, sweet girl. A woman of deep passion is to be treasured.

Seek out your treasure now, lovely one. Let your fingers glide across your stomach to the swell of your womanhood. How beautiful the shadow of your curls must be beneath the silk. Pull your heels close to your bottom, then let your knees fall wide. Open yourself to me.

She drew her legs up, the slip bunching and gathering over her mound. As she opened her legs to her imaginary lover, heat that had nothing to do with the temperature of the room rushed to her cheeks. She'd never exposed herself to anyone this way, not even her ex-husband. She imagined Jimmy Doyle looking at her. Would his eyes light with desire? Would he touch her the way she longed to be touched?

Does it excite you to think of me between your legs, looking upon your most secret places? I could not bear it if you were to hide your body from me. I am so hard for you, my darling. Even though my discomfort is near impossible to bear, I will continue, for leaving you unfulfilled would pain me more than anything.

Explore farther, sweet Evelyn. Make a V with two fingers and press the silk into the secret recesses so your pearl is held prisoner by the fabric.

She followed his instructions, forcing the slip into her creases, rubbing up and down a few times. The friction of her fingers sliding against the trapped skin brought a moan to her lips. Her hips moved, seeking more.

Does your clitoris throb against its confinement? The little jewel needs attention, my love. Use your thumb to tease it. Flick it. Scrape your fingernail over it, then press down and rub your thumb in a circular motion.

She knew the right amount of pressure to apply and had discovered the technique of a circular motion on her own, desperately seeking relief on many dark and lonely nights. But this felt different. Maybe it was the silk organza or that tonight, she had a face to put with the anonymous man she imagined doing these things to her. Every tiny flick, every circuit of her thumb felt more intense, more insistent. She could hardly breathe. Need coiled tight and low in her belly.

Yes, like that, darling. I can see your breath growing short. I can smell your heightened arousal. You need to come, to feel the exquisite release from earth's bonds.

59

Do you feel wicked, my passionate one, sitting there, your legs open, playing with yourself? I can't imagine anything lovelier, sweet one, unless it was my hand between your legs. My fingers moving lower to find the gate to your treasure. Do it for me, lovely Evelyn. Press the silk past the inner gates. Drive it deep inside you so your honey soaks through to your fingers.

Evelyn hesitated. Wetting the organza would ruin it, but he knew it would. Just as he had known what it would do to the handkerchief. An image flashed through her mind—Jimmy Doyle bringing a scrap of cloth to his face, his eyes closing, a smile curving his lips as he inhaled her scent.

The image broke down her resistance. Evelyn bit her lower lip for courage, then plunged her cloth-wrapped finger into her channel.

She moaned, relaxing back on the bed to enjoy the new sensation of silk sliding along her inner walls. It added a new, exciting dimension to the finger play she'd become accustomed to in her masturbation sessions.

As wonderful as it felt, there was more. With Jimmy Doyle, there was always more, and wasn't that the reason she had given him the handkerchief? Because he promised more than she could even imagine?

Evelyn read.

Do it again, my love. Harder. Faster. Two fingers now. Fill yourself as I long to.

I can almost see you, my darling. How beautiful you look, fucking yourself with the slip I bought you. Your lips are parted, begging to be kissed. Wet them, Evelyn. Beg me to kiss you. Ah, yes, like that. I cannot deny you anything, my sweet. I feel your muscles tightening like a spring. Your eyes are growing soft as your every thought is centered on the need growing desperate between your legs.

Add another finger, darling. Stretch your treasure hole. Fill it. Fuck it hard. God, you are fucking beautiful like this, all sensual woman bringing yourself pleasure. If I could paint, I would paint you like this for the world to see. Beauty such as this should not be hidden behind closed doors. It should not be reviled, but celebrated for the miracle it is.

Come for me, my precious love. Let go of the invisible shackles binding your pleasure. Break free, dear one.

Evelyn worked her fingers, pushing in, pulling out, fluttering her fingertips against the sensitized walls. Her hips rode her palm, rhythmically pressing her clit against the heel of her hand. The bedsprings screeched with every movement, but she was beyond caring if the other tenants heard and guessed what she was doing. Relief was one, two plunges away.

The orgasm broke over her like a wave, rolling her under, stealing the air from her lungs, and battering her body. She closed her legs tight, holding her hand captive as she rode out wave after wave of pleasure so intense they brought tears to her eyes.

Long minutes later, the tension eased, leaving her feeling euphoric and wrung out all at the same time.

She'd almost forgotten Jimmy Doyle's letter.

Yes! My God, it is beautiful to witness such a sacred thing as a woman being the sensual creature she was born to be.

Can you breathe again, my darling? Close your legs so your fingers are trapped inside you. Rub the heel of your hand over your clitoris and your mound. Ah, your flesh is so sensitive now, the lightest touch is almost more than you can bear, isn't it? You think touching yourself is torture, but there are ways to draw more pleasure from your sated body. I promise to show them to you someday soon.

When the ache subsides, my beautiful love, tug the silk free from your treasure hole. Smooth it over your body and let the fabric dry. I can hardly wait to see the splotches, badges that represent your passion, covering the most womanly parts of your body.

I return to Washington later this week. Take a drive with me, sweetheart. I want to be alone with you. I'll pick you up Sunday morning at nine. Wear the dress I asked you to purchase, and the slip you are wearing now. Do not try to clean it. I want to see the evidence of your passion.

Until we are together,
Jimmy Doyle

CHAPTER SEVEN

Smoothing the expensive fabric over her body brought a rush of memories to the forefront—thoughts she'd tried to put out of her mind since the night she'd first worn the slip. She'd worn the soiled garment until the damp spots had dried, then folded it and placed it, and the accompanying letter, in the bottom dresser drawer that was rapidly filling with gifts from Jimmy Doyle.

The stains over her nipples where he'd taken her into his mouth had grown faint, hardly noticeable unless she turned just so. She placed her hand over the splotch marking the juncture of her legs. The organza had dried opaque, somewhat crusty, and wrinkled where she'd forced the fabric inside her body. The garment was positively indecent. She'd be humiliated beyond belief if anyone saw it.

Jimmy Doyle wanted to see it. She imagined lifting her skirt for him. Would he be pleased she'd followed his instructions? Or would she be subjected to another rejection? Old memories filled with the pain of being called a slut, a whore, overlaid her imaginings. Fear racked her body. She'd sacrificed her entire life for a few moments of pleasure.

The bedsprings creaked beneath her weight. She wiped her clammy palms on the bedspread while she stared at the new button-down frock hanging on a peg next to her Sunday best. If she closed her eyes, she could see his hands working the buttons free. Or would he want her to undress for him? She grabbed the pillow and clutched it to her chest as memories rushed in.

Her father had preached another of his put-the-fear-of-God-in-you sermons on the evils of sodomy. As long as she could remember, he'd postulated about that particular sin, more than any other. As a teenager with an awakening body, she'd been curious, wondering what made that sin worse than others. One day when her father and mother were attending the funeral of one of the parishioners, Eve sneaked into her father's library to search for answers to her questions. She'd been shocked to discover the nature of the sin, and intrigued too. That night, alone in her room, she'd touched that part of her body for the first time. She could still remember her surprise at finding out how sensitive the area was.

She'd been innocent on her wedding night. Her new husband had made her wait long minutes for him to come to their bed. When he did appear, ready to consummate their vows, he'd wasted no time. He pushed her nightgown to her waist and shoved his member inside her. The excruciating pain of his penetration had eclipsed all her anticipation of becoming a woman. For the next two years, he rarely demanded his husbandly rights, and when he did, he'd demanded she take his member into her mouth until he grew hard. Then it was her wedding night all over again. He didn't look at her body, didn't touch her other than to shove inside her. A few quick thrusts and he was done.

Evelyn had learned to pleasure herself during the lonely days she spent at home while he worked their small farm.

They'd been on their way home from church. The silence between them had become deafening the past few months, but she'd been brought up to believe marriage was sacred. Unable to fathom a lifetime of silence, she had decided to engage her husband in conversation.

"Father preaches often on the sin of sodomy. I'm not sure I even know what it is. I mean…I think I do, but—"

Curtis grabbed her arm, pulling her to a stop in the middle of the dirt road leading to their house. *"What do you think you know?"*

His eyes were alight with something, she didn't know what. He'd never looked at her that way before, as if he wanted to shake her or worse. She tried to back away, but he tightened his hold on her upper arm. *"Tell me, Eve. What do you know of sodomy?"*

"Nothing. Just what I've read." In retrospect, she'd been stupid. She should have kept her mouth shut. *"It's like making love, but…not. I don't understand what is so wrong about it."*

"You don't, do you?"

She shook her head. *"No. I know it's a sin, but I can't help but wonder what it would feel like."*

"Do you really want to know, Eve?"

He was close to her now, towering over her, pressing his body into hers. He was hard, and she hadn't even had to help him get that way. Excitement and desire made her reckless. *"Will you show me?"*

God help her, she fluttered her eyelashes at him, flirting with him as she never had before. He wasn't a particularly attractive man; being nearly thirty years her senior, he had always reminded her of her father—same build, same smooth skin, same full lips and thinning hair. But he was her husband. The Bible commanded her to lie with him, and she had always been obedient to the Lord. She'd remained quiet, never asking for more than he was willing to give, but her body was starved for attention.

"You don't know what you're asking, but you're going to find out." He practically dragged her up the front steps, then paused before opening the door. *"Just remember, you asked for this."*

Like she could ever forget her fall into disgrace.

After hauling her by her arm into the bedroom, he released her. *"Take your drawers off and lay on the bed, face-first. I'll be right back."*

Eve removed her shoes, then her drawers, folding them neatly and setting them on the ladder-back chair in the corner of the room. Curtis was in the kitchen. She could hear him opening and closing cabinets, looking for something. She had no idea what, but desire had a hold on her. As long as he came back to her, showed her what she had fantasized about for years, she didn't care what he did to her kitchen.

When he returned, shutting the door behind him, she was face down on the bed, the chenille spread making dents in her cheek. Her sex had become wet, something she understood went along with her arousal. She wondered if he would notice since she'd only experienced the telltale moisture when she fondled herself.

Something landed on the nightstand with a clatter. Eve jerked her head up to see the tin of lard she kept next to the stove. *What?*

"Scoot to the edge, feet on the floor." Curtis grabbed her ankle and pulled her toward him. In the process of getting her feet on the floor, her skirt rode up to her waist. Her husband's hand on her back pinned her torso to the mattress. *"Spread your legs."*

Aided by his kick to her instep, Eve moved her feet. Rough hands grabbed her buttocks, prying the globes apart. Curtis grunted something unintelligible before he released her. His suspenders snapped, a sound she'd become familiar with listening to him undress for bed. A moment later his hairy legs brushed the insides of her thighs, and his hard, heavy erection rested along the upper crest of her bottom.

Eve clutched at the bedspread and listened to the sounds of her husband's preparations. The scrape of tin on wood. The squishing of fingers digging into the thick goo. The rattle of tin settling back on the nightstand.

She gasped when he smeared a glob of lard down the seam of her ass. *"It's still gonna hurt like hell, but this will make it better—at least for me."*

Eve tensed at the mention of pain. She'd thought she knew what sodomy was, but now that she was on the brink of the act, she wasn't entirely certain she wanted to go through with it. Would his member even fit in her backside?

His staff slid between her cheeks, up and down until he found her hole and fitted himself against it. She thought her heart was going to beat out of her chest. He felt impossibly hard, a sign he physically wanted her. The power in knowing her husband desired her allayed her fear of the actual act. She wanted this. She'd never been so excited in her life. Moisture slicked the insides of her thighs. He pressed harder against her opening.

The pressure of his member seeking entrance stole her breath. Her intimate parts tingled, begging for attention. For the first time ever, she desired her husband. She wanted him to join with her, to make the ache between her legs go away.

He breached the tight ring of muscles with one powerful stroke. Eve screamed as he drove his thick rod deep inside her. His balls ricocheted off her clit, then came back to rest against her wet folds. The pain blinded her, but only for a moment. Then she began to feel the fullness, the stretch. His balls hanging loose against her throbbing sex excited her. She hoped to heaven this wasn't all there was, and she said so. *"Please."*

"You want more?"

"Yes." The word was barely a whisper, but he heard. He pulled all the way out, then slammed back in, filling her, tapping her clit with his heavy sac. Her eyes rolled back in her head, and she moaned her satisfaction.

He drove into her, again and again until she was delirious with the feel of being taken so thoroughly. The coil of tension she'd come to know on her own began to build deep in her gut. A few more strokes was all it took. The orgasm was the most powerful she'd ever experienced. Moisture flooded her legs, coating Curtis's balls. In her euphoric state, she heard him speak, but surely, she'd misheard.

Curtis came, spewing his seed and curses in equal measure. *"Fucking whore. Going to hell. Sodomite. Devil's temptress. Evil Satan's wife."*

Before she knew what was happening, she stood in her father's office, head bowed, arousal and semen running down her bare legs while her husband accused her of being in league with the devil. She thought she'd known shame, but not until Curtis lifted her skirt, swiped his fingers between her legs, and presented the evidence of her depravity to her father. Only a whore's body craved a man's.

Curtis got on his knees to beg forgiveness for being weak, for letting himself be led down the sinner's path.

When the two of them were done with her, her knees bled from hours of kneeling to pray on thorns her father said reminded him of Christ's crown. She'd prayed for forgiveness, for cleansing, for salvation of her soul, for release from Satan's harem.

It had all been in vain. Years later, she still craved the sins of the flesh. Still craved a man's touch. Still felt the wicked desires that had been the end of her marriage.

The guilt of being a sinner, beyond redemption, still weighed on her. But for the first time since that horrible day, she was beginning to think perhaps her desires weren't sins at all. Jimmy Doyle had opened her mind to the possibility that pleasure wasn't a mortal sin, but a blessing.

But what if he was like her ex-husband? What if he led her down the road to wickedness only to leave her there all alone when he was done with her? The first time had rocked her to the core—a second time would destroy her.

The sound of an automobile stopping in front of the boardinghouse drew her back into the present. She peeked through the curtains. He stood on the sidewalk in front of an older-model Ford. He was dressed for either church or sin. She suspected the latter was the case, and the thought shot through her, straight to the flesh between her legs. Her heart lodged in her throat at the decision facing her. She could sit in her room and pretend he wasn't there until he gave up and went away. Or she could put on the dress he wanted to see her in and spend a few hours with the man she craved with her body and soul.

As if he sensed her watching him, he glanced up at her window. His gaze was direct, open, and honest. If she left with him, he would expect to see what she'd done to the slip, and possibly more. Though she was naive in many ways, she understood he wanted more from her than polite friendship. And if she was honest with herself, she needed more from him.

Evelyn hurried away from the window to finish dressing. Her hands trembled as she fastened rayon stockings to her garter belt. The buttons on the front of her dress were easier. She slipped on her best shoes and grabbed her pocketbook and gloves from the dresser as she raced out the door.

"Evelyn." The way he said her name, as if he were claiming her, sent a bolt of awareness through to her body. His gaze held hers, but she sensed he saw past her clothes, past her fears all the way to her core.

"Jimmy Doyle."

He smiled at her proper tone, then extended his hand. She ducked her head and, placing her hand in his, let him lead her to his automobile. He settled her in the passenger seat as if she were someone special, then came around to the driver's side and started the car.

He navigated the busy streets until they were out of town, traveling dirt roads lined with plowed fields and the occasional row of trees marking property lines. Farmhouses dotted the landscape but grew fewer the longer they drove. With every mile they put between them and the city, Evelyn felt more tension leave her body. The rumble of the engine coupled with the air blowing through the open windows made it next to impossible to talk, but every so often, her skin would tingle and she'd glance around to find Jimmy Doyle looking at her.

He made no apology for his brazen behavior. His lips would quirk up in a lopsided grin; then he'd turn his attention back to the road. By the time he steered the automobile down a narrow path through a grove of trees, her body hummed with anticipation.

"It's not much farther," he said, slowing to avoid a deep rut carved into the lane. "I think you'll like it here."

"Where are we?"

"A friend of mine owns this place. Hardly anyone knows about this access to the river, so we'll have the place to ourselves."

A few minutes later they emerged from the woods onto the

bank of a wide river. He parked beneath the branches of an oak that was a century old, if it was a day. Its limbs extended out over the water, shading the bank. The summer heat had dried most of the grass to a crispy brown, but here, it was soft and green, thanks to the benevolent tree and the river.

"It's beautiful," she said, admiring the scenery as she climbed from the car. She breathed deep, taking in air laden with moisture. "Thanks for bringing me here."

Jimmy Doyle wrestled a picnic basket from the backseat. He set it beside the car, then spread a blanket on the grass next to the front wheel. Evelyn walked closer to the water. Every cell in her body vibrated with awareness, but the fear she'd thought she put to rest back in her room was rearing its ugly head again.

As beautiful as this place was, she was alone with a man who wanted to do things to her body. She'd gone back and forth so many times—her body warring with her mind—that she was tired of thinking. She wanted to feel. She wanted to go to a place where there was no uncertainty, where there were no decisions to make. She wanted to feel alive but know, no matter what, she was safe.

She sensed his presence before he wrapped his arms around her waist from behind and pulled her back snug against his front. He'd taken off his suit coat and rolled the sleeves of his shirt to his elbows. Evelyn placed her hands on his very masculine forearms. Lightly dusted with hair, the muscles felt like thick strands of rope.

"Relax, sweet one. I won't hurt you." His lips nuzzled her neck just below her ear. His warm breath feathering over her skin made her shiver all the way to her toes. She tilted her head, allowing him better access. "Remember, we do nothing you don't want to do."

How was she supposed to know if she wanted to do something or not? She knew next to nothing about what men and women did together. Since he knew she'd been married, he probably assumed she had more experience than she did. She should tell him the truth before things went any further.

"Do you want me to do this, sweet Evelyn?" One hand

skimmed upward to close over her breast.

Evelyn closed her eyes and let her head fall against his shoulder. "Yes," she whispered. Her breast grew heavy; her nipple thrust out, begging for attention.

"And this?" His thumb brushed the hard peak, eliciting a moan from her. "I'll take that as a yes." He switched hands, giving her other breast the same attention while his mouth roamed up and down her throat, stealing her inhibitions one nibble at a time.

"You need more, sweetheart."

Yes. Oh, yes. More.

"Say it, Evelyn. Ask for what you want."

"Touch me. Please."

He squeezed her breast hard. Evelyn cried out even as she arched her back, pressing her bosom into his hand. "When you speak to me, you will do so with respect. Try again, Evelyn. *Touch me. Please, Sir.*"

Her mind whirled, processing the change in his voice and demeanor. He'd taken charge in the span of a minute. A frisson of fear racked her body.

"I won't hurt you, precious girl. I only want to make you feel good. Now, ask me politely for what you want."

Her fear dissolved under the spell of his voice and the way his hands were making promises she prayed they'd keep. "Please, Sir. Touch me."

"Much better. Good girls are to be rewarded." His praise felt like a baptism, washing away the past.

His hand slipped inside her bodice, beneath her slip to find her tender flesh. "Your breasts are perfect." His fingers explored, brushing over her nipple, varying the sensation from hard to a butterfly touch. As before, he switched sides, repeating his movements until he knew every inch of her bosom. When he withdrew his hands, she whimpered at the loss of contact.

"Shh, sweet girl. We're not through." With his hands on her waist, he held her upright while he circled around to face her. "Look at me, Evelyn."

She tilted her face up to meet his implacable gaze. "Unbutton the dress for me. I want to see what you've done to my slip."

His slip. Yes, it was his. He had a right to see what she'd done to it. Would the evidence of her depravity change his mind about her? Would he reject her once he saw for certain how her body craved the sins of the flesh?

Her hands trembled on the top button. She jerked her gaze from his as the fastener slid free. Suddenly, one of his hands covered both of hers, stilling her movement. His other hand went to her chin, lifting her face to his. "Don't hide anything from me. No matter what. I will never punish you for something I told you to do, and I will never punish you for something you have no control over." His eyes searched hers. "Do you understand, Evelyn? You are safe with me."

Her bottom lip quivered, and tears blurred her vision. She'd once thought she was safe in her marriage, but that had been an illusion. She'd thought her father would protect her, but that too had been false. She shouldn't believe Jimmy Doyle's promises, but she did. "Yes." His eyes narrowed. "Sir," she added.

The smile he gave her weakened her knees. She leaned into him, their hands clasped between their bodies. He placed a hand on the small of her back, lending her his strength. "I need to see you, sweet one. Be strong and complete the task I gave you. I promise to give you what you need, but you have to trust me."

CHAPTER EIGHT

"I do." Evelyn pushed away from him to stand firm on her own two feet. His steadying hand and his words helped her find her courage.

"Eyes on me," he said, taking a step backward. "Don't look away from my face. I want you to see me when I look upon what is mine."

What is mine. He might have been talking about the slip again, but she didn't think so. It was almost as if he owned her. As she slipped the next buttons loose, she thought about his comment and decided she liked the idea of being possessed by a man who didn't see a sinner when he looked at her.

She had to bend at the waist to reach the last few buttons, but she kept her gaze on his face the entire time. When she straightened, the dress open but revealing nothing but a thin band down the center, he stood statue still, his gaze riveted on her chest.

"Grab the lapels and pull the dress down your back, but only to your elbows. Don't take it all the way off."

She did as he said, letting the summer-weight cotton slide off her shoulders, revealing her upper torso and most of her lower body. His gaze darted back and forth across her chest, then slid lower, stopping over her crotch and the jagged-edged opaque spot, the evidence of her sinful conduct. His face was a mask she couldn't interpret. Her earlier confidence fled, leaving her shivering with anxiety.

His silence was killing her. She moved to cover herself.

"Don't." Evelyn stopped. "Never hide yourself from me." His gaze had gone from stone to desire in a flash, chasing away the chill of apprehension.

He closed the distance between them, pulling her against his hard body. Her arms were trapped by the dress, but she managed to put her hands on his waist to help steady herself. His erection branded her belly through the thin layer of silk organza. The thrill of his desire shot through her, filling her heart with joy. When he lifted her, fitting his mouth to hers, she surrendered. Other than once at the altar following her wedding, Curtis had never kissed her. Up until today, she hadn't thought she'd been missing anything. Now she knew differently. Jimmy Doyle's lips moved over hers, tutoring her in an act he had mastered—seducing her in ways she had never imagined in her solo explorations. Lost in the new sensations, she didn't realize they'd moved until he sank to his knees, taking her to the quilt with him. He broke the kiss to strip the dress from her, tossing it in a heap next to the picnic basket. On her knees, wearing nothing more than an indecent slip, garter belt, panties, and stockings, she crossed her arms over her stomach and prayed no one would come upon them.

Already bearing the stain of a sinner, her reputation would never recover if she were discovered in such a compromising position. Even as the warning raced through her mind, she knew the chance of ruin was one she was willing to take. The way he looked at her, the way her skin tingled when he touched her, the promises he'd made to her. She couldn't walk away from those things, not until she knew what they all meant.

"Look at me."

Evelyn looked up from the quilt square she'd been studying. The fire blazing in his eyes burned all her doubts to cinders. Like a starving woman at a buffet, she wanted whatever he was serving up. She might go to hell for it, but she was headed there anyway, so what was the difference?

"I will never hurt you." His gaze darted to her arms crossed protectively over her middle, then back up. "I only want to see you, touch you."

The sincerity in his voice, coupled with his calm demeanor, soothed her fears. Keeping her chin up, she focused on his face and let her arms fall to her sides.

His gaze traveled her torso as it had before, stopping on her breasts and again on the embarrassing patch lower down. Without looking back up, he reached for her. Hands on her waist, he drew her lower body against his. "Perfect. Absolutely perfect."

When his eyes met hers, the look of approval she saw there was like a balm to her soul. No one had ever thought she was perfect. It wasn't true, of course, but just for today, she wanted to believe him. She smiled. "I'm not, but thank you anyway."

He leaned in to nibble at her neck. "Let me show you, sweet Evelyn." He cupped her breast, gave it a light squeeze that sent a wave of need to the place between her legs. His breath was hot against her skin. "Lie back, arms over your head."

She hesitated. Then he nipped at her collarbone. "Do it, Evelyn."

She wasn't sure if he followed her down or if she went under his weight, but as soon as she was stretched out beneath him, the how of getting there no longer mattered. The feel of his body pressing against hers, all hard planes and angles fitting perfectly with her softer counterpoints, made her dizzy with desire.

One big hand pinned her wrists together above her head while the other explored along the side of her body, teasing her curves with a light touch from shoulder to midthigh. When she groaned, shifting beneath him in a wordless plea for more, he switched from nuzzling her neck to devouring her mouth.

His tongue stroked the seam of her lips. What was that for? She started to ask, but his tongue pushed inside, answering the question before she could ask it. Oh, sweet heaven! His hips and mouth worked in tandem, letting her know exactly what he wanted to do to her, promising her wicked pleasure like she'd never known. Evelyn picked up the rhythm, her tongue dancing with his until her entire body felt ready to explode.

When he broke the kiss, she moaned, struggling against his restraining hand. She wanted to touch him, to feel his skin against hers, to take him inside her and let him ease the burning need his kiss had stoked to roaring flames.

"Shh, sweet Evelyn." He calmed her with tiny kisses over her face, neck, and chest. "Still, girl, and I'll take care of you. I promise."

Evelyn closed her eyes and willed her body to cease struggling. Once she lay meek beneath him, he rose to his knees, straddling her, his weight pinning her hips to the ground.

"This is new to you, isn't it?"

Shame nearly choked her. "Yes."

"One of these days you're going to tell me about your marriage, but not today. Today, I want you to learn that you can trust me."

Her eyes popped open. She met his tender gaze with a fierce one of her own. "I do. I trust you."

He shook his head and began to unknot his tie. "Saying you trust and giving your trust are two different things. You have no idea what it means to trust a man like me. I'm going to show you." He leaned down, bracing himself over her on outstretched arms. The necktie he held in one hand trailed over her breasts. "I'm going to tie your hands to the wheel of the car."

Evelyn gasped and tried to twist out from under him, but she was no match for a man his size and strength. He had her arms pinned instantly in a firm but gentle grip. "Relax, Evelyn. Remember? I promised I would never hurt you."

She met his gaze again. Honesty reflected back at her, calming the fear his words had incited. "You're hurting now, aren't you?" He reached between them, brushing the fingers of one hand over the tender flesh at the juncture of her thighs. "Let me make it go away. I promise you will feel nothing but pleasure." Removing his hand, he backed off so he once again sat straddling her. "The decision is yours, as always."

She couldn't think with him staring at her. Evelyn closed her eyes, blocking out everything in order to choose a path. His promises repeated on an endless loop. The idea of being tied up, unable to escape if his assurances proved hollow, frightened her. Reality crashed in. Even without her hands tied, she stood little chance against him, or any man. And if she were to get away from him, she had no way to escape, no place to go. She'd put herself into a situation she had no control over.

Only she did have control. She could say no. She'd made the mistake of trusting a man before, but there was something about this one that made her believe he was a man of his word. He would respect whatever decision she made.

He stroked her mound again, reminding her of all she'd be giving up if she decided to end their encounter. With a resigned sigh, she opened her eyes. "You'll let me go if I tell you to?"

"All you have to do is say the word, and I'll stop." He fixed her with a stern look. "But don't say stop if you don't mean it."

"I won't."

Leaning over her, he wound one end of his tie around her wrists, then secured the other to a spoke in the front wheel of the car. She tugged on the bindings, and when there was no give, her heartbeat raced.

"It's a simple knot, sweetheart. If you needed to, you could release yourself, but you won't need to. I'm here." With one hand, he stroked along her jaw, down her neck and chest. He cupped her breast, massaging the mound until she moaned and arched her back, begging for more. "I'm going to make you feel so good you'll forget all about your hands being tied."

An argument formed in her mind, but his thumbs brushing over her distended nipples commanded her attention. He'd shifted to the side, leaving her fully exposed to him. She closed her eyes again, wanting to concentrate everything she had on his touch.

"Watch me, Evelyn. One of these days I'll blindfold you, but today I want you to know it's me touching you. I want you to see how pleased I am with your body." He ran his hand down her midriff to her stomach. "I knew this slip would look like this on you—decadent. Like a sweet treat all wrapped up, waiting for me to taste it."

His hand moved lower to cover the crusty patch of fabric—proof of her wickedness. "Did you enjoy masturbating, sweet one? Did the silk feel good inside you? Did you wish it was something else? My cock, for instance?"

"I-I don't know."

"Yes, you do. When I ask you something, I expect an answer. In the future, you might be punished for keeping things from me, but since you are learning what to expect from me, and I am learning about you too, there will be no punishment. However, there will be no pleasure either. Not until you answer all my questions."

Punishment? Evelyn couldn't stop the shiver of fear racking her body. She'd endured mental and physical punishment at the hands of her father and her ex-husband—enough to last a lifetime. No one was going to punish her again. Not if she could help it. "I want to stop. Now."

Jimmy Doyle's gaze held hers so long she began to squirm, working her fingers against the knot at her wrists. She almost had it free when he clamped a hand over hers. "No punishment today, Evelyn. Only pleasure."

"No punishment ever." She put every bit of conviction she had into her words and her expression. There wasn't enough pleasure in the world to make up for the humiliation and degradation of being punished for things she couldn't control.

His gaze searched hers for what seemed like an eternity before he released her hands. He didn't help her release the knot, but he didn't stop her either. She sat up, rubbing her wrists and arms. Jimmy Doyle sat with his back to her, one hand draped over his raised knee.

"I'm sorry."

"No need to be." He twisted around to face her. "I didn't realize you had issues with punishment. That's my fault. I want you so bad that I'm rushing you."

Evelyn ducked her head. "I wanted you too. It's just..."

"You've been punished before."

"Yes."

"I need to explain some things. All I ask is for you to listen. Afterward, if you want me to take you home, I will. Or we can stay here and continue."

She felt self-conscious having a rational conversation with a fully dressed man while she sat on the riverbank in nothing but her underclothes, but he was being perfectly reasonable about her calling a halt to their encounter. The least she could do was hear him out. "Okay. I guess."

"One of these days, I want to hear everything about your marriage, but I already know more than you would think. I know you were hurt, emotionally and physically."

Evelyn jerked her gaze up to his. "How?" No one knew what she'd been through. No one.

"Anyone who really sees you would know. You've built barriers around yourself so no one can get too close. Because of the walls you've put up, you're lonely—and alone. They aren't the same thing, you know?"

She nodded her understanding.

"You're afraid too. You don't trust anyone, especially men. I wasn't sure at first what exactly you were afraid of, but now I know. You're afraid of letting anyone close enough to hurt you, emotionally and physically." When he reached for her hand, she let him take it in his own, surrounding her with his strength. "I don't want to hurt you, Evelyn, but I can't make any promises regarding your heart. Just know that you are already precious to me, and though I have no idea where our relationship will go from here, I know where I want it to go. I want to be with you. I want to show you who I am, and I want to get to know you too. I'll do anything in my power to make you happy."

He squeezed her fingers. "I don't know what you were searching for at that tent revival, but I know you didn't find what you were looking for. I have a theory about that. Want to hear it?"

"Yes."

"I think the reason people like you and me don't find what we're looking for in those places is because we're looking for something that doesn't exist. There's no such thing as forgiveness for something that isn't a sin."

"But—"

"Your sexual needs are not a sin, Evelyn. It's not a sin to enjoy sex. It's not a sin to need sex. Joining your body with another is an expression of who you are. I've learned more about you by holding your hand than by all the conversations we've had. You are a passionate woman. Whatever you do, you do it with your whole heart, whether it's taking an extra shift to help out a coworker or opening your body to me. Everything you do, you do with passion. That's what I saw in you that first day. You'd made up your mind about that preacher, and you followed your heart right out the door. I had to follow you. There were plenty of other people in that tent who didn't find what they were there for, but they didn't have enough fire in their bellies to walk out. You did. I think I might have fallen in love with you right then."

"What?" Evelyn straightened as tingles shimmied down her spine. "You love me?"

He nodded. "I think I do, and it pains me that you don't think you're worthy of love—mine or anyone else's."

"I don't—"

"Yes, you do. Let me prove you wrong, Evelyn. Let me love you today."

Oh, how she wanted to believe him, but she'd never heard those words before and she was afraid she didn't know what they meant. Her ex-husband had vowed before God and everyone to love, honor, and cherish her, but he'd never told her he loved her.

She felt something for Jimmy Doyle, but was it love? Perhaps it was only lust, and wasn't that a sin? Her head spun trying to make sense of everything.

"What did you mean by punishment?"

He drew his shoulders back, and for a second she thought he was going to release her hand, but he didn't. He let out a long breath and met her gaze. "I would never punish you for something you have no control over. You can control many things in your life—the places you go, the books you read, the food you eat. But you can't control the things your body needs in order to be whole. You can't control whether you breathe or if your stomach gets hungry any more than you can control your sexual desires. They're all physical needs, and if not met, your body suffers."

He looked down at their clasped hands, then back up, capturing her eyes with his. "If you are mine, I will require you to follow certain rules. The letters I sent were a test to see if you would submit to me as fully as I desire. So far, you have done everything I have asked of you, so I have no reason to punish you. In the future, you might find reasons to ignore my commands or disobey me in other ways. For the decisions you consciously make, you will be punished. Depending on the infraction, your punishment could be corporal—a spanking, sitting in a corner, performing some task you dislike. Other times I might withhold sexual gratification in order for you to reflect upon what you've done. But no matter what form your punishment takes, my feelings for you will not change. Everything I do will be to strengthen our relationship, not break it down."

"What if you're wrong? Will I be allowed to defend my actions?"

His smile was so quick and so genuine she felt it like a lightning bolt. "I'm far from perfect, as you'll learn soon enough, but yes, you will always be given an opportunity to explain. Sometimes there are extenuating circumstances I am unaware of. I'm a good listener, Evelyn. You can always tell me what you are thinking and feeling. In fact, I encourage you to share everything with me. The more I know about you, the better I will be able to care for you."

"Care for me?" She'd been caring for herself for so long the idea of someone else taking on that role seemed foreign.

"Yes, sweetheart. Protect you. Provide for you, mentally and physically. Care for you. Love you. Those are all on my shoulders. I might fail at them on occasion, but the one that will always be constant is my love."

His shoulders appeared broad enough to carry more than the paltry list he'd made. She'd done a good job of all those things except the last one. She couldn't even remember when she had loved herself—it was that long ago. Vanity had been drummed out of her at a young age.

"Have I allayed your fears?"

She glanced at his discarded tie. "I'm sorry I acted like a child."

"It's my fault you didn't understand. I still want to see to your pleasure, if you'll let me."

"You want to tie my hands again?"

"Yes. I know I'm asking a lot of you. The binding is for me, something I need, but it can be freeing for you. It sounds crazy, but if you'll trust me this one time, I think you'll understand. We'll talk afterward. I promise."

CHAPTER NINE

She held her free hand out alongside the one he held firmly in his grip. "Please?" That one word was sweeter than any benediction he'd ever heard. When she'd put a stop to his lovemaking and released herself, he'd been sure he'd lost her forever. But she was stronger than he'd given her credit for. As he wrapped the tie around her slim wrists, he sent a silent prayer of thanks out into the universe. He had underestimated the trauma in her past—a mistake he didn't want to make twice. She still had no idea what kind of things he needed from her or the heights of pleasure his needs could take them both to.

He'd always planned on taking her on the journey slowly, initiating her into the life he led one small step at a time, but her fears had forced him to admit a great deal more than he'd planned today. That she was still here, allowing him to restrain her again, spoke volumes about her needs. Today, he'd taste her and, in so doing, give her a taste of what it would be like to submit completely to him.

"Too tight?"

She tested the silk binding and shook her head. "No."

When she turned her face up to his, the fear in her eyes stabbed at his heart. Cupping her jaw, he pressed a reassuring kiss to her lips. "You have nothing to fear. I'll tie the same knot as before so you know you can free yourself at any time." He nibbled down her neck, the thrill of victory coursing through his veins when she angled her head to one side, allowing him better access. "I promise you'll forget all about being bound in a few minutes. If you don't, I'm not doing my job well enough."

"Jimmy Doyle." His name was nothing more than a breathless whisper on her lips as he gently leaned forward, pressing her back to the quilt.

"Hands above your head, sweetheart. Give yourself to me."

His dick was so hard he could drill for oil with it. Once again, she lay before him like a feast for the gods. The dappled sunlight played over her silk-clad body, casting shadows and light here and there like a stage spotlight searching for a place to land. The proof of her submissive nature was right there, written in three strategically placed stains. Some might say the slip was ruined, but to him it was more beautiful than the day he'd purchased it. If he had his way, she'd wear it like this every day as a reminder of whom she belonged to.

"No pain, sweetheart, unless you beg me for it." He sat beside her, stroking her breasts. She shook her head, her eyes wide with certainty that she'd never beg for pain. She had so much to learn about the nature of pain and pleasure. He could tell she'd already forgotten about pinching her nipples. A reminder was in order, but first, a little pleasure.

He moved to her feet. She was wearing too many clothes. He explored every inch of her legs, then slipped beneath the silk covering to find the waistband of her panties. She gasped and clasped her thighs tight.

"Don't deny either of us, Evelyn." The scent of her arousal went straight to his libido. She wanted him. The knowledge brought his dominant nature out in force. "I'm going to take these off you, with or without your help."

He curled his fingers around the top edge. He could see her internal struggle. Then, like the perfect submissive he knew her to be, she lifted her hips. He pulled the garment free and lifted the crotch to his nose and drank in her scent. "Ah, Evelyn. I could never get enough of your scent. It intoxicates me."

She groaned and tried to cross one leg over the other. He stopped her, easily overpowering her by wrapping his fingers around her ankles, anchoring her to the quilt. "Remember what I said. No hiding from me." Using his knees, he spread her legs wide. The slip rode high, dipping between her thighs to curtain her pussy. He was dying to see that part of her, touch her, taste her, but she wasn't ready for that yet. By the time he put his mouth on her, she would be begging him to make her come. He'd see to it.

Lowering his body over hers, he took her mouth in a kiss that foretold everything he wanted to do to her. She was a quick learner, opening for him, her tongue sparring with his until they separated, both panting for breath. "I can't wait to taste your pussy."

His admission sent a shudder through her body that he felt all the way to his toes. He worked his way down her neck to the ruffled edge of the slip. Resting on one elbow, he took her breast in hand. The sheer silk made her nipple look like a watercolor painting, softening the color to a pale rose. He licked it. The perfect nub stood at attention. He licked again, then sucked the bud, silk and all, to the roof of his mouth.

Evelyn moaned and arched her back, offering him more. He took, pulling harder until she writhed beneath him in invitation. Her response emboldened him. Shifting his weight, he gave the other breast the same attention before sitting back on his knees to admire the wet fabric clinging to her flesh.

"So beautiful. But it's not enough. I need to see you." He took the slip in both hands and yanked, tearing the thin fabric down the center, exposing her breasts to his gaze. Evelyn cried out, but he shushed her by taking her flesh in his palms. She was even more beautiful than he'd imagined, and he told her so. She made a whimpering sound, but when he bent to take her in his mouth without the silk barrier, the whimper turned to a moan.

God, she tasted like candy. Melt-in-your-mouth sweet. He feasted until he had his fill and her nipples were pebble hard. He cradled one in his hand, learning the feel of her, testing her response. Her breathing evened out as she relaxed beneath him.

"Do you own a brassiere?"

She nodded and hummed a yes.

"You bought it yourself?"

Another positive response as she wallowed in his soft caresses. He could imagine the contraption she'd purchased. "I'll send you one of my choosing. You'll wear it every day to remind you of my hands touching you."

He grabbed each nipple between a thumb and forefinger, giving them both a quick pinch. A strangled scream erupted from her throat, dying suddenly when he released her. Her nipples now resembled the bruised rosebuds he'd imagined in his letter. Evelyn's chest rose and fell rapidly, her lips pressed in a thin line as she processed the pain.

"So beautiful." He toyed with her nipples, rubbing his thumbs over them, pinching lightly to see how she handled the sensation. "You're doing fine, sweetheart." When the tension left her face, he bent and took her nipples in his mouth again, pleasuring each one in turn with his tongue.

"Are you still with me, Evelyn?" Eyes scrunched tight, she nodded.

"Very good. You liked the pain, didn't you, sweetheart?"

Tears leaked from the corners of her eyes. "Yes."

He brushed the moisture from her temples. "I'm so proud of you. One more time, my brave girl, and I'll ease the ache between your legs." He positioned his fingers on her nipples again. "Focus on your pussy—on the need there, sweetheart."

He pinched harder and longer this time. Evelyn arched her back and screamed. She drew her knees up, let her legs fall open as her hips rose in invitation. God, she was magnificent.

Releasing her, he fell upon her, taking first one breast, then the other in his mouth, soothing the pain before he began working his way down her torso, leaving hot, wet kisses in his wake. At her mound, he pushed the hem of the slip up to her waist and, with his hands on her inner thighs, opened her wide.

The heady scent of her arousal went straight to his brain, drugging him with the need to taste her. He closed his eyes for a fraction of a second, letting the crazy whirl of emotions settle before he opened his mouth over her pussy.

"Oh my God!" She tried to scramble away from him, but he wrapped his arms around her thighs and pressed her hips down with his hands. "Jimmy Doyle!"

She was able to form words, which meant he wasn't doing it right. He lapped at her slit, pausing at the top to flick at her clitoris. The unintelligible sounds emerging from her throat made him smile with satisfaction. A few more strokes with his tongue, then he plunged inside her. Sealing his lips to hers, he kissed her pussy until she writhed beneath him in a dance of passion as old as time.

His head buzzed like he'd been hit with a fastball. Everything about her blended together into an elixir custom-made for him. His cock protested, wanting to see if she felt as good as she tasted. He knew she would. His cock could wait awhile longer. Convincing Evelyn to trust him had to come before his own needs.

She was struggling against her bindings, but she wasn't trying to get loose. She was trying to get closer, to force him to end the sensual torment he inflicted on her. As much as he wanted to keep her at his mercy, he couldn't keep her on the edge forever. He'd promised to end the aching need, and he wouldn't ever go back on a promise to her, especially one that would be as much about his pleasure as hers.

Shifting his attention to her clitoris, he licked and sucked at it, occasionally raking his teeth over the sensitized nub.

"Please," she begged for the promised orgasm.

He smiled against her pussy, then thrust two fingers into her hot channel. Her hips rocketed upward as she absorbed the shock of his entry. He fastened his lips over her clitoris and sucked hard.

She came in a series of discordant contractions that rocked her torso and threatened to dislodge him from his mission. He drank in the honey pouring from her, never having tasted anything sweeter in his life. A wave of possessiveness washed over him as he nuzzled her pussy until the last tremor shook her.

Mine.

He'd known it from the moment he saw her in the godforsaken tent. Now that he'd tasted her, had her scent in his nostrils, he didn't want to let her go. But the decision wasn't his. Even though he preferred to be in control, when it came to the type of relationship he wanted with Evelyn, he had to let her decide if she wanted to continue.

When her body stilled, turning to putty beneath his hands, he moved to sit beside her. He gently nudged her legs together, then pulled her slip down to cover her. She looked up, meeting his gaze as he reached above her to release her. A tiny smile curved her lips, which he returned with one of his own. "Better now?"

"Much." She sat up, rubbing at her wrists.

"Here." He took her hands, examining the red marks where his tie had abraded her skin. The sight thrilled him, but he kept that thought to himself. Instead, he ran his thumbs over the abused flesh. "Sorry about that. Does it hurt?"

"No. I guess I pulled too hard, huh?"

He tried to hide a satisfied smile. "Maybe. It wasn't too tight, was it?"

"Not at all. These are entirely my fault. I— You— It—"

"Was intense?"

She ducked her head, turning her face away from him. Her pulse jumped beneath his thumb, but he kept her hands in his. "Yes. I've never…" She took a deep breath, then let it out. "I've never experienced anything like it."

"Did you like it?"

He held his breath, waiting for her answer. If she said no, he'd know she was a liar. If she said yes, he might still have a chance to make her his. She lifted her chin but kept her face averted. She closed her eyes, took in another deep breath through her nose. "Yes. God help me, I want to do it again and again."

His smile came from deep inside but barely broke across his

face before shattering.

"Why did you tie my hands?" She looked him square in the eye. The sated woman was gone, replaced by the practical woman who, out of necessity, chose her steps wisely.

"Get dressed, and we'll talk." Jimmy Doyle released her hands and stood. He walked the few steps down to the river, letting the motion of the gently rolling water calm his soul. He'd never told anyone what had led him down the path he'd taken. The few people who knew of his sexual inclinations weren't the kind to judge or to question. They accepted him for who he was, and he afforded them the same courtesy.

Since he'd connected with the underground group in Washington that shared his perverse nature, he hadn't had a sexual partner from outside the closed society. Life was easier that way. But then he'd met Evelyn.

He couldn't let her go, but there was a real possibility she wouldn't want to see him again once she knew the whole truth. He'd planned all along to introduce her to his lifestyle gradually, and he wasn't going to change his plans at this stage of the game. He'd tell her a little, help her understand what had happened today. If that didn't scare her off, he'd reveal more.

As much as he wanted to take her to the farm where he'd worked as a laborer during his five-year suspension in return for room and board and the freedom to hone his skills as a dominant lover, she wasn't ready to meet his friends in the lifestyle or for complete immersion. *One baby step at a time*, he reminded himself.

He turned. Evelyn, dressed once again, knelt beside the picnic basket, removing the contents as if a few minutes ago she hadn't been restrained and screaming her lungs out as he made her come with his mouth. The longing in his heart almost took him to his knees. He wanted a lifetime with this woman who one minute gave herself to him with beautiful abandon and the next became the nurturing individual he wanted for the mother of his children.

He had to keep her. And to do that, he had to tell her the truth.

"I didn't know what you liked, so I asked for an assortment," he said. She looked up as he joined her on the blanket.

"I'm hungry enough to eat the back end of a horse." She smiled as she examined one waxed-paper-wrapped sandwich. "Ham and cheese?"

"I'll eat anything. You choose first."

She opened another. The way she scrunched her nose was cute. "Here. Give me that one. You take the ham."

Handing the offensive item over, she asked, "Are you sure? There are more to choose from."

"I'm sure." He peeled the paper back and laughed. "Not a fan of egg salad?"

"No. You?"

"I'll eat anything that doesn't eat me first." He took a big bite, illustrating his point.

Evelyn picked up the ham and cheese and settled back to eat. The marks on her wrists were already growing faint. By the time he returned her to town, they would be completely gone. The need to somehow mark her as his flashed like fire through his system. He couldn't stomach the idea of another man looking at her and thinking he had a chance with her.

"Did I get something on my dress?" She looked down, brushing at invisible specks.

"No. Sorry. I didn't mean to stare."

She relaxed, placing what was left of her meal on the quilt beside her. "You were looking at my wrists, weren't you?"

"Guilty." He nodded toward her hand. "In a few more minutes no one will suspect."

She twisted her arms, checking out the damage. "Almost back to normal." She took a drink from the bottle of pop he'd brought for her. "Are you going to tell me now why you tied my hands?"

Jimmy Doyle crumpled his empty sandwich wrapper into a ball and tossed it into the picnic basket. "I owe you that much," he said, making himself comfortable. "Ever since I was a teenager, I've had this thing about restraining my sexual partners. I like to do it. I like to be in charge."

"I know I'm naive, but I never heard of anyone doing such a thing."

"It's more common than you know."

"Really? How do you know?"

"I didn't at first. But I saw something when I was kid that opened my eyes to the way things are in the real world. Since then, I've learned a few things."

"What did you see?"

"I grew up on a dirt farm in Texas. We didn't have much other than some worn-out land and family. My Uncle James and Aunt Sally owned the land next to ours. Their kids were still too young to help with the hay, so when we were done with ours, my dad would send me over to help. Jim always wanted to start at the crack of dawn, so I'd go over after supper and sleep in his hayloft. That way, I'd be there, ready to go in the morning.

"When I was sixteen, it was late when I decided to go over, so I let myself into the barn and climbed up into the loft. I was just about asleep when I heard someone open the side door. I figured it was my aunt or uncle, come to make sure everything was right and tight for the night before they went to bed. I started to reveal myself when I heard them talking."

He paused to let the memories flood back in. "I'll never forget that night. Sally was laughing, but in a coy way, like they were teenagers sneaking out to the barn or something. I didn't know what they had to sneak around for. They were married, and they had a big ole farmhouse that was all theirs, but it was clear they were up to something, so I kept quiet.

"There was a knothole in the floor beside me, so I looked to see what was going on. They'd brought a lantern out, and Jim lit a couple more he kept hanging from the crossbeams, so the place was lit up pretty good. Aunt Sally had on a housecoat, and she was barefoot. Her hair was down, loose, and it hung nearly to the small of her back. I'd never seen it down before, and it struck me how pretty it was. How pretty she was. Every time I'd seen her, she was busy corralling their three young'uns, which, in my opinion, did nothing for her—looks-wise. But in the lantern light, with her hair down and a smile on her face, she was about the most beautiful woman I'd ever seen. Jim was mighty protective of her, and that night, I understood why."

"What did you do?"

"I should have called out, told them I was there, but everything happened so fast. One minute Sally was laughing; then the next, she was standing stark naked in the center of the barn, and Jim was wrapping rope around her wrists.

"I was terrified. I'd been raised to treat women with respect. I was a teenager. I had all kinds of fantasies about touching girls. Mind you, I didn't have a clue how to convince one to let me touch, but that didn't stop me from coming up with ideas on how to make it happen."

He laughed at the distant memory. "I sort of knew a wife would have to do what I wanted, even if she didn't like it—that's what the Bible said. It never occurred to me I might have to tie a wife up in order to do my husbandly duty. But there was my uncle, tying up his wife."

He shifted to a more comfortable position on the blanket. "I remember trying to find my voice, to yell at Jim, make him stop before he hurt her, but something stopped me. Looking back, I remember hearing Jim's voice. It was low, and not at all threatening. Sally could have run, but she stood there and let him tie her hands. The more I watched, the more I became convinced it wasn't the first time they'd done it, and to my surprise, my aunt appeared to be helping Jim. She certainly wasn't resisting him."

"Oh, my heavens!" Evelyn's eyes were as wide as his must have been on that long-ago night.

"I kept quiet and watched. I figured if things got out of hand, if Sally made a single move or said anything to indicate she didn't want to play along, I'd reveal myself."

"But she didn't."

"No, she didn't." Jimmy Doyle picked an apple from the

picnic basket, rolling it around in his palm like a baseball. "Once Uncle Jim had her hands secured to the beam, my aunt could barely touch the floor with her toes. He had some old leather rigging he put around her waist. Then, using rope through the rings at her sides, he pulled her higher, taking the weight off her shoulders and wrists. There was an old sawhorse in the corner of the barn. He brought that over and tied her ankles to it so she was sitting in midair with her knees spread wide. All that, and not once did she beg or plead with him to stop. I didn't know what to do. What goes on between a man and his wife is private, and from what I could see, it appeared to be consensual, so I held my tongue." Jimmy Doyle smiled. "That was the first time I'd seen a naked woman—in the flesh. She was so beautiful I got hard the minute she dropped her robe over the stall door, and by the time Jim had her strung up, I had my dick in my hand.

"I was mesmerized, and horny as hell. I had no idea couples did the things those two did that night. When he took a horse flogger to her, I almost gave away my hiding place. How could Jim strike a woman? But after the first time or two, I could see he wasn't hurting her. At least, it didn't seem like he was. She was moaning and begging for more.

"He played with her breasts—put clothespins on them, then flicked them with his finger. He did things to her—between her legs." He shook his head at the memory. "I got quite the education."

EVELYN PICKED A blade of grass and began shredding it with her fingers. She imagined herself in his Aunt Sally's place, and Jimmy Doyle doing *things* to her. Those things had to be sins, didn't they? "They'll burn in hell."

"You wouldn't say that if you knew them. They're two of the most loving, generous Christians you'll ever meet. Jim is a church deacon, and Sally has taught Sunday school for twenty years."

"But—"

"But nothing. What they did was beautiful to see. Two people bringing each other pleasure, loving each other. Does it matter how they do it as long as they both want it?"

Taking a deep breath, Evelyn closed her eyes, then let it out on a sigh. Did it matter? She was sure her father would say it did, but for the first time she wondered if he might be wrong. Tilting her face up to the sun, she relished the feel of the rays on her skin.

"I want to believe you. I want to believe the things my body wants don't make me a sinner—don't condemn me into Satan's hands for eternity."

"If they do, then we'll both be in good company."

She jerked her gaze to him. "How do you know?"

He shrugged, not looking at her. "I know."

They sat that way, both absorbing the fresh air and the import of their conversation, until a cloud obscured the sun, casting them in shadow.

"There's nothing wrong with you if you like being tied up during sex."

"I can't help but believe it's wrong."

"There's nothing wrong with feeling good, is there?"

"I-I don't know."

"I loved seeing you restrained, at my mercy while I made you feel good. I did make you feel good, didn't I?"

"Yes. You know you did."

"You could have freed yourself, but you didn't. How did it make you feel, Evelyn? Did you feel as if you had no choice but to experience the pleasure?"

The rush of helplessness came flooding back in, along with a host of other feelings she didn't understand.

"By tying your hands, I gave you the freedom to feel completely, to experience the most pleasure I could give you without feeling any guilt for liking it. I decided how much pleasure you could stand. I decided when, and if, you could orgasm. Being in control of your body pleases me, sweetheart. It excites me to force pleasure on you, to plumb the depths of your passion. You were magnificent today, but there is so much more for you to experience, and I want to be the one to give you those experiences."

"Your aunt—she liked what your uncle did to her?"

"If you could have seen the look on her face or heard the way she screamed his name when he finally let her orgasm, you wouldn't have to ask. When Jim released her, she was all over him. Took him down to the barn floor, and well, I had a new cousin nine months later."

"I can't imagine… You were so young."

"I was old enough, I guess. I knew about sex, even if I hadn't experienced the real thing. I'd been pleasuring myself for years, in bed, in the barn, behind the barn, out in the fields. Anywhere I could put my hand in my pants and not get caught.

"Anyway, a few years later I signed a contract to play baseball in Washington. On the day I left, my uncle took me aside at the train station and told me he and Sally knew I was in the hayloft that night. He said he always figured I was going to go places, and he didn't want me to go there without knowing something of the world." Jimmy Doyle chuckled. "He also thanked me for keeping my mouth shut. Seems that being watched was one of Sally's fantasies. If I'd spoken up, I would have ruined the whole thing for her."

Suddenly aware of all they'd done out in the open where anyone could have come upon them, Evelyn wrapped her arms tight around her middle.

"Don't worry. No one saw us. Though I would have been proud of you if they had. You did very well for your first time being restrained."

His praise warmed her from the inside out. After stopping him once, she had recovered nicely. Memories of the things he'd done to her played like a movie reel in her mind. "You ruined my slip."

"I want you to wear that slip to bed every night and remember my hands on you. The tear is there to remind you not to hide your body from me."

"I don't know about all this. The things you say make sense, but I can't help but think it's wrong to want the things I want."

"Your desires are natural. If you'll let me, I'll show you that you aren't alone, that what you feel, what you need and desire, doesn't condemn you. It only makes you human."

"I need some time to think about it. Please?"

CHAPTER TEN

The air in the downstairs parlor felt as if the room sat above the pits of hell. Not even the oscillating fan sitting atop the radio made a difference. Every breath seemed to steal more oxygen than it provided. Lying all but naked in the dappled sunshine on the riverbank, gasping for air as Jimmy Doyle did magic things to her body felt like a dream compared to the nightmare of being trapped indoors listening to the baseball game with her fellow boarders.

He hadn't pressured her to do anything more after she'd asked for time to think about everything she'd learned about him, and from him. After they'd packed up their picnic, he'd kissed her gently, then settled her in the car for the drive back into town. He'd dropped her off in front of the boardinghouse, waving good-bye as he headed to the stadium for the afternoon game.

Mrs. Rubenstein had provided glasses of lemonade and tea cakes to lure the women together for what was supposed to be a social gathering but felt more like a funeral as the afternoon wore on. Evelyn didn't know much about the game, but in the past few weeks, she'd read enough newspaper accounts to decipher most of the announcer's words. Jimmy Doyle played first base and had moved up to the fourth spot in the batting order after beginning the season batting last. The sports reporters seemed to think that was pretty remarkable for someone who had been out of the game for the past five years.

They talked in vague terms about his time away—time she realized she knew nothing about. Why should she? There was much about her past she hadn't told him too. Unlike her untold stories, whatever had kept him out of baseball for five years wasn't a secret to those who followed the game. She tuned out the announcer's words, preferring to hear the details from Jimmy Doyle himself, when, and if, he chose to tell her.

Evelyn sipped at her tepid drink, letting her mind wander back to the morning. The temperature, though warm, had been mild in comparison to the afternoon. Lying on the blanket wearing nothing but her underclothes, she'd been cool on the outside, but on the inside her blood had felt like molten lava. It was wrong to do the things they'd done outside of wedlock, but who was to know besides them? God had apparently abandoned her marriage before the wedding was over. Maybe he'd known all along that a union without passion couldn't last. Or maybe he'd glimpsed the beast living within her and sanctioned the actions of her ex-husband and father. In the eyes of God, she deserved what they'd done to her. The Holy Spirit was no match for the devil making her crave the sins of the flesh.

The spot between her legs still throbbed from having Jimmy Doyle's mouth there. Just thinking about him touching her so intimately made her skin grow hot, and that was the last thing she needed at the moment. She pressed her handkerchief to her forehead, her cheeks, her neck. The bottom of the lace curtains stirred on a tiny breeze. Evelyn stood. "I think I'll sit on the porch."

Even though there were several chairs on the wide veranda, no one followed her out. Evelyn chose the seat nearest the window and sat. Without the oppressiveness of the parlor to dampen it, the announcer's voice came through the open window clearly. Evelyn closed her eyes and let her head drop against the high-backed rocker. With a gentle push, she set the chair in motion, stirring a breeze where there was none.

The game droned on in the background, overlaid with the perfunctory conversations of the other boarders. Most of the girls worked as waitresses, but a few had found employment behind shop counters. Evelyn was the only one with a skill. She'd been fortunate to find a paying apprenticeship at the phone company when she first arrived in Washington. Over the years, she'd worked her way up to the day shift on the board that handled most of the calls in the downtown area. The pay wasn't great, but she made enough to pay rent and set aside a few dollars a month for the future. She had her eye on a small apartment near DuPont Circle. If she could save enough for the security deposit, the three-room flat would be hers. She'd thought about getting an apartment with a second bedroom she could rent out, but after years of living in a tiny space surrounded by other women, she just wanted to be alone.

She wanted to cook her own meals and decorate the rooms without having to take anyone else's taste or comfort into account. She wanted something she could call her own. Animated voices inside the parlor snapped Evelyn from her reverie. Craning her neck, she listened to find out what had everyone so excited.

"Turn up the volume," one of the boarders said.

"And he does it again!" The announcer's voice rose above the noise of the crowd attending the game. "Jimmy Doyle Walker sends another one out of the park! Three runs score, putting the Diplomats up by four runs here in the sixth inning. Man, oh man, are the fans glad to have Mr. Walker back in the lineup. I tell you, folks, the Diplomats did the right thing by bringing him back this season. The fans have their eyes on the pennant this season, and beyond. Can this last, boys and girls?"

The broadcast faded to a normal level as someone inside adjusted the volume. Evelyn relaxed back in the rocker, the happiness she felt for her friend making her glow inside. He never talked about his job, but clearly he was good at it. She imagined the fans on their feet, cheering for him. Did he like to be singled out that way? If the announcer was correct, a lot rested on the first baseman's shoulders this season. How did he deal with that kind of pressure?

With her, he seemed calm, always in control of himself and the things around him. Was that how he felt on the field? Did the other players look to him to lead? He was very good at getting what he wanted, at least from her.

"The Diplomats have this one won." Evelyn thought the comment came from Laura, a wide-eyed girl fresh out of high school who waitressed at a mom-and-pop restaurant a few blocks away. She shared a room with one of the other women who couldn't afford a single room on what they made.

"I don't care how good he is; he shouldn't be on the team." Evelyn bit her lower lip. Madelyn was one of the oldest women in the house and had an opinion on everything from the cost of buttermilk to the trolley schedule. Evelyn steered clear of her whenever possible, afraid the woman's negativity might rub off on her. "They say he wasn't involved in the scandal, that it was all a mistake, but mark my words, he's as guilty as the rest of them."

"The charges were dropped against him," Suzanna, Laura's roommate, argued.

Evelyn's heart nearly stopped. *Charges?* She couldn't imagine the man she knew being accused of any kind of criminal activity. He was too open, too honest. Or was that a game he played with her? He certainly hadn't been forthcoming about criminal charges!

"I heard there wasn't enough evidence against him." Evelyn leaned closer to the window. She wasn't sure, but she thought the comment came from Wanda, a mouse of a woman who worked as a file clerk at a legal firm or something like that.

"Where did you hear that?" Madelyn's voice was laden with skepticism.

"I overheard some of the lawyers talking one day. They said the league had to reinstate him since no one could prove he'd done anything."

"Poppycock!" the older woman said. "If they looked hard enough, they'd find the rotten core, I'm sure."

"All men aren't rotten at the core, Madelyn." Tilly was the only one in the house brave enough to challenge Madelyn on her frequent rants regarding the male species. "Just because you bit into a ruined one doesn't mean the whole barrel is bad."

"Why— I never— Hmph!" Evelyn imagined smoke billowing from the bitter woman's ears as she stomped out of the room. Heavy footsteps sounded on the stairs, followed by a door opening, then slamming shut on the second floor.

Tilly was right to call Madelyn on her belief that men weren't to be trusted. Even though Evelyn's personal experience with men led her to think along the same lines, she wasn't ready to condemn every male the way the older woman was. Though today's conversation gave her pause. Had she been too quick to trust Jimmy Doyle? Was he one of the bad apples in the barrel?

He'd certainly won her over with his gifts and assurances that she was in charge. Like a marionette, she danced to his tune.

Someone changed the radio to a gospel-music station, and the conversation inside subsided. Evelyn twisted her handkerchief into a tight rope. What did it say about her that she couldn't remember feeling as happy as she had in the few weeks since she'd met the baseball player? He'd made her feel special from the very first. Her body hummed with life when he was around, though she had to be honest—he frightened her too.

She rocked, letting the motion lull her into a peaceful state. She'd been scared when he first tied her hands this morning. He'd mentioned punishment before, but threatening to punish her while he had her restrained had triggered something inside her. He hadn't helped her out of the bindings, but he hadn't stopped her from untying her wrists either. He'd been patient, explaining what he'd meant and letting her decide for herself is she wanted to continue. When he'd asked her to trust him again, she'd been more than willing to lie back and let him tie her hands.

Evelyn opened her mind to the feelings she'd experienced that morning. She'd been frightened, but only for a moment. She'd already released the bonds once, so she knew she could do it again.

So it wasn't really fear that drove her emotions. It was the thrill of giving him complete control, even if it was an illusion, that had excited her.

Yes, that was it. She'd been excited. Aroused. She'd consented to let him do as he pleased with her body. The bindings compelling her to experience every touch, every sensation. In a convoluted way, tying her hands gave her more freedom.

She wouldn't have believed it if she hadn't experienced it for herself. And now that she had, she wanted to experience it again. Jimmy Doyle had awakened things inside her she hadn't known were there.

≈∾≈

"Whatever happened with that girl from the revival?"

Jimmy Doyle tied his cleats. He knew it was only a matter of time before Harvey got around to asking. It had been nearly two months, but the second baseman was that kind of guy, not slow, but methodical. Jimmy Doyle would bet the man had thought about that day more than once, mulling the situation over, biding his time. His interest in Evelyn had been easy to see, but being an honorable Christian, he wouldn't poach another man's girl. "I've seen her a couple of times. You know how it is, not much time for a life with our schedule."

"What was her name again?"

"Evelyn."

"Pretty name for a pretty girl."

Jimmy Doyle stood, adjusting his pants. Harvey was right. Evelyn was pretty. And nice too. She probably deserved someone better than him. "See you out there." He grabbed his glove out of his locker, nodding to Harvey.

He stood in the dugout, looking out at the field. Five years ago, he thought he'd never see this view again. He didn't know which had hurt worse, being accused of something he hadn't done or walking away from the game he loved—possibly forever. Hell, it would have been forever except for a friend of his. He'd met Judge

Hallstead a year after being banished. The man had listened to his story, then questioned every one of their mutual friends as to Jimmy Doyle's character. Once he'd assured himself that his new friend was a man of honor, the judge had gone to bat for him. Jimmy Doyle owed him. He had no idea how he could repay the man's kindness, but he'd find a way. Someday.

The afternoon sun began its slow descent, casting half the field in shadow. His mind drifted back to the morning and how lovely Evelyn had looked lying in the dappled shadow, her hands tied above her head, her body writhing, then quaking under his touch. She was perfect for him. She had a body made for lovin', and though she didn't see it in herself, she was submissive to the bone. Circumstances had forced her to rely on herself, but deep inside, she needed someone to take charge, to guide her and give her the freedom to explore her sexuality. He wanted to be that man.

He wanted her more than he'd ever wanted a woman in his life.

"Thinking about ways to sabotage today's game?" Jimmy Doyle continued to gaze out at the field, ignoring the asshole beside him. He'd done all he could to convince his teammates of his innocence, though he'd clearly failed with this one.

"What's the matter, cat got your tongue?"

Jimmy Doyle stepped out of the dugout, then turned. "Nope. But I did just figure out how to improve our game today."

"How's that, wise guy?"

"Trade you to St. Louis." With that parting remark, he trotted out onto the field, eager to work the tension out of his body that had begun to build up the minute Ray Snodgrass opened his mouth.

He stretched, then ran a lap around the deserted field to clear his head of negative thoughts. There would always be people who didn't believe him when he said he'd had nothing to do with betting on games. Officially, he'd been cleared of all charges, but anyone who cared enough to look deep would find the charges had been dropped for lack of evidence instead of a belief in his innocence. Judge Hallstead used all his influence to get the league, and the Diplomats, to reverse the lifetime ban they'd imposed on him. Proving to everyone Jimmy Doyle Walker still had what it took to play the game had become his only goal.

Before, he'd had a solid fan base. Fathers had brought their sons to see him play and hung out before and after the games to get his autograph. Now he was lucky to get a wave from a fan, and the only ones seeking his autograph were punks who figured it would be worth something when he finally did go to jail.

Not that he'd ever faced jail time. In his mind, being incarcerated couldn't possibly have been any worse than being cut off from the game he loved.

The other players began to make their way onto the field for batting practice. He exchanged pleasantries with some who weren't afraid their reputations would suffer for being seen talking to him, then took his place in the line of players waiting to swing the bat at a few balls. He'd long since come to the conclusion he couldn't change anyone's mind about the accusations attached to his name, but he could prove he was still worthy of being on the team. He worked harder and longer on his skills than anyone else.

During his exile, he'd managed to stay in shape doing manual labor on the farm. If anything, he was in better condition now than he had been when he was forced to leave the game. Farmwork wasn't for slack-abouts. He'd built more muscle and toned ones he already had. As a result, he was stronger than before he'd left, and his batting stats reflected that.

He was good. He had one of the best averages on the team, and he intended to keep it up all the way to the World Series. Sure, he was playing first base now instead of shortstop, a definite concession to his age, but one he was willing to make to stay on the field. Hell, he'd have agreed to just about anything to play again.

Jimmy Doyle powered through batting practice, using the time to narrow his focus to the game. Judge Hallstead had convinced the Diplomats to take him back for one year with the provision he had to prove himself in order to extend his contract once the season was over. He couldn't let anything, not gibes from his teammates and opponents or the beauty of Evelyn's submission, distract him from accomplishing his goal.

After his single in the first inning was for naught, he connected with a ball in the third, putting the Diplomats up by one run. When he came to bat in the sixth with two runners on and two outs, the tension in the dugout was palpable. It was time to rally or risk letting the game slide out of their hands. They needed runs on the board, and they needed them now.

Jimmy Doyle stepped into the batter's box, working the toe of his right foot into the soft dirt, looking for purchase. Memories of the last time he'd faced this pitcher flashed through his mind. The situation had been different—no one on base, and the Browns had a commanding lead. The situation was perfect for the pitcher to express his opinion regarding the batter's character. He'd caught Jimmy Doyle square in the hip with a fastball.

It hadn't been the first time he'd been hit by a pitch this season, but Caldwell threw a wicked fastball. Jimmy Doyle had limped to first base, then limped everywhere else for a solid week. He wasn't looking forward to a repeat. Fortunately, St. Louis needed to get out of the inning without letting the Diplomats score runs. Caldwell would pitch to him, and he was ready.

As ready as he'd ever be, he raised the bat to his shoulder, relaxed into his batting stance, and waited. The first pitch broke inside. Jimmy Doyle made an evasive move, though it was clear the pitcher had only wanted to remind him of their last meeting.

He went through his prebatting ritual, then stepped back in the box. He knew the mental game as well as he knew the physical game. Putting the previous pitch out of his mind, he focused on the next one.

Patience was a virtue in this game. Waiting on the pitch you wanted could mess with a pitcher as much as seeing a fastball whizzing past your nose could mess with a batter. If there was one thing he had in spades, it was patience.

Some of the best treasures in life could be had if one possessed the patience to wait for them.

Just like that, an image of Evelyn popped into his mind. He'd have to take his time with her. Bring her along one tiny step at a time. But in the end, the reward would be worth it. She'd be his. Just like the pitch hurling toward him at that moment.

He smiled on the inside as he cocked his muscles and fired. He swung the bat in a perfect arc, meeting the ball in front of home plate. God, he loved the sound of a bat connecting solidly with a ball. There was nothing like it in the world, and only one sound more satisfying—the sound of a woman coming apart at his hands.

He took a moment to admire the graceful rise of the ball as it headed for center field. Assured it wasn't going to drop short of the outfield wall, he tipped his hat to the pitcher, then took off to round the bases.

He'd done his part. The Diplomats had a four-run lead, thanks primarily to him. He couldn't produce results like that every game, but if he managed them often enough, he would have a decent chance of signing a multiyear contract at the end of the season. And if the Diplomats didn't want him, he'd bet someone else would.

CHAPTER ELEVEN

She hadn't seen or heard from Jimmy Doyle for five days. The Diplomats were winding up a weeklong home stand and would be going back out on the road soon. Talk around the dinner table for the past few days had centered on the team's winning streak, and despite herself, Evelyn had listened intently as the women discussed the team's chances of winning the pennant. She wished she knew more about the game so she could contribute to the conversation, but what could she say? *Jimmy Doyle Walker likes to tie women up and do sinfully wicked things to their bodies?*

She couldn't see that going over well at the dinner table. Nor could she mention the letters he wrote to her or the gifts he sent her. They were private—her own little secrets she cherished. She might not know much about the game, but she knew more than she ought about the Diplomats' star first baseman.

And she missed him. It seemed silly to miss someone who lived in the same city. If he wanted to see her, he could. He'd asked for the phone number of the boardinghouse, and she'd given it to him—for emergencies, she'd said. Now she wished she hadn't said it that way. Wanting to see her was not an emergency. He could have come by, knocked on the door, and asked for her. Mrs. Rubenstein would have an apoplexy if she found him on the doorstep.

The thought of that made Evelyn smile as she went up the

back staircase to her room. The old house was solid, but more than a few floorboards and stair treads creaked. Over the years, Evelyn had learned how to avoid most of them, but on nights like tonight when her mind was too cluttered with other things, she couldn't bring herself to care how much noise she made.

She trudged the length of the hall to her room at the front of the house. Avoiding the upstairs heat, she'd lingered at the table, sipping cold lemonade and nibbling on tea cakes, the shortbread cookies Mrs. Rubenstein kept on hand all the time. Once the sunlight faded from the west-facing windows, she'd said good night to the others.

The moment she opened the door to her room and stuck her head inside, she knew something was wrong. The room was cloaked in darkness, except for a faint sliver of light coming from beneath the closed bathroom door. Had she left the light in the bathroom on? Mrs. Rubenstein was adamant about turning out lights when they weren't in use, so Evelyn never left a bulb burning when she wasn't in the room. Not to mention, adding the heat from a bulb to the already sweltering temperature in her room wasn't a good idea.

Had the nosy old woman been in her room again? Maybe one of the other boarders? She tried to remember who had been downstairs and who might be unaccounted for, but her brain wouldn't go there. She slipped inside, closed the door, and leaned against it, giving her eyes time to adjust to the darkness.

"Come here, Evelyn." The deep, masculine voice nearly made her jump out of her skin. She covered her mouth to hold in the scream-turned-gasp as her brain matched the voice to the person.

Jimmy Doyle. In her room. On her bed, if her hearing hadn't failed her. She bit her bottom lip to keep from shouting at him. If anyone found him here, she would be out on the street before she could explain.

But what was there to explain? There was a man. In. Her. Room. A man every woman in the house thought they knew. A man they'd been discussing over pot roast and root vegetables a few hours ago.

She had to get him out before he was discovered. Before she was ruined and homeless.

"How did you get in?" Though she wanted to scream at him, she kept her voice low.

"Did you know there's a very sturdy oak tree on the side of the house?" He spoke just above a whisper, but the walls of her room were as thin as tissue paper. What if someone heard him? There would be no way to explain away a voice as rich as his.

"Shh! Keep your voice down."

"Come stand beside the bed, sweetheart. Do as I say, and I promise to be as quiet as possible."

She'd do anything to keep him quiet. A few steps brought her to the side of the bed where he sat, legs splayed, waiting for her. He rested his hands on her waist. Hardly able to believe he was really there, in her room, on her bed, issuing orders she had little choice but to obey. Her body swayed toward his.

She leaned over him, and he raised his hands, holding her hair back from her face with his fingers as he drew her face to his. Cocking his head to one side, he covered her mouth with his, his soft lips commanding hers in a way she had no power to resist. Placing her hands on his shoulders to steady herself, Evelyn gave in to the need coursing through her body.

She'd spent countless lonely nights awake, wearing her torn slip and dreaming of his kisses. His letters had become a game she played with herself, resisting as long as she could before extracting one from the drawer and reading it over again. She knew them all by heart now, knew the excitement of touching herself guided by his instructions. But it was never enough—would never be enough. She would always want more, and the time she'd spent with Jimmy Doyle beside the river had only shown her how much she needed a man's touch.

His tongue demanded entrance, and she complied, opening for the erotic exploration. He was every bit as thorough as he had been when he'd kissed her pussy. Every thought left Evelyn's head except that she needed more from him. Kisses and touches weren't enough. Her body ached to take him inside her, to feel him stretching her, filling her.

She tried to close the distance between them, only to have him break the kiss. "I need to make love to you, but only if you promise not to make a sound." His hot breath tickled her ear. "Can you do that for me?"

Evelyn pressed her lips together, silencing the hallelujah threatening to escape, and nodded.

"Good girl." The openmouthed kiss to her neck sent a shiver along her spine. "Take all your clothes off and lay on the bed, on your back. Remember, not a sound."

She nodded again, and he let her go. She'd taken one step back when he reached for her hand, stopping her. Her eyes had adjusted to the darkened room. A faint glow from the streetlight a few houses down allowed her to make out his intent. He wanted her to undress right there.

Her hands trembled as she worked the buttons loose on her shirtwaist bodice. After working one arm free, then the other, she hooked her thumbs at her waist and pushed the dress past her hips. She had a brassiere, but she saved it for special occasions, so she stood before him wearing nothing but panties, a garter belt, stockings, and shoes.

The slightest pressure from his fingers on her hips brought her forward. Then his mouth was on her breast, his tongue teasing her nipple to a tight peak. Evelyn cradled his head in her palms. Her legs turned to jelly, and she would have sunk to the floor had he not wrapped one strong arm around her waist to support her. With his free hand, he covered her other breast, kneading, then pinching and tugging the nipple until she had to bite her lower lip to keep from screaming. Just when she thought she couldn't take any more, he switched breasts, sucking on the one he'd tormented with his hand, while he tormented her other one with his fingers.

Her head spun trying to process all the sensations at once. It was all too much, yet nowhere near enough to satisfy the hunger raging through her body. Her channel clenched, and she caught the scent of her arousal, musky and heavy in the air. She dug her fingernails into his scalp to get his attention.

His mouth left her breast with a tiny, wet *pop*. Evelyn sighed against the top of his head, certain he would end the ache between her legs now. When he began placing light kisses across her stomach, she had to stifle a groan of protest. Desperation clawed at her insides, but he acted as if he had all the time in the world.

It took her a moment to realize his reason. She was still wearing too many clothes. One by one, he released the clips holding her stockings up. The thin fabric slid down her legs, pooling around her ankles and shoes. She lifted one leg, intent on pushing the garments off, but his hand against her thigh stopped her.

He looked up at her, caught and held her gaze with his blazing one. She didn't need spoken words to know he was asking her permission to continue. Knowing she would die if he stopped, she bent and took his mouth in a scorching kiss. He hooked his thumbs beneath the waistband of her panties. Evelyn shuddered as he shoved the plain cotton past her mound, his work-roughened hands sliding along her thighs, slowly removing the last barrier to her womanhood.

The panties joined her stockings around her ankles. It seemed like an eternity that she stood there, knees knocking, breath held captive in her lungs just as she was held captive by his gaze. Muffled voices and footsteps sounded in the hallway as the other ladies went to their rooms. An automobile rattled past on the street. The groan of chains as the old porch swing took someone's weight. People went about their lives, unaware of the secret rendezvous going on a few feet away from them. A slow smile crossed his face. She was crazy to be doing this. Here. The thrill of possible discovery shot through her. God, she wanted this man. Wanted him with an intensity she had never experienced before. She answered his smile with one of her own.

Holding her gaze, he lifted her off her feet as if she weighed no more than a fly. In the blink of an eye, she sat in the very spot he'd vacated. A finger to his lips reminded her of her vow of silence. As if she were fragile, he laid her back so her head rested on the pillow, then lifted her feet, swinging them to the mattress. Silently, he removed her shoes, placing them beneath the bed. Next came her panties, which he brought to his nose, inhaled deeply before placing them on the nightstand.

When his hands smoothed her stockings back up her legs, she closed her eyes and concentrated on breathing—something that had become increasingly difficult to do with him looking at her exposed body. No man had ever seen her like this, not even her ex-husband. The few times he'd come to her, she'd removed only what clothing was necessary to get the job done, and he'd barely looked then.

The hunger in his eyes burned away any worries she had about him finding her unattractive. His gaze roamed her form, lingering on her breasts and the thatch of dark curls covering her mound. He reminded her of the art enthusiasts she'd seen in the National Museum, studying the paintings as if to memorize every detail.

After a long while, he took her hands, lifting them above her head. Then he positioned her legs with her knees bent, her thighs spread wide. Again, he took his time while Evelyn wavered between total embarrassment and feeling like a priceless piece of art. As he looked his fill, she studied him. The few times they'd been together, she'd never had the chance to just look at him. He was far too handsome to be real—sophisticated yet rugged. His face held too many worry lines for someone his age, but the imperfection suited him. There was a lifetime of wisdom in his eyes, as if he had lived more in his thirty years than most did in twice that. Yet he smiled easily, and when he looked at her, his face lit up with desire.

She had spent many nights imagining what he would look like beneath his clothes. She'd caught glimpses of her ex-husband during their short marriage, but he'd been careful never to be entirely undressed in her presence. The other women in the boardinghouse liked to look at the Sears catalog and point to the pictures of men in their underclothes, but she'd never found those illustrations to be interesting. Not like Jimmy Doyle. Having never seen him any way but fully dressed, she knew he'd put them all to shame.

He lifted his hands to his necktie. She watched as his long fingers worked the knot loose. As he pulled the fabric free of his collar, she glanced up at his face. The utter calm she saw there sent a shiver through her body. He knew what he was doing. Had calculated and measured out exactly what he would do to her. Liquid heat pooled low in her belly and trickled between her legs. This would be no hurried coupling that left her feeling cheap and unwanted. Jimmy Doyle knew how to make a female feel like a woman.

He draped his tie over the footboard of her iron bedstead, then slipped the straps of his suspenders off his shoulders. Without taking his eyes off hers, he worked the fasteners free of his waistband, front and back. When he leaned over her prone body to fasten the strips of webbing around her wrists, she closed her eyes and let the heat from his body warm her. He smelled of sunshine and something heavier, headier that had her straining to get closer to him.

It didn't take him long to secure her wrists, one to each side of the headboard. Then he lowered himself slowly to the edge of the bed. The soft wool of his trousers brushed her hip. She didn't own anything as fine as the clothes he wore, and feeling the expensive fabric against her skin was pure bliss. But she would rather have felt his skin. As if in slow motion, he removed his cuff links, placing them on the nightstand next to her panties. Then he went to work on the buttons on the front of his shirt, carefully draping the discarded garment over the footboard next to his tie. Evelyn stared, wide-eyed, as he pulled his undershirt over his head, revealing his upper body in all its male glory.

She strained to lift her head to take in the sight she'd only imagined up until now. Clearly, her imagination had been lacking.

She licked her lips, gone dry from taking shallow breaths through her mouth.

The muscles in the arm she could see and his back bunched and shifted as he unfastened the buttons on his fly. He stood then and, facing her, made sure he had her complete attention. One eyebrow rose in silent question.

This was it. Though bound to the headboard of her bed, she alone controlled what would happen next. If she nodded, he would drop his pants and make love to her. If she shook her head, it ended here. She appreciated that he'd stuck to his promise of letting her decide what they did and did not do, but there was no decision to be made here. She had made up her mind the second she recognized his familiar figure sitting on her bed. She wanted him. Pulling her heels closer to her bottom, she opened herself wider and at the same time nodded.

Gaze still fixed on hers, he pushed his trousers and undershorts down and stepped out of them. When he stood, his powerful erection bobbed straight out from his groin like a knight's lance ready for battle.

Suddenly, she wished it were daylight so she could see everything the shadowed light promised was there. Hard planes and ridges. Solid sheets of muscle across broad shoulders and tapering down to a trim waist. And his massive member. Larger by far than her ex-husband's, and from the looks of it, hard as rock. Jimmy Doyle didn't need to coax his to attention as Curtis had.

He reached for something on the nightstand. A small packet he ripped open, then discarded after removing the contents. Evelyn watched, fascinated, as he sheathed his member from tip to base. She had no idea what it was, but she didn't care once he moved toward the bed.

His strength was never as evident as when he lowered himself onto the bed, taking care to move slowly so the old rusty bedsprings didn't make a sound as they gave beneath their combined weight.

He held himself above her, the muscles in his arms bulging

under the strain. Evelyn didn't know where to look. Her gaze flitted from his arms to his chest hovering above her, to his shoulders to, finally, his face. The instant her gaze met his, she felt him nudge at her core. He rocked his hips once, twice, opening her, then lodging the tip of his penis inside her.

A crash sounded in the hallway—someone scuffling around to pick up whatever they'd dropped. All the while, she and Jimmy Doyle remained frozen in almost copulation. Sweat beaded on her lover's face and neck as he held himself in check, waiting for the hallway to quiet. Evelyn willed her lungs to operate. Then, taking in a deep breath and letting it out, she met her lover's gaze once again and nodded.

He entered her bit by bit, stretching the long-neglected tissues lining her channel, filling her to capacity as he went. When he was fully inside her, he lowered his chest to hers, supporting himself with his forearms on either side of her head.

Nothing had ever felt as good as his penis felt inside her. He was big but oh, so perfect. It was as if he filled every empty spot in her. His heat warmed every cold place inside her. The hard planes of his body fit like puzzle pieces against her curves. A strange emotion swirled through her, wrapped itself around her heart, and squeezed. She'd always believed God created one man and one woman whom he meant to be together, but she'd never believed she would find the one he'd made for her. Until now.

Her heart swelled against the strange emotion banding it. Love. She loved Jimmy Doyle Walker. God had made him just for her, and her for him. The church said what they were doing was wrong outside of wedlock, but hadn't said a word when she'd married a man old enough to be her father—a man who didn't love her, didn't want her. A man so clearly not the one God had intended for her. In her mind, the church had lost its right to condemn her for loving the right man.

A song rose in her throat, but before it escaped her lips, Jimmy Doyle kissed her, swallowing the notes of her love even as he flexed his hips and, ever so reverently, withdrew and filled her again.

The household moved around them. People settling into bed, making preparations for the new day while the man of her dreams made slow and deliberate love to her. The creaky old bed knew better than to protest, it seemed, as it remained quiet. Sounds drifted in the window from the street, cars passing, footsteps advancing and retreating along the sidewalk. The porch swing giving up its burden for the night.

Inside Evelyn's room, the only sounds were of lovers expressing the inexpressible with their bodies. Sweat aided the slip and slide of skin on skin. Jimmy Doyle entered her at a steady pace, stoking the fire in her belly while his hands skimmed her body, teasing every inch as he went. He took all her cries into himself, drinking in her passion with his kisses, drugging her with his love.

Tension coiled in her womb, familiar only because she'd brought herself to this point while reading his letters. But this was different. This was frightening in its intensity. Evelyn fought against her restraints as the orgasm built. When she jerked her mouth away from his, he held her face in his hands and silently commanded her to meet his gaze.

Understanding shone in the depths of his eyes. He knew the struggle she was going through. Here, in the dark silence, he demanded she give him everything—her heart, her body, her trust, her orgasm. Stripped of every defense save one, the word *no*, she felt the syllable form in her throat. One whispered word and he would end it. He wouldn't take what he'd come there to claim.

As he stroked her forehead with his thumbs, his gaze bored into her, allowing him to see clear to her soul. He acknowledged what he saw there as something worthy of love. Her fear ebbed and slowly morphed into something else. Acceptance.

Jimmy Doyle owned her. She willingly gave him her body, but he'd come for so much more. He'd come for her.

Keeping a steady rhythm, in, out, he arched his back, bringing his face down to hers. His lips brushed the shell of her ear. She closed her eyes, shutting out everything but the man who held the power to create her or destroy her. "Give it all to me, sweetheart. I want it all."

Some would say she'd been seduced by Satan, but she knew better. This was a baptism of sorts, cleansing her of the guilt she'd carried away from the church where her marriage had taken place. She was one orgasm away from the gates of heaven. All she had to do was embrace the truth of her existence and submit fully to Jimmy Doyle. Once past the gates, he'd guide and protect her. His promise was in his tender lovemaking, and in the way he let her decide her own fate.

When she opened her eyes, he once again gazed at her, a serene expression on his face that belied the strain of holding off his own release. Pure love filled her heart and radiated throughout her body. He filled her again. She let him see everything in her heart through her eyes. "Take me. I'm yours."

CHAPTER TWELVE

He pulled out of her. With one hard thrust that forced a groan from the bedsprings and sent the headboard against the wall with a thud, he took her. He claimed her mouth, taking her cries of pleasure into himself, as was his right. Her channel clenched around his stiff member, until he panted hard and ground against her in short, jerky movements, giving her his heart in hot spurts.

Jimmy Doyle held his breath as he listened for the sound of someone coming to investigate the noise they'd made. When all remained quiet, he allowed himself to relax.

He'd waited longer than he wanted to make love to Evelyn, but now that he'd claimed her body, he wanted more. Passion ran deep in his Evelyn, deeper than in any woman he'd ever had the pleasure of fucking. Beneath him, her heart beat a crazy rhythm, and her inner walls clenched his dick in irregular spasms— aftershocks from her intense orgasm. He'd done everything in his power to woo her—the letters, the gifts—in the place of actual time spent together. Never before had he resented baseball for keeping him away from a woman. There was always another one willing to fall into his bed, but few understood his need to dominate the way Evelyn did.

When he'd seen her bow her head in that godforsaken tent, visions of her on her knees, bowing to him had filled his mind.

How he'd known she was the one, he didn't know. He hadn't been looking for "the one," or any woman, for that matter. When the pressure became too much, he knew where to go to find the kind of companionship his body craved. But there she was, so sad, so lost, looking for something he knew she'd never find in a church.

Perhaps God had been present after all, bringing two people together even if most would label them both sinners.

He knew the exact second when Evelyn's spirit returned to her body. One second she was soft and pliant beneath him, a serene smile on her lips. The next, her body tensed, and her eyes grew wide. He hated that the old hurt still lived inside her. He'd have to work at getting her to open up to him, to tell him what lurked in the shadows. Only then could he banish the demons. Only then would she be completely his.

Once again, he stroked her forehead with his thumbs, splaying his fingers across the back of her head, massaging gently. Some of the tension left her body, but something ugly lurked in her eyes. He whispered in her ear. "You have nothing to be ashamed of, sweet Evelyn. Your body and your orgasm are the most beautiful gifts I've ever received. I'll cherish them forever." The whimper that passed her lips nearly broke his heart. He kissed her, trying to take her sobs into himself. He'd do anything to take her pain away. If only she'd tell him where it stemmed from, he'd do whatever it took to banish it. That time would come. He just had to be patient. He had to show her what he already knew—she was one of God's most wondrous creations. Made for him and no other.

He held her, their bodies joined as one until her tears were spent. Then he eased from her, careful to make not a sound. He slipped the condom off, wrapping it in his handkerchief before he released her from the makeshift restraints. As he rubbed feeling back into her arms and tucked her into bed, he imagined her properly restrained and all the things he would do to her lovely body. If he mastered her skillfully, she would tell him what he needed to know to banish the demons stealing her happiness.

He dressed quietly, lingered over her lips one more time,

pouring all his love for her into the kiss before leaving the way he'd arrived—through the window opening to the side of the house and the ancient oak.

Alone in his bed later on, thoughts of her sweet surrender, however fleeting it had been, kept him awake late into the night.

God, the way she surrendered to him was fucking beautiful. She didn't yet understand what her submission—or his dominance—meant, but she would. He could see it in her eyes when he restrained her. Her heart raced, but it was with excitement, not fear. There was so much she didn't know about herself, but he would teach her. Soon, he'd take her to the farm where he could show her who she was. Hell, *he'd* learn who she was. He'd see exactly what she was made of.

He already knew she was strong. There was steel in her. Had to be to live the life she did, alone in a big city, making her own way. But when he had her tied up, beneath and open to him, she was soft and pliant. The pain he'd seen in her eyes when she'd come down from her orgasm ate at him. He'd been raised to protect the women in his life. Her problems were his, and whatever burdens she carried, it was his duty to eliminate them—carry them if he had to.

If the Diplomats didn't have out-of-town games coming up, he'd find a way to take her out to the farm this week, but that wasn't an option. After tomorrow's game, he'd be away from home for the next two weeks. Leaving her so soon after claiming her would be hard on both of them, but he'd make sure she felt his concern from across the miles. She'd know she was always on his mind, and that he was coming back for her. She'd know she was his.

He'd had a few minutes to look around her room before she'd come upstairs tonight. Looking through her dresser drawers might have been out of line, seeing as he hadn't been invited, and he hadn't claimed her yet, but he'd gone there to do the claiming. Learning everything he could about her beforehand made sense.

She was his now. Soon, he'd know everything there was to

know about her, from the brand of soap she used to where she kept her most precious possessions. He'd been pleased to find the letters he'd sent, worn from repeated handling, in the bottom drawer beneath her winter stockings. Tucked safely away were the gloves he'd sent, the fingertips soft and supple still, but the doeskin had molded itself to the shape of her hands—a sign she'd worn them often. He liked knowing she pleasured herself with the items he'd provided for that very purpose. One of these days, he'd be the one seeing to her pleasure, often and thoroughly. Though he wouldn't mind watching her accomplish the job wearing the gloves. God knew he'd imagined it enough times.

He'd found the handkerchief and the torn slip, still stained where she'd pressed the silk inside her body. The linen square appeared unused, but when he'd held the slip to his face, it smelled of Evelyn, and he'd gotten hard as a post. After placing everything back exactly as he'd found it, he'd noted the contents of the other drawers. Serviceable undergarments, carefully mended in some cases, and a few more recently purchased. She wasn't frivolous with her money. When she did buy for herself, she bought quality over quantity. He liked that about her.

He glanced around his darkened room. His gaze landed on the photographs of his family and mementos of his life. He'd moved several times since he'd left the family farm in Texas to pursue a career in baseball, but no matter where he went, the keepsakes went with him. As he'd stood in the center of Evelyn's small room, he'd noted the lack of personal items. There had been no photographs of her parents, her siblings. No personal mementos of any kind. If he hadn't known she'd lived in that room for several years, he would assume she'd just moved in.

It was that barren.

His heart ached as he realized her family was most likely the cause of the shame she carried inside her. Had they turned her away following the divorce? He knew she'd been raised in the church; why else would she have been at the tent revival? Lots of folks, church types or not, didn't cotton to divorced women.

Marriage was supposed to be for life—no matter how miserable two people were together—and when the union went south, it was generally believed to be the woman's fault.

He'd been around long enough to realize sometimes people weren't who you thought they were. He'd paid a price for believing people he called friends were honest folk. The mistake had cost him five years of his life and his good name.

Whatever Evelyn's reason for ending her marriage, he'd be willing to bet the blame didn't rest on her shoulders. Any man with a woman like Evelyn in his bed would have to be insane to let her go.

≪୨≫

He put everything he had into the afternoon game, but when it came time to board the train for Philadelphia, he did so with less enthusiasm. They'd spend four days in Philly; then the team would go on to New York and Boston before returning to Washington. Two and a half weeks without seeing Evelyn. Most of the other players had wives or girlfriends they would miss, but unlike him, many also had women they visited while on the road to take care of their baser needs. Before the scandal he'd known a few women, but after five years out of the game, they'd moved on and so had he. If he was really desperate, he knew of private clubs in a couple of the larger cities where the mention of mutual friends would gain him entrance and guarantee him whatever variety of companionship he wanted. The problem was, he didn't want anyone but Evelyn. Which meant he had a long, lonely stretch of time ahead.

The games in Philly exhausted him, and though he had a few hours free, he spent most of that time alone in his hotel room thinking about Evelyn and how to convince her to tell him about her life before she came to Washington. If he were there, he'd visit her room every night and slowly introduce her to the world of submission he knew she was born to. But since he couldn't do that, he'd have to hope his gifts and letters would be an adequate stand-in. By the time they reached New York, he had mapped out a plan.

As soon as he stepped off the train in Grand Central Terminal, he waved off his teammates who wanted to party and went in search of a store he'd heard about through his connections at the farm. Evelyn was in need of some proper undergarments, and the proprietress he sought was well-known in certain circles for her exquisite handmade items.

He found the storefront on Thirty-Sixth Street near the intersection of Tenth Avenue. Surrounded by showrooms on either side, the place was as respectable as any other. He admired the garments on display in the window before he entered. There was one in particular, a dusky rose nightgown that would look lovely on Evelyn. It was feminine and classy—two things that reminded him of the woman he had claimed for his own. She was beautiful in anything—or nothing—but she deserved to wear only the finest of fabrics against her skin.

An older woman wearing a smart suit pushed through the curtain separating the front of the store from the workroom. "May I help you?"

"I'm looking for something special for a special kind of woman." He repeated the phrase exactly as he'd been told. If he was in the right place, he'd be shown into a private room to view the designer's exclusive collection.

Her gaze raked over him as if she could discern his sexual interests from his outward appearance. Jimmy Doyle fought the inclination to squirm, squaring his shoulders and staring her down. When her gaze returned to his face, she smiled. "Follow me, Mister…"

"Smith."

She dipped her chin, accepting the false name readily enough. He'd passed the test, it seemed, as he was led through the curtains, past a cramped workroom where several people working at sewing machines and giant worktables paid him no mind. He guessed they were used to the owner escorting special customers through to view the unadvertised collection. She unlocked the door with a key she removed from the broach she wore at her waist and ushered him inside.

"Have a seat, Mr. Smith." Jimmy Doyle sat in the plush chair she indicated. "What, exactly, did you have in mind?"

She listened as he listed the garments he wanted. Then, after asking pertinent questions regarding the size and shape of the lady in question, she opened another door and disappeared for a few minutes. When she returned, she laid out an assortment of items for him to choose from. He selected several, then inquired about the gown he'd seen out front. He paid, leaving specific instructions regarding the shipment of the items. Assured his instructions would be carried out, he left in search of another gift.

The address on the Upper West Side was a brownstone with a stoop and a massive carved wood door. He knocked on the door and waited. A man about his age and build answered, ushering him into a parlor lined with display cases filled with glass figurines. They were beautiful, but not what he'd come for. "I'm looking for an obelisk. Do you have any?"

The man's lips quirked up on one side. "Something for yourself?"

"No. For a lady."

"I think I have just what you need." He crossed to a cabinet on the opposite wall. He withdrew a key from his pocket and unlocked the intricately carved doors. Inside, on tilted display shelves lined with velvet, lay the smooth glass objects he'd come for. "As you can see, we have many sizes to choose from."

The clerk waved his hand to indicate an upper shelf. "Some of the ladies prefer the colorful ones."

Jimmy Doyle scanned the offerings, zeroing in on a clear one with a raised ribbon of red swirling from base to tip. "That one." He motioned to it, and the salesclerk removed it from the display, handing it to him for a closer look. Using his hand to gauge the size, he determined it to be close in size to his cock. The raised ribbing would add to Evelyn's pleasure. In moments, the item was paid for, the shipping arrangements made.

⊱⊰

He wasn't going to let Ray Snodgrass get to him. The man never missed an opportunity to jab at old wounds, and today was no exception. Jimmy Doyle rubbed his rib cage where an earlier pitch had caught him as he attempted to move out of the way. The team doctor had checked him out, declared his ribs to be fine, but the diagnosis didn't ease the pain. It would take a while for this one to heal, but he'd be damned if it kept him from doing his job.

"I thought every one of their pitchers had already had a go at you. Guess I was mistaken." Ray's gibe was accompanied by a snicker of disgust.

"At least I got on base. That's more than I can say for you today." In fact, it was the middle of the eighth inning, and he had been the only Diplomat to make it to first base. He didn't like the way he'd gotten there, but it was better than not. If any of his teammates had been able to hit a pitch, he might have scored. As it was, the Diplomats were losing by four runs with little hope of digging themselves out of the hole. He had a whole string of things he wanted to say to his teammate, but none of them would improve the man's opinion of Jimmy Doyle or raise him up in the eyes of the rest of the team.

Harvey moved in between them, steering Jimmy Doyle to the other end of the dugout where he'd left his glove when he'd gone out to bat. "One of these days he'll wake up and figure out who's scoring all the runs on this team." The second baseman slapped the heel of his hand against his forehead. "Wait. What am I saying? Everyone with half a brain already knows this season would be in the toilet if not for you. They also know Ray only has a quarter of a brain."

Jimmy Doyle tried to hide his smile but failed. They retrieved their gloves and walked out on the field. "I appreciate the pep talk, but it isn't necessary. We're all contributing to the success of the team, including Snodgrass. Nothing gets past him in center field, and he has a strong bat." He watched the man in question break into a run, headed for his position in the outfield.

"Man, you're awfully generous to someone who hates your guts."

Ray was one of the few players on the team who had been playing five years ago. He'd known the players involved in the scandal as well as Jimmy Doyle had, yet no one had accused him of betting on the games. Not that he thought Ray had pointed a finger at him. He knew who had pointed his direction. Fat lot of good it had done him. A couple of months after claiming Jimmy Doyle's field position as his own, Bucky Holden had stepped off a curb in his hometown of Chicago and been flattened by a car. The driver wasn't charged, but many people thought the timing suspicious. Jimmy Doyle didn't know if the incident had been accidental or just made to look that way. Bucky had pissed off more than his share of people in his twenty-six short years on the planet.

"He loves the game." Jimmy Doyle scooped up a ground ball, then took his time to examine the orb before tossing it up in the air and catching it. "I can't blame him for wanting to protect it. Besides, he'll eventually figure out that our goals are the same. I'll still be here when he does." And he had more important things to worry about—like getting the next three outs, and maybe scoring a run in the ninth so they wouldn't start this series out by being skunked. Besides, team management was well aware of his contribution to the game, but a few were watching to see how he handled situations like the one with Ray. He wasn't going to give them a reason not to renew his contract at the end of the season.

That had always been his goal, but his motivation for reaching that pinnacle had changed the minute he laid eyes on Evelyn. Yeah, the extended contract still represented everything he'd worked for the past five years—restoration of his reputation, acknowledgment of his skill on the field—but there was more at stake now.

Working as a farmhand was fine for a single man, but he wasn't going to be a single man much longer. He thought about the ring he'd purchased for her. It was too soon to give it to her, to pledge his life to taking care of her and ask her to be his. Evelyn deserved so much more than a poor dirt farmer for a husband. Her satin skin should be wrapped in the finest fabrics. When she opened herself to him, she deserved a man with enough self-respect to understand what a precious thing her submission was. She deserved a hero, and he was fuckin' going to give her one.

That feeling stayed with him as he fielded the last out of the inning, and followed him out to the field in the top of the ninth. Ray had miraculously managed to get on base, then had stolen second. The Diplomats needed more than one miracle to get back in this game, but every rally had to start somewhere.

Jimmy Doyle stepped up to bat. He went through his familiar ritual, stretching to loosen muscles grown tight from the tension of remaining vigilant through eight grueling innings in the unrelenting heat. If he could bring Snodgrass home, maybe some of the others behind him would get inspired to hit the ball. He'd seen more games than he could count come down to the last six outs. Fatigue claimed even the best players. Not to mention the heat. It was like having a woman tied spread-eagle in the middle of the diamond, her pussy glistening and open. A player couldn't ignore it, no matter how hard he wanted to concentrate on the game.

It all came down to which team wanted the win the most.

Jimmy Doyle backed out of the batter's box. The umpire called time, allowing everyone to take a breath. He took one himself, then focused on the dugout. Standing at the rail, Harvey was the first to notice. He tapped a guy on the shoulder, who tapped another. When Jimmy Doyle stepped up to the plate again, every single member of the Diplomats stood along the rail—a united front against defeat.

Smiling to himself, he raised the bat to his shoulder. The first pitch came dangerously close to his sore ribs. He danced out of the way. Yeah, he wanted on base in the worst possible way, but a walk wasn't going to do it. He fuckin' wanted to send the ball out of the stadium. There wasn't anything like the slow, easy lope a player indulged in when he'd hit a homer. He only knew one thing to compare it to—watching a woman's orgasm claim her body, then taking a victory lap in her pussy while her screams cheered him on.

He fouled the second pitch into the right-field bleachers.

He had everyone's attention now—both dugouts, the crowd. Power surged through him the same way it did when he restrained Evelyn with the intent of blinding her with pleasure. He was in control. No one else. The ball would dance to the tune of his bat just as Evelyn would dance to the tune of his whip.

Jimmy Doyle focused everything he had on the pitcher. The man was breathing harder now than he had been earlier in the game. A trickle of sweat rolled unimpeded down his temple. In his years away from the game, Jimmy Doyle had not only honed his physical abilities, but he'd spent a great deal of time learning to interpret a person's body language. Male or female, it didn't matter. Fatigue was fatigue. Nerves were nerves.

He should call it quits—tell his master it's time to end the session. A good master would see the signs and put a stop to the session before it went any further. But no one in the opposing dugout was thinking about his pitcher. They were too busy wondering what Jimmy Doyle was going to do.

Watch and see. Watch. And. See.

Given the pitcher's motion and the way his fingers were wrapped around the ball, he expected the pitch to curve away from the plate at the last second. Patience was another skill he'd learned from playing at the farm. He waited. Infinitesimal seconds ticked silently by.

He loosened his fingers around the handle of the bat, clenched them tight, then eased off, holding the lumber as he would a flogger. Just enough pressure to retain control, but not so much that the muscles in his arms wouldn't respond when called upon.

He extended his hands, throwing them at the ball, reaching out for it like it was the sweetest snatch and his if he could only touch it.

It was almost as if he'd called the ball to him.

Come.

Now.

A flick of the wrist. The bat swung into the path of the speeding orb. The instant of contact hummed through his body like a current of electricity, spreading lightning fast, leaving in its wake a warmth and a certainty that something momentous had happened.

His feet instinctively moved toward first base. His gaze never left the ball as it soared high into the glare of the stadium lights, descending again in a high arc that would carry it over the left-center-field wall.

Every footfall ricocheted up his legs, vibrated through his dick and across his lower back before traveling up to his shoulders and along his arms, which still tingled from the impact. The screams of the crowd were music to his ears. He measured his steps out in his mind, drawing out the pleasure as long as he could before it was all over.

He counted the bases in his head—one, two, three. Home. The Diplomats dugout emptied out as every single player came out to greet him at the plate—all except Ray Snodgrass, who, having crossed home plate ahead of him, continued on into the dugout. Satisfaction raced through his blood, but as wonderful as it felt to be in charge on the field, it paled in comparison to his relationship with Evelyn.

He would have her. In every way possible. Her pleasure was his pleasure.

CHAPTER THIRTEEN

Evelyn was tempted to leave the packages on the hall table with a note for the postman—return to sender—but there was no way they would go unnoticed by her fellow boarders. Deliveries were an occasion for the women of the house who mostly lived day to day. Refusing one would invite questions she didn't want to answer. Her landlady already gave her disapproving looks every time they met in the hall and across the table at supper. If the woman had any idea what had gone on in Evelyn's room a few nights ago, she'd be looking for another place to live.

She snatched up the packages, tucked them under her arm, and went upstairs to her room. She dropped them on the bed and covered her face with her hands in an effort to block out the images the bed invoked. Shame burned through her, heating her skin. She never should have allowed Jimmy Doyle to make love to her. It was one thing to let him look upon her nakedness. Allowing him to touch her intimately had stretched the bounds of decency, but taking him to her bed. Fornicating with him. That had been indecent. Immoral. A sin.

She was nothing more than the slut her father and ex-husband accused her of being. She'd tried so hard to cleanse her soul of the wicked desires harbored there, but from the moment the baseball player had touched her arm outside the tent revival, the needs had come roaring back like a runaway freight train, obliterating her good sense and setting her body on fire.

Maybe if he'd left her alone, she would have indulged in a few fantasies, then purged him from her mind, but he hadn't. Her heart sped up each day as she approached the boardinghouse, anticipating another letter or package from him. Days would go by, a week, crushing her spirit and driving her to reread the missives she kept secreted away.

The moment she'd seen him sitting on her bed, she should have shoved him out the window, but the demon lust had gripped her hard, demanded she feed it.

Evelyn slipped her hands down her face, along the length of her neck as her head dropped back. Eyes closed, she brushed her fingertips across her chest, dropping lower to tease at her nipples— which were already hard and aching from the memories of Jimmy Doyle's hands and mouth there—demanding her surrender. Cupping her unbound breasts, she pressed the mounds flat, remembering the feel of his chest hard against hers, his weight pressing her into the mattress.

She bit her lower lip to stifle a moan as she skimmed her hands across her belly to the juncture of her thighs. Not an hour went by when she didn't think of his mouth on her, his manhood spearing into her. Slow. So slow she thought she might die from the wanting. She'd never known coupling could be like that. The Bible spoke of two becoming one, but until Jimmy Doyle had filled her body with his, she hadn't known what it meant to be so close to another that you didn't know where he ended and you began.

Ever since, she'd ached to have him inside her, to feel that connection again. She was finding it harder and harder to believe that anything so wonderful as two souls connecting as they had could be wrong.

Wrapping her arms tight around her middle, she backed away from the bed. Shame gnawed at her gut. Like Eve of old, she was cursed to desire men. She physically ached to feel a man joining with her, but the Bible said copulation was for the purpose of procreating, and according to her father, lust and desire were the sins of a whore.

Her body on fire, both from remembering what she and Jimmy Doyle had done in her bed, and from the oppressive heat in the room, she undressed down to her panties. A damp washcloth applied to the back of her neck helped cool her outside temperature but did nothing to extinguish the flame of desire deep inside.

Approaching the bed again, she sighed, her resistance melted in the heat of her longing. She would open the packages after supper. And whatever instructions were in the accompanying letter, she would follow and deal with the shame later on.

Evelyn put on her at-home dress and went down to supper. She ate in silence, her thoughts completely focused on the boxes sitting on her bed upstairs. The one was too heavy to be another garment. Perhaps he had sent her a souvenir from his travels. She wondered what it was like for him, going from city to city by train, staying in hotels, and eating in restaurants—seeing all kinds of sights. The farthest she'd ever been from her hometown in central Virginia was Washington, DC.

Whatever was in the boxes, she would be glad to have, because it meant Jimmy Doyle thought about her while he was gone.

The second it became okay for her to leave the table, Evelyn excused herself. As soon as she closed and locked her door, she stripped to her panties, then sat cross-legged on the bed and drew the packages to her. The postmark indicated they had been mailed from New York. She'd seen newsreels about the city and couldn't imagine walking the streets. She'd be lost in no time, but her lover had braved the massive city to buy something for her.

One was both smaller and lighter than the other, and for no particular reason, she decided to save it for last. Beneath the outer wrapping was a plain but distinguished-looking cream-colored box that bore no name to indicate the shop it had come from. Her curiosity piqued, she removed the lid. Inside was a beautiful blue lace brassiere. She pressed her fingers to her lips to contain a gasp.

Handling the garment as if it might shatter, she held it up. It had to be the most beautiful thing she'd ever seen. She set it gingerly aside and removed the next layer of tissue paper to reveal matching panties. Digging deeper, she found another set in pink, garter belts to go with both, and last, two pairs of silk stockings.

The expensive garments looked out of place against the worn chenille spread covering her bed, and she thought they would look even more out of place on her. These were garments for a queen or, at the very least, a fine lady. Not a divorcée working as a switchboard operator.

The string holding the wrapping on the smaller package was done up tight but, after some tugging, gave way. Evelyn peeled back the brown paper to reveal another plain box—this one was an elegant dark green and, like the one before, bore no markings.

Evelyn took a deep breath, then let it out before lifting the top. Crinkled packing material of the type used to cushion fragile items filled the inside. She carefully removed the top layer and placed it inside the lid. Nestled in shredded paper was the most scandalous thing she'd ever seen in her life. She froze, fingers pressed to her lips to seal in her laughter.

Oh, Jimmy Doyle. What is this?

Afraid she might break it, she traced the raised ribbon of colored glass with her fingertip. It was cool to the touch, sending a shiver along her spine. What in the world was she supposed to do with it? It was a work of art, to be sure, but she couldn't very well display it in her room. What if someone were to see it? A giggle escaped her lips before she could stop it. It would almost be worth getting thrown out on the street to see her landlady's face when she saw the glass penis.

Evelyn stared at the object a few seconds more before reaching for the letter that had arrived along with the packages. Her lover had some explaining to do! What had the man been thinking to send her something like that?

My dearest Evelyn,

I miss you more each day I'm away, darling girl. I have only to close my eyes to see you in all your glory and to remember your heat welcoming me home. I can't tell you how much I long to be inside you again, my love. The remembering is both sweet and painful, causing me no small amount of discomfort. I take matters into my own hands often, but the temporary cure for what ails me is nothing compared to being inside you.

Do you ache for me, sweet Evelyn? Do not lie to me or to yourself. I've seen your passion, my dearest, and know your needs are as great as mine.

I must tell you, love, how very proud you made me the other night. You were so beautiful in your submission, and you followed my instructions so well. The next time I am inside you, bringing you to the peak of pleasure, you will be free to make all the sounds you want without fear of discovery. It was all I could do to remain quiet as well. Moving inside you so slowly was the most delicious form of torture I have ever experienced, and believe me, I know much on that subject.

Being away from you is the worst kind of anguish. My hands long to touch you. My lips long to kiss you. My tongue longs to taste you. My cock swells with the need to fuck you.

I can almost smell your arousal, darling. You need me as much as I need you, don't you, my precious one? Go ahead, touch yourself. Dip your fingers inside your sweet pussy and spread your juices around so you are slick and wet between your legs. Do it again, dear one, but this time, bring your fingers to your lips and coat your plump mouth with the warm liquid.

God, to be there with you! Taste yourself, darling girl. Lick your lips, then your fingers. This is the taste I'm addicted to. It is yours, and yours alone. It is mine.

Your body is mine. Whatever your needs are, I will be the one to meet them. From the first moment I saw you, I sensed that you were meant to be mine, and once I tasted you, I knew for certain. All that was left was the claiming. You were so brave, so magnificent while I staked my claim. You offered your body, and I took it, every last inch of it, for my own.

Does that frighten you, my love? It shouldn't. The control is always in your hands, though I confess, I will push your boundaries in an effort to help you find the greatest pleasure possible. Always know I cherish what is mine, which brings me to my latest gifts. Did you receive the packages, darling girl? Please do not be mad at me for wanting you to have nice things. Your body is a work of art, and everything that touches it should be art as well.

I couldn't decide which color would look best on you, so I purchased them both. Choose the one you prefer and put it on for me. I want to finish writing this while I imagine you in one of those beautiful creations.

Evelyn let out an exasperated breath. She shouldn't keep the garments, but she didn't want to hurt his feelings either. Still, he had to quit sending her things. Sooner or later someone in the house was going to wonder why, all of a sudden, she was receiving packages every few weeks, and then what would she say?

She fingered the blue lace brassiere again. There was no way she could return the items to the store, and she felt sure returning them to the man who'd purchased them would do no good. What was done was done. They were hers now, so what harm would there be in trying them on?

"Oh, my!" Evelyn wished she had a full-length mirror to see herself. If she stood just right, she could see her lace-clad chest in the one over the bathroom sink, and that was enough to give her pause. She'd never dreamed anything so luxurious even existed, yet clearly it did, and Jimmy Doyle thought *her* worthy of wearing it. She didn't know what to say to that.

Deciding some things couldn't be explained, she returned to the bed and picked up the letter.

My imagination is running away at this moment, beautiful woman, creating images of you in blue lace. Is that the one you chose? The color reminded me of your eyes when you find your pleasure, so I had to get it. I expect you to wear them often, and to think of me when you do. Do not argue with me on this, my Evelyn. I want to think about you sitting at your workstation, looking for all the world like any other switchboard operator, but underneath your working dress, you and I will know you are like no other. It will be our secret.

Now. About the other package...

Forgive me for smiling at the image that comes to mind when I think of you discovering what I have sent you. Do not be scandalized, dearest one. It was purchased with your needs and your pleasure in mind. I wish I could be there to show you how to use it, but my absence is the reason for the gift in the first place. If I were there, you would have no need of it, except that it would give me great pleasure to watch you use it to bring yourself to completion.

Yes, my sweet one, that is exactly what it is for, if you have not figured that out for yourself. The artist I purchased it from had many to choose from, but this one made me smile when I saw it. All I could think about was how the raised ribbons would add to your pleasure, and then nothing could have prevented me from making the purchase.

I need you so badly, sweet Evelyn. Allow me to bring you pleasure and, in so doing, ease my need to provide for you.

So, it wasn't a piece of art—or rather it was, but it had a function too. Evelyn felt her skin heat from the inside out. She closed her eyes, imagining putting the glass penis inside her body. Then she saw herself doing it while Jimmy Doyle watched from the foot of the bed. He said he'd like to watch her, but where would she find the courage to allow that? She remembered the heated look in his eyes when he made love to her, and she knew she'd do whatever it took to see that expression on his face again—even pleasure herself with a piece of glass.

She made herself comfortable on the bed, the gift in one hand, her lover's letter in the other.

I can see you, sweet Evelyn, lying on your bed, your legs spread, your woman's flesh swollen and wet—need making your eyes darken. I want nothing more than to give you the pleasure you seek, but first, there is something else I want you to do.

I chose the dildo in part because it is very close in size to my cock when my desire for you is at its peak. Remember that I have claimed your body, and that there are many things I will ask you to do, in the name of your pleasure and mine, in the future. One thing that will greatly please me is to fuck your mouth. In order for me to do this, it will be necessary for you to become accustomed to taking as much of my length into your mouth as possible. Each day, I want you to set aside ten minutes to practice taking the dildo into your mouth. Learn to suck it, sweet darling. Tease it with your tongue. Learn to graze it lightly with your teeth. But most important, learn to take it to the back of your throat. It will be necessary for you to learn to breathe through your nose and to swallow while the dildo is in place.

While you do these exercises each day, imagine the pleasure it will give me when you sink to your knees and take me into your mouth.

Try it now, lovely one. Kneel facing your bed, back straight, knees shoulder width apart. Place one hand behind your back and use the other to hold the dildo.

Oh, God. Evelyn's heart thundered. Memories of taking her ex-husband's penis in her mouth made her want to vomit. She paused a moment to calm her nerves before rereading that part of the letter. On the third time through, she realized what was different about it. He wasn't suggesting she suck him until he became hard. He was saying he wanted to use her mouth the way he would her pussy—putting his already hard penis inside.

When she was around, he always seemed to have an erection. Unlike her ex-husband, he'd never needed her assistance to achieve one.

She remembered the pleasure he'd given her with his mouth. He was asking her to do the same for him. Could she go to her knees for him? She closed her eyes and tried to imagine herself on her knees, taking his hard penis in her mouth. He would look at her with love in his eyes as he slipped his erection between her lips.

The erotic image helped ease the pain in her stomach. She could do it. She wanted to do it. She slid off the edge of the bed and assumed the position he'd indicated. With the glass object in hand and his letter on the bed, she read.

I am hard, imagining you positioned to take me into your mouth, sweet woman. Sometimes I will stand while you suck me; other times I will be seated or lying down. Regardless, it will give me great pleasure to watch my cock slip past your lips. Imagine I am standing before you, darling. Take me in hand and taste me with your tongue. Yes, swirl it around the head. Do not be surprised if it weeps for you. That pearl of fluid is because I want you so badly, woman of mine.

Open your lips now, my precious. Take me in as far as you can. Yes, like that. Swallow, Evelyn. Take me in a little more. Breathe, darling. Yes, look up at me. See how much you please me? I am at your mercy, my love. My pleasure is yours to give or withhold. I am yours as you are mine.

God, Evelyn, my love, I don't know how long I can continue to write to you this way without filling my hand with my seed. Oh, how I would love to shoot it down your throat, but that will have to wait. One day soon, I promise. You have given yourself to me, and I will return the favor. In the meantime, enough of that. Daily practice until I return will have you ready to accept my cock in your mouth. Let's return to your pleasure, lovely one.

I'm afraid you'll need to remove those lovely panties now so they don't get in the way. Do that, and then return to your place on the floor. I only ask this because I want you to have the freedom to move without worrying about the springs on your bed making noise you would have to explain later.

Place one hand on the edge of the bed for support. Rub the dildo through your folds until it is coated in your juices. Yes, I know it's cold. In the future, soak it in warm water to heat it, but today, the cold will be a reminder that I am a lonely man without you.

Spread your knees wider if you need to, sweet darling. Bring the head of the dildo to your opening. Nudge it inside. Do you feel the stretch? Give yourself time to adjust to being filled, then press it in deeper. Slowly, Evelyn. Savor the feeling of being filled with my cock.

Does it feel good going in? Does it remind you of me? You have my permission to do this as often as needed, but only when I am out of town. If I am there, you will save your orgasms for me. I will not share them, even with an inanimate object.

Is it all the way in, darling? Pull it all the way out, then shove it back in, faster this time. Hold it there. I want you to fuck yourself, my love. Think of me as you work the dildo in and out of your pussy. You set the pace. Hard and fast or easy and slow. It is up to you to decide what you need. When I return, I will require you to tell me about each time you have given yourself an orgasm.

They are mine, after all.

Set the letter aside, my love, and pleasure yourself. Go ahead, lovely one. Imagine me standing behind you, watching. Enjoy the orgasm. I'll be here when you are done.

Evelyn leaned her forehead against the mattress. The dildo, cold at first, had absorbed the warmth of her body. She closed her eyes and, breathing deeply, scented her arousal. She imagined Jimmy Doyle, naked, standing behind her, waiting.

She pulled the glass phallus to the rim of her vagina, then inserted it again. She repeated the process, faster and harder this time, gasping at the pleasure of being filled and the friction added by the raised ribbon swirl. It felt good. Incredibly good. After she established a rhythm, the tension built until she was on the brink of release. She bit her bottom lip and quickened the pace, faster and harder so the heel of her hand slapped against her clitoris. Her breath grew shallow. Her thighs trembled with the movement of her hips and the effort needed to keep her aloft.

Time slowed. Her body drew within itself like an overwound clock spring. One more thrust of her hips. One more thrust of the glass cock and the tension released in a violent eruption that made her inner muscles quake and grip the dildo in arrhythmic convulsions. A shudder of satisfaction rocked her from head to toe as she pulled the object free of her body and curled up on the floor. As soon as her breathing returned to normal, she sat up, leaned against the bed and reached for the letter. The thin paper fluttered in her trembling fingers like dry leaves in the wind. She didn't have a firm bone left in her body, it seemed.

Light from the windows had grown dim by the time she felt steady enough to finish the letter.

Ah, my sweet love, I cannot tell you how much I wish I had been there to witness your orgasm. Was it wonderful, my darling? Are you sleepy, drugged with pleasure? I hope so. I'm sure you need your rest now, so place the dildo beneath your pillow. The morning will be soon enough to clean it and put it away. Remove your lovely new garments and sleep nude tonight, lovely one. I won't sleep a wink thinking of you sated and naked.

> *Until next time,*
> *All my love,*
> *Jimmy Doyle*

CHAPTER FOURTEEN

He couldn't seem to think of anything but her. Every time he closed his eyes, he saw her slim fingers wrapped around the glass dildo he'd sent her as she worked it in and out of her body. The image was driving him out of his mind.

The only good thing he could find about being in Boston was that just three games stood between him and being with Evelyn again. Christ, when his fingers weren't dealing with his constant hard-on, they were itching to touch her skin. He'd fucked plenty of women, had tied them up and played with their bodies for his satisfaction and theirs. But nothing compared to the time he'd spent with Evelyn.

He couldn't wait to have her beneath him again. Making love to her in her bed, slow so the rusted bedsprings wouldn't give them away, had been pure torture as well as the single most satisfying sex he'd ever had. Sinking his dick inside her felt like coming home, and once there, he hadn't wanted to leave.

But leave he did. Physically, at least. Nearly two weeks had passed, and when he took his dick in hand to find relief from the constant need to be with her, it was her slick heat he dreamed of. It was her scent he imagined. It was her soft, welcoming body he slammed into. It was her name on his lips when he erupted.

Three games, he reminded himself. Twenty-seven innings

until he could take her to the farm.

He'd wanted to take her there since the day in the park when she'd handed him a soiled handkerchief, but that wasn't a decision to be taken lightly. He owed it to everyone who belonged there to exercise caution, and he expected no less from them. Revealing the secret club to the wrong person could mean disaster for everyone involved. So, he'd waited until he was sure she was the right sort of person to understand what was going on there, and that she could keep the secret. Hell, one of the reasons he most wanted to take her there was to have the means and the privacy necessary to pry secrets from her.

Never before had he felt the need to know everything about a woman. Not until Evelyn. She was a mystery to him in so many ways. Yes, he knew how to make her body sing—though he'd only begun to explore and catalog every little spot that drove her wild. He figured it could take a lifetime to discover them all.

Choosing his seat on the train with an eye for privacy, Jimmy Doyle sat and pulled a folded newspaper from beneath his arm. Inside the daily edition, he'd carefully hidden a smaller, lesser-known periodical only available in New York. Before his banishment from the league, he'd picked up a copy for his friend, Grace, every time he was in the city. Since his return to the game, he'd resumed the habit. Grace had more friends than anyone he knew, but she rarely left the farm, so it was the least he could do for the woman who had taught him so much. She said that keeping up with news and trends among people who practiced out-of-the-ordinary sex made her feel less isolated. He supposed he understood that.

No sooner had he opened the paper than he was joined by the team's manager.

"Jimmy Doyle," the man said, taking the facing seat. "Mind if I sit?"

If he'd been in a better position regarding his future with the team, he might have pointed out that it was a bit too late to ask since the man had already sat down, but instead, Jimmy Doyle folded his paper, tucked it between his hip and the wall of the car, and said, "Not at all."

There were several empty seats between him and most of the rest of the team, so there was little doubt Toby Grant had chosen that particular seat for a reason. Jimmy Doyle pretended interest in the platform outside, where travelers struggled with luggage, hurrying to get aboard before the train departed. Whatever the manager had come to say, he'd spit it out, eventually. Being as it was a short ride between New York and Boston, Jimmy Doyle figured the mystery would be solved soon enough.

"How's it going?" They'd just pulled out of the station when Grant spoke. "You doin' all right?"

He shrugged. "I have a few more bruises than I would like, but otherwise, I can't complain."

"Everyone on the team treating you well?"

He lifted his shoulders again, choosing not to make an issue of the lingering animosity between him and his teammates. It was what it was. They were entitled to believe what they wanted. As long as he got paid and had field time, he was good.

"We've been impressed with how you've handled the situation. Personally, I'd hoped that some of the more vocal players would have come around by now, but they haven't. Any ideas on why that is?"

"Not a one." Was the man hoping he would say something stupid like, *Maybe because I was guilty as sin, and they know it?*

This time, it was the older man who shrugged. "I guess some people are more attached to their opinion than others. Me? I never did think you were the type to do something like that. You love the game too much." He slapped his hands on his thighs. "Well, just wanted to check in with you and let you know the owners are impressed with your statistics. They want to see you when we get back. And just so you know, I've recommended that they do whatever it takes to keep you for the next few years. You've been an asset to the team, and I think you'll continue to contribute."

Jimmy Doyle stood when he did, quietly thanking him for his

support. Resuming his seat, he replayed the conversation in his head. For the first time since he'd put the uniform back on, he allowed himself to think beyond this season. A few more years, guaranteed, would replenish the savings he'd used to defend himself and to live on while in exile. When he was too old to play, maybe he could get a coaching job. Providing for Evelyn was his number one priority.

⁊⁊⁊

Jimmy Doyle dropped his duffel in his room, then went back down to the bank of phone booths lining a hallway off the main lobby. After placing a call to Grace to let her know he planned to bring Evelyn to the farm, he allowed himself to relax. He hadn't expected his friend to question his judgment, and she hadn't, but she asked plenty of questions. A decade his senior, she had been his first partner at the farm, teaching him the art of domination through her patient submission. He'd moved on to other partners, and she'd taken to looking out for him like a big sister. At times, that was both annoying and comforting. He could talk with her about things he could never express to his real family, so he didn't take offense at her curiosity. In the five years he'd lived and worked on the farm, he'd never been with a woman from outside, so he supposed she had a right to worry.

Grace had a responsibility to the other members of the exclusive private club that operated at the farm too. They trusted her to keep their secrets, so naturally, she'd want to know everything about Evelyn before allowing her membership. He hadn't expected special treatment and was assured there would be none.

With his plans in place, he focused on the games ahead. The Diplomats needed to win the series to maintain their standing in the league. Winning the pennant was a real possibility if they didn't fall apart in the last few weeks of the season. Despite what the manager said, this could very well be his final season, and he wanted to go out on top. Or as close to the top as possible. He

144

couldn't afford to let his personal life intrude on his job. Not now, when he was so close to getting everything he'd worked for.

The next day, he went out to play with a clear head and a fire for winning in his gut. Early in the season, he'd taken a few hits from the Red Sox pitchers, but like most teams, they'd voiced their opinions of him, then moved on. He could only wish his own teammates would do the same.

"Hey, slugger." Harvey paused at first base. "Nice hit. Wish I could have followed through."

Jimmy Doyle shrugged. "It's only the first inning. Plenty of time left." He adjusted the glove on his left hand.

The second baseman glanced at the outfielders, sprinting to their positions. "Did you see his face when he struck out? That man has anger issues."

He could only be talking about Ray Snodgrass, who was the sole outfielder in the top of the batting order. "He's hard enough on himself without us being on his case. Don't forget, there's a reason he bats third. He gets on base."

"So you can bring him in."

"I understand the way he thinks. He wants to contribute to the team, and when he doesn't, he gets angry at himself. Sometimes all that anger comes out in inappropriate ways." Jimmy Doyle had more in common with Ray than he was willing to admit. Thanks to his control issues in other aspects of his life, he'd learned to let the anger go and focus on more important things.

Harvey tapped him on the shoulder with his glove. "I can see I was wrong taking you to church. You're a saint, man. Snod treats you like shit, and you defend him." He trotted over to his position in time to field a warm-up ground ball.

Jimmy Doyle went through the warm-up routine by rote. If Harv knew how far from a saint he really was, the man would drag him to church seven days a week. He'd come to terms with Ray's behavior months ago. He couldn't say it didn't still bother him, but he felt sure the man would come around, and bring the younger players who looked up to him with him. Jimmy Doyle just had to continue working toward his goal of getting the team into the play-offs and securing a new multiyear contract for himself. Everything else would fall into place—eventually.

✌᠔

Evelyn looked around for a familiar landmark, but like most farm country she'd seen, everything looked pretty much alike. If you'd seen one barn, one farmhouse, one dried-up field, you'd seen them all. Jimmy Doyle had promised to take her somewhere they could be alone, and in his words, *"You can make as much noise as you want when you come."* He'd also promised a day full of surprises, but so far, the only surprise was how far they'd driven. The heat of the day made minutes seem like hours. If not for the breeze blowing through the open car windows, depositing a fine layer of grit in every crease and pore, there would be no relief. "Do you know where you're going?" she asked with a smile.

He glanced in her direction. His lips quirked up on the corners in a way that said he knew all too well her impatience had to do with her need to be with him as much it did with the drive. She'd been in a state of need ever since she'd received his last letter telling her he'd be by to pick her up on his day off, and to wear nothing but the frock he'd bought her and her shoes. Everything else she would need for their day together, he would provide.

"Yes, sweet one, I do." His gaze darted to the road, then back to her. "You'd be cooler if you weren't wearing that dress. Unbutton it."

"What?" Her hand automatically went to the collar as if the buttons might pop open of their own accord.

"Unbutton your dress, Evelyn. I want to see you."

She hesitated, searching his eyes for any indication that he was joking.

"Remember when we talked about punishment?" Evelyn nodded, clutching the top of her dress in her tight fist. "Today, you will do as I say without question or hesitation or suffer the consequences of your actions. Just so you know what you are

146

facing, if you don't unbutton your dress by the time I count to ten, the first thing I'm going to do when we reach our destination is bend you over the hood of the car, raise your skirt, and spank your ass twenty times."

While he gave his edict, he kept his gaze on the road, but she knew in her bones he was aware of the way her heart beat against her chest and the way her core responded to his authoritative voice. "Do you understand?"

"Yes."

"Sir. You'll address me as Sir today."

"Yes, Sir. What if someone—"

"No one will see you out here." He nearly barked the comment at her, then flexed his fingers on the steering wheel as if he'd been holding on too tight. "I said, no questions. You have to trust me, Evelyn. There will be times when I will want others to see you, but they will be people I know and trust, not complete strangers. I would never put you in a situation that would compromise your reputation."

Her mind was still reeling from his comment about other people seeing her naked, when he began to count. A glance out the windshield assured her no other cars were on the dirt road they traveled. By the time she'd worked the top three buttons free, she'd convinced herself no one in a passing car would see anything. She popped the last button free just as he said, "Ten."

"Spread the dress open, then put your feet up on the dashboard, shoulder width apart."

As soon as she parted the fabric and the warm breeze brushed over her skin, her nipples hardened into tight points, and she broke out in gooseflesh all over. She felt wicked and wanton, and she couldn't remember ever feeling the rush of excitement she did when she placed her feet on the dashboard, allowing the air to swirl between her legs.

"Let your knees fall open, sweetheart. I want to see you."

She was crazy to do as he said, but he seemed to know every sinful thing she'd ever thought, and not only allowed her to do them, but encouraged her. She relaxed her thighs, and her knees dropped, exposing her private parts to the world.

"You're so beautiful. Hang on, we're turning here."

Evelyn gripped the edge of the seat on one side and the armrest on the other as he turned the steering wheel with one hand and worked the gearshift. The car bounced and groaned in protest. Once they were going steadily down yet another dirt road, he turned his attention back to her. "Spread yourself open, baby girl. Dip a couple of fingers inside and show me how wet you are."

Doing as she was told, she showed him two fingers dripping wet.

"Excellent. Lick your fingers clean, then put your hands on your thighs. Keep your knees apart."

They rode along in silence. His gaze heated her skin more than the dry breeze blowing through the windows. She tried not to think about what would happen if they passed another car. He was probably right—they wouldn't see much, if anything, but that was little comfort. She felt exposed in a way that was both disconcerting and exhilarating. No one in her adult life had seen her completely nude except Jimmy Doyle. Thoughts of others seeing her, perhaps watching while she touched herself, flitted through her mind. The flesh between her legs tingled, arousal building as the fantasy formed in her mind. She squirmed in the seat, allowing her fingers to dip closer to her pussy.

"Go ahead. Touch yourself."

Evelyn jerked her hands back to their original places higher on her thighs. Embarrassed at being caught in a fantasy, she felt a blush sweep over her face.

"I don't suppose you've ever had anyone watch, have you?"

She closed her eyes. How had he known what she was thinking? At times, it seemed as if he could read her mind. "No."

"No, what?"

Electricity skated along her skin, then settled into her core where it ignited a blaze of yearning. "No, Sir."

"Thank you."

She popped her eyes open to see the smile on his face matched the one she'd heard in his voice.

"No matter what happens today, calling me Sir will guarantee no one else will touch you."

Evelyn sat up, reaching for the buttons on her dress. He stopped her with a firm hand over hers. "I didn't tell you to move. Resume the position."

Again, his tone left no room for argument. Evelyn parted the sides of her dress and placed her feet on the dashboard. "Who will be there?"

"I don't know for sure. It might just be us and the owners. Few people come out on weekdays."

"Come out to where? Where are we going?"

"We're going to a farm I used to work at."

"While you were suspended from the game?"

His gaze darted to hers, then back to the road. He gripped the steering wheel until his knuckles turned white. "You know about that?"

"I heard some people talking about it."

"What did they say?"

"Not much, except that you were accused of gambling."

"I was accused of betting on games. A lot of the people I called friends were involved. I was guilty by association. It took me five years to prove to the league and the courts that I had nothing to do with the gambling ring. In the meantime, I worked out here on the farm. I put up hay in the summer, fed the livestock in the winter, and in general, kept the place running year-round. They paid me in room and board and waived my membership fees. The work kept me from going insane." Jimmy Doyle eased the car to a stop in the middle of the road, and for a few minutes he simply stared out the windshield. "The people you are going to meet today are my friends. Some of them are like family to me. I want you to know that. Most folks would call them deviant or perverted, but they aren't. They're just like everyone else, only they don't judge people based on their sexual inclinations."

He relaxed his grip on the steering wheel, then turned to face her. "You can live out every fantasy you've ever had without censure. You can be who you are, Evelyn. No one will condemn you for what your body needs. Sex is not a sin at the farm. Sexual pleasure is *not* a sin."

Her body felt like it was on fire from the inside out. Her pussy throbbed in tandem with her heart beating like she'd run a marathon. She opened her mouth to speak, but nothing came out.

"Do you understand?"

Evelyn nodded, though she wasn't sure she had a grasp on all he'd said. He was taking her to a farm, but people went there to have sex? He'd worked there for years, which meant he'd probably been with all the women there. Were there women there? Would other men want her? Yes, but as long as she called Jimmy Doyle Sir, they would leave her alone. Unless—

"I need to hear you say it, Eve. Tell me you understand. What goes on at the farm remains there. I'll see to your needs in every way, and you will see to mine. Nothing you say or do at the farm is wrong. Even if you see someone you met here on the streets of Washington, they won't acknowledge knowing you. You and your sexual needs will be completely safe."

A large blackbird landed on the hood ornament, flapped his shiny wings a few times as he looked about, eventually doing an about-face. He blinked his beady eyes at the people behind the glass wall, or perhaps he was only viewing his reflection. Evelyn didn't know which, but to her it seemed as if the bird was looking straight at her. Her mind replaced beady bird eyes with human ones. She groaned and clutched at her thighs as arousal clawed at her insides.

"I understand." She said the words he needed to hear. She closed her eyes. Biting her lower lip, she rocked her hips. "Please, Jimmy Doyle. I need…"

"Does the bird watching excite you, little one?" He let go of the steering wheel to stroke her pussy. "You're swollen and wet." His fingers spread the evidence around. Evelyn moved her hips, seeking relief from the storm building inside her. She was going to die if the storm didn't break soon.

"Ask me nicely, sweet Evelyn, and I'll make you come."

"Please…"

"Please, what?" Her brain scrambled to find the words he was looking for.

"Please, Sir."

"So sweet." Two fingers speared her. Her hips shot off the seat, rocking to find the rhythm he set. In. Out. In. Out. "He's watching you, sweet one. He wants to see you come. We both want to see you come."

Oh, God. Her mind conjured a mystery man in the shadows, watching Jimmy Doyle bring her to orgasm. Never in her wildest fantasies had she ever imagined such a thing, but now that it was in her head, the image wouldn't go away. She didn't want it to. Her fingers dug into her thighs.

"Come for us, Evelyn. Let go, baby. It's okay. Scream if you want. No one but us will hear you."

He pressed deep inside her again. The tension coiled in her womb unwound, fast and hard. She tried to clamp her legs together, but a strong arm braced between her knees prohibited it. Pain, sharp and insistent, pulsed through her, followed by the most intense pleasure she'd ever known.

"Oh, God!" Evelyn thrashed beneath him. Somehow, he'd wedged himself across her so all she saw when the orgasm eased and she opened her eyes was his back. She loosened the tight grip she held on her thighs, sighing as her body melted in the aftermath of her orgasm.

"Beautiful." Warm lips nibbled at her inner thigh.

"Jimmy Doyle!" Evelyn squirmed, but her arms were trapped beneath his torso draped across her midsection. She couldn't possibly dislodge him. He placed another kiss, this one lower.

"Beautiful." He moved his fingers, still inside her, she realized. "Now that I know you like being watched, I'll have to indulge you in that particular fantasy as often as possible."

Evelyn groaned. He kissed his way to her center. When his tongue flicked at her clitoris, another orgasm jolted her so hard she cried out.

"I've got to get you to the farm." He rose, licking his fingers before putting the car back in gear and accelerating down the dusty road. Evelyn lay like a limp dishrag on the seat, her legs splayed, exposing her sopping-wet folds. Her body hummed with satisfaction, but her mind raced. Only a very wicked woman would do what she had just done. Shame drained the last dregs of pleasure from her body.

She moved, trying to push herself upright. He placed his hand over her pussy, stopping her. "Don't think that's all there is. You're going to come over and over. I'm going to see to it."

What had she gotten herself into?

Evelyn fastened the last button, then straightened in her seat moments before he steered the car along what appeared to be a dirt driveway lined with trees on either side. They'd gone maybe fifty yards when a man stepped from the tangled brush into the middle of the road. Evelyn gasped. The man wore striped overalls and a hat that shadowed most of his face. He held a shotgun in one hand, the barrel lying casually in the crook of his arm.

Jimmy Doyle stopped the car, then leaned out the window. With a friendly wave, he called out through the billowing dust, "It's just me, Lloyd, Jimmy Doyle."

"Long time, no see." Lloyd appeared at the side of the car. Smiling, he bent, his gaze sweeping the interior. "Who ya got with you?"

Jimmy Doyle gave her a reassuring look, then turned back to the man with the gun. "This here's Evelyn. I'll vouch for her. Grace is expecting us."

Evelyn started, hearing the woman's name roll so casually off her companion's lips. Whoever she was, mentioning her name seemed to carry more weight with the gun-toting man than her escort's good opinion.

Lloyd nodded. "Good to see you again, Mr. Walker." He

stood away, then leaned back down. "Meant to tell you I've been following the team. Keep up the good work."

Jimmy Doyle inclined his head, accepting the veiled compliment. "I'll try and do that, Lloyd. Thanks."

The guard walked back to the tree line where he'd come from. As Jimmy Doyle wrestled the car into gear and drove off, Evelyn returned the man's wave. "What was that all about, and who is Grace?"

"Just a precaution against unwanted guests." As they went farther along the road, Evelyn glimpsed fenced acreage beyond the tangle of trees and wild vegetation lining the roadway. The only person they'd seen for miles was Lloyd.

"What guests? We haven't seen anyone for miles."

They came to a stretch shaded by limbs overhanging from both sides. Jimmy Doyle stopped the car, and with one wrist dangling over the steering wheel, he turned to her. "No matter what you see, hear, or do at the farm, you can't speak of it to anyone, ever. Things go on here that most folk wouldn't understand. All newcomers have to have the approval of at least three members of the club in order to participate in any activity. I'm a member, so you have my vote." His smile, and the way his eyes undressed her with just a look made it clear why he approved of her. "I spoke to Grace on the telephone the other day. She and her husband, Carl, own the farm. If they agree to accept you, she'll give you a tour of the facilities. Once that is out of the way, we can play."

"How long will that take?" She hated the way her voice shook, but it couldn't be helped. Her whole body was trembling like a plucked guitar string. The orgasm he'd given her in the car still resonated in her body, and though it should have been enough to squelch her sexual needs for a month, it had only whetted her appetite for more.

"Not too long. Grace will have some questions for you. Don't answer the way you think she wants you to; just be honest. Having doubts and concerns is natural for someone with as little experience as you have."

"Has anyone ever been turned away?"

"I don't know. The members are extremely careful about bringing new people in." He took her hand in his, rubbing his thumb across the back. "I know you have issues, Evelyn. I see the way you shut down after every orgasm I give you. If you'll let me, I can help you get past that, but first, you have to trust me enough to tell me what puts those shadows in your eyes."

Evelyn glanced at her white-gloved hands clasped in her lap. She wanted to tell him, but she couldn't. How many hours had she prayed to God to cast the demon lust from her, to no avail? Jimmy Doyle really believed he could help her, but she was flawed at her core, the shame buried too deep. "I wish you could help me, but there's no help for someone like me."

As they sat there, the thick silence between them drowned out the rumble of the idling car engine. "You're wrong, and I'm going to prove it to you."

He put the car in gear. Several minutes later, a large, white clapboard farmhouse came into view. Behind it and off to either side sat an enormous barn and a smaller shed. The biggest oak tree Evelyn had ever seen shaded the front yard of the house. A few patches of green grass had survived the summer heat along with a row of four-o'clocks mashed up against the base of the wraparound porch. A man and woman occupied rocking chairs beneath the wide veranda. Once he killed the car engine, the drone of a tractor in a nearby field filled the air. If not for her companion's warnings, she would have thought this was a farm like hundreds of others in Virginia.

"This is it?"

Jimmy Doyle nodded. "Yep. Are you ready?"

"No. But I don't think I ever will be, so we might as well get this over with."

His smile held a hint of uncertainty. "I think you belong here, Evelyn, but if you don't want to stay, I'll take you back to town. Say the word, anytime, and I'll take you home. Like I told you before, you control how far we go—not me."

CHAPTER FIFTEEN

"Do you really think I belong here?"

"I do. You're a passionate woman, Evelyn. I've restrained you twice now, and each time you responded better than I expected. You've followed my instructions even when I haven't been there to make sure you do. I have the evidence to prove it." He pulled a crumpled handkerchief out of his back pocket, held it to his nose, and inhaled deeply. "You can't tell me you don't respond to my commands. If I told you to strip naked and walk up the porch steps, you'd do it. You wouldn't like it, but you would do it."

Evelyn shook her head, not daring to meet his eyes. Shame weighed heavy on her shoulders. He was right, but she prayed he wouldn't tell her to do something so humiliating.

"You can get your shoulders out of your ears, sweet one. I won't ask you to parade around nude today, but one day soon, I hope you will trust that if I did, it would be because I knew what was best for you at that time."

Evelyn closed her eyes and pinched her lips between her teeth. She could see herself striding naked across the lawn, her head held high while Jimmy Doyle stood on the porch, smiling at her progress. She'd do almost anything to see pride on his face. She wanted to make him proud of her.

She'd failed miserably at making her father and ex-husband

proud of her. Everything she'd done had brought them, and her, nothing but shame.

"Would you be proud of me if I walked to the house naked?"

"Today?"

"Today."

"No, I wouldn't. You'd only be doing it to prove something—to me or to yourself. When I ask you to bare yourself to others, it will be for the right reasons."

"What could ever be right about something like that?"

"People hide their true selves behind clothing. When you take that away from them, when you strip them down, they're vulnerable. You aren't ready for that. Yet. When you have nothing left to hide from me or from the world, then you won't care who sees you. Until that time comes, you'll keep your clothes on in public."

"But you had me undress in the car."

"That was for me, and to see how you would react to the possibility of having an audience. I admit, I was surprised at how easily you went into the fantasy. Just another reason you belong here. I can indulge that little fantasy of yours as often as I want."

"You said I should keep my clothes on in public."

"One or two people watching you come or be fucked is not public."

The low hum in her belly ramped up to a full-blown symphony, complete with crashing cymbals and kettledrums beating loud enough to drown out what he was saying. "Huh?"

"Are you ready to go inside?" Evelyn took a deep breath, then let it out. She glanced at the couple on the porch. They hadn't moved since she and Jimmy Doyle had driven up. "Grace and Carl understand what a big step this is. They won't come to you; you have to go to them. The choice is always yours, remember?"

"Yes."

"Yes, what?"

"Yes, Sir."

❧❧

After introductions were done, Jimmy Doyle took Grace's vacated seat while the older woman led Evelyn through the house to the kitchen. "Would you like something to drink? We have a new Kelvinator—keeps everything cold as a well digger's dangler."

Evelyn blushed at the ribald comment. "Water would be nice. Thank you."

Grace filled two glasses from a pitcher, returned the container to the refrigerated box, then joined Evelyn at the massive, rectangular wooden table. "I was surprised when Jimmy Doyle called to ask if he could bring a woman out. He's a very cautious man."

Evelyn thought back to the way he'd approached her at the tent revival meeting and the way he'd continued to pursue her ever since. *Cautious* wasn't a word she would use to describe him. "How do you mean?"

"I mean, he's careful about who he associates with, and he doesn't trust easily. After what happened…well, and with his proclivities thrown in, who could blame him?"

"He said the people here at the farm are his friends."

Grace smiled. "Yes, we are. He means a lot to everyone here. As much as we wanted him to move back into the life he loves, we were sad to see him go. He lived with us for most of the five years he was banned from baseball."

Evelyn sipped her water and waited for the woman to continue. It wasn't long before the older woman broke the silence. "He told me he restrained you. How did that make you feel?"

She stared at the woman across the table. She didn't know what surprised her more, that Jimmy Doyle had spoken of their intimate encounters with this person, or that the woman wanted to know something so personal.

"Come now. Were you frightened? Excited? Shocked? There's no wrong answer, just your answer."

Evelyn wrapped her hands around the cool glass and focused on her fingers. "All of those things, I guess." She swirled the glass around on the table, watching the ring of water beneath it growing wider. She had felt all those things, and something more. "I felt safe. I know it sounds crazy."

"Not at all, Evelyn. Did you at any time experience a feeling of freedom? As if you were free to enjoy what was happening to you?"

Evelyn jerked her gaze up to her inquisitor's. "Yes! But how can one be imprisoned and be free at the same time?"

"It's a question that has no answer." Grace tapped the side of her glass with her fingers. "Let me ask you something else, if I may?"

"Go ahead."

"You acknowledged your fear. What were you afraid of? Jimmy Doyle?"

"No. I knew he would never hurt me. I-I don't know what I was afraid of, but I'm sure I never worried for my physical safety."

Grace smiled. "You trust him that much?"

"I do. He's always been gentle with me."

"Has he ever caused you physical pain? Even in a small amount?"

Evelyn felt heat creeping up from her chest to her cheeks. She splayed her hand protectively in front of her. "My nipples," she whispered. "He pinched me. Hard."

"You were restrained?"

"Yes." Memories of that day played like a cinema through her mind. He'd done many things to her that day, all of them new to her, all of them exciting and shamefully arousing.

"You liked what he did?"

She stared at the rim of her glass. "Yes." *God, help me. Yes.*

"I'm sure that must have been painful, so why did you like it?"

"I can't explain it. My body— I wanted...more."

"What kind of more?"

"I wanted him inside me."

"Why?"

"Why?" Evelyn looked up, catching a glimmer of compassion

in the woman's eyes.

"Yes, why, Evelyn? What was your ultimate goal that day? Just to have him inside you or something else?"

She remembered the day by the river as she lay exposed to him while he did wicked, wondrous things to her body. She'd needed... "I wanted to have an orgasm. I needed to come so badly. When he pinched my nipples, it was like they were attached to something down there."

"Say it, Evelyn. We don't mince words here."

"It was like my nipples were attached to my vagina. I needed to come."

"He let you orgasm?"

"Yes. He put his mouth on me, on my pussy." The slang word made her blush even more. She had to be as red as a ripe strawberry by now.

"Cunnilingus. Oral sex."

Evelyn absorbed the words. "Yes."

"You were married."

There was only one way this woman could know that. Jimmy Doyle had told her. A rush of annoyance, coupled with the sharp knife of betrayal, jolted her. Her marriage was something she didn't talk about with just anyone. Tilting her chin up, she summoned every ounce of control she had. "Yes."

"What happened?"

"We divorced."

"That must have been very difficult for you." The compassion in Grace's voice was unexpected. Most people, especially women, saw divorce as a failure on the woman's part and never took her feelings into consideration.

"It was. It still is."

Grace nodded. "Whose idea was it to divorce?"

"My ex-husband's." The pain of that day still had the power to cripple her. She closed her eyes against the emotions being scraped raw once more.

"Did you love him?"

Evelyn had married to please her father, assuming love would naturally grow between two people who were as intimate as marriage required. But the intimacy and the love had never materialized. "No. I never did."

"Well, that's good."

Evelyn's eyes popped open. "What?"

"I said, it's a good thing you didn't love him. Jimmy Doyle is a wonderful man, and I'd hate to think he had fallen for a woman whose heart was with another man."

"But—"

Grace slapped her hand on the table. "No, don't try to say he hasn't fallen for you. I've known him for years, watched him sate his needs with a number of women, but in all that time he's never trusted anyone the way he trusts you." The older woman crossed her forearms on the table and leaned over them. "Just tell me one thing. Do you think you could love him?"

She'd never felt as close to her ex-husband as she did to Jimmy Doyle. The man seemed to know her better than she knew herself. Could she fall in love with him? In a heartbeat. "Yes."

The smile on Grace's face was filled with understanding and compassion. "That's good enough for me. Don't you worry. My husband, Carl, goes along with everything I say." She stood. "Let me show you around the place."

Evelyn followed the other woman, stopping first to put their water glasses in the sink for washing. The farmhouse, built over a century ago for a large family boasted numerous bedrooms on two upper floors. The kitchen, parlor, dining room, library/office occupied the main floor. Grace pointed out the door leading to the basement but said the special facility belowground was currently in use by another member, and promised to show it to Evelyn another time.

They exited the house via the front door. Jimmy Doyle stood the moment she stepped out on the porch. Gathering her in his arms, he kissed her hard on the mouth while his hands roamed her body, staking claim to her ass, her breasts, and anywhere else he could reach. Having never been kissed, much less groped in the presence of others, she found she didn't mind at all, as long as it was Jimmy Doyle's hands on her. His touch spoke of possession and passion, two things that awakened matching feelings in her.

"Let her be, Jimmy Doyle." Grace's no-nonsense voice broke them apart. "She's seen the house. I'm going to show her the barn, explain a few things to her. Give us about half an hour, then come on over. She'll be all yours then."

Not daring to look in his eyes, Evelyn flattened her palms against Jimmy Doyle's shirt and stared at his tie. It was the same one he'd used to secure her wrists to the wheel of his car on their first real date. Her nipples pebbled as the memories of that day, revived anew by Grace's questions, flitted through her mind. Jimmy Doyle tightened his hands on her hips to get her attention. She looked up into his smoldering eyes. "Do you want me to go with you?"

She was grateful he was willing to push the rules in order to comfort her, but whatever was in that barn, she felt sure she was ready to face it. "I'll be fine."

"Of course she will be. I'm only going to show her around, Jimmy Doyle. I'll leave the tying up to you." Grace moved to the top step, then paused to look back at them. Evelyn stepped out of Jimmy Doyle's embrace.

"I'll see you in a few minutes?"

He glanced at Carl. "You got a pocket watch?" The older man fished a gold-cased one out of his front pocket and held it up for all to see. Jimmy Doyle turned his attention to Grace. "Half an hour. Then I'm coming for her."

The barn appeared as normal as any other similar building she'd ever been in, but once Grace began the tour, it became apparent that there was nothing normal about this particular barn. Relics of days gone by, hand plows and other primitive implements, now had new uses as creative as the minds of the club members. Seemingly innocent items had been rigged as restraints. Sawhorses, with and without saddles, were scattered about. The stalls, once used to house horses and cattle, looked ready for their four-footed inhabitants to arrive, but as Grace elaborated, eyebolts screwed into the wooden walls could tether a horse for grooming or a human for whatever their partner had in mind.

The tack room sported the usual array of saddles, harnesses, and such, but behind false walls rested a second collection meant for human use. Her guide pointed out a stack of horse blankets. "Never been on a horse. Lots of people are shaky afterward, so we have blankets to wrap them in until they come back to their senses."

She indicated a box sitting on a shelf. "There's bandages and basic medical supplies in there. We don't hold with drawing blood, but sometimes it happens. Everything needed to care for that type of injury is in the box." Evelyn's head swam imagining some of the items hanging about causing that kind of injury.

"Here." Grace steered her out of the tack room to sit on a wooden bench against the wall. Evelyn sat forward, resting her face in her hands. "I didn't show you that to scare you. Everyone should know the medical supplies are there, for peace of mind. Back at the house, you told me you liked a little bit of pain. Mistakes happen, dear. A whip applied too hard, skin abrasions from rope or leather. We urge our members to use caution, but sometimes that isn't enough."

Blinking against the bright sunlight shining through the wide door open to the world, Evelyn breathed deep. Her first inclination was to run as fast and as far from this place as possible, but something else held her there as surely as if she'd been lassoed by one of the ropes hanging on the far wall. She drifted back to the picnic and the story Jimmy Doyle had told her about witnessing his aunt and uncle having sex in the barn. It all seemed so foreign to her, sinfully wicked, but maybe it wasn't. She'd always heard about teenagers sneaking off to the hayloft for hanky-panky, but with her present knowledge, she wondered if barn high jinks wasn't exclusive to the younger set.

"He told you about his aunt and uncle, didn't he?"

"Yes. He said the experience changed his life."

"He can change yours too, if you let him. Trust him, Evelyn. Jimmy Doyle is a good man. He'd never cause you harm."

Evelyn picked at a piece of straw she'd found on the bench. He wouldn't harm her, but hurt and harm weren't the same thing. Remembering the pain shooting through her body when he'd pinched her nipples made her breasts ache. She straightened her spine and, raising her eyes, locked gazes with Jimmy Doyle.

CHAPTER SIXTEEN

"She's all yours," Grace said, rising from the bench and walking past Jimmy Doyle to the open door. "I'll see that you aren't disturbed."

The shaft of light narrowed to a sliver slicing across the packed dirt floor as Grace slid the door closed, leaving Evelyn alone in the barn with the man she was becoming more and more certain she was in love with.

He'd left his suit jacket and tie somewhere. His suspenders hung loose on his hips. He looked as if he'd begun to undress on his way to the barn and only gotten so far. He'd tucked his hands into the front pockets of his trousers, striking a pose that should have been casual but looked anything but. Tension radiated off him like heat waves off a paved road.

The only thing that moved for the longest time were the particles of dust drifting through the band of daylight, stirred by invisible currents. Evelyn wondered if, perhaps, she should be afraid. But the tremors rocking her body had nothing to do with fear and everything to do with the barely banked flames of desire shining in the man's eyes. He'd brought her to this place in order to do wicked things to her body. He'd promised she could make all the noise she wanted and no one would care. If she screamed, not a soul would rush to save her from him or from herself.

"I'm not afraid of you," she said, as much to reassure herself as to break the silence.

"Grace was right. I would never cause you harm."

"You told me that before. I'm not stupid, Jimmy Doyle. I know the difference between hurt and harm."

"I'm not going to hurt you. Not today. Today is about pleasure, yours and mine, and nothing more."

"But someday, you plan to inflict pain, is that right?"

"Yes. Unless you tell me not to. There are things you aren't telling me—things that make you unhappy. I want you to tell me everything, but I realize that your secrets might be buried so deep inside that you can't release them. Pain can be cathartic."

She knew about pain—knew how it could scar a person for life, but cathartic? She'd never heard of such. "You mean you'll beat me until I tell you."

"No. There are other ways to force people to look inside themselves and see the truth. I've had years to master the skills necessary to bring you to that point."

"But if I say no?"

"Then we stop. Always. I won't push you to go someplace in your mind and heart that you don't want to go. One of these days, you'll trust me enough to let me try."

"Some things are best left buried."

"Not the ones that poison your life."

Evelyn looked at the piece of straw still clutched in her fingers. She ran her fingernail along the length of it, splitting the stalk in half. He was right. The wounds left from her short marriage had festered and were slowly poisoning her from the inside out. They'd taken away her happiness and her dreams of having a husband and family of her own. No decent man wanted a woman like her for a wife.

"If you think you can do it, why not do it today?"

"Because you aren't ready." He shifted his weight from one foot to the other. "What do you think of the farm?"

She glanced around the barn, noting things she ordinarily

wouldn't have thought twice about, but now that she had been clued in, she understood why they were there. "It's wicked. People come here"—she waved her hand around—"and do things to each other."

"They come here seeking to give and receive pleasure in a place where no one judges them based on their sexual needs. Everything that goes on here is consensual. If I hurt you, it will be because you allow me to do so. If I give you pleasure, it will be because you allow me to do so." Evelyn's breath froze in her lungs. How many times had she been told it was her decision to make? And here he was again, desire lighting his eyes, yet he hadn't made a move toward her. He stood between her and the door. If she ran, he could easily block her path and overpower her.

"If you want to go home, leave now." He stepped aside, clearing the path for her to leave. "I'll give you time to get to the car; then I'll drive you back to town." Evelyn eyed the space between the doors. Freedom was just beyond.

"I'm going to go into the tack room. If you decide to stay, remove all your clothes and stand over there facing this way." He pointed to the first stall. "It's up to you."

Without another word, he left her sitting there holding a piece of straw that was as shredded as her thoughts.

❧

Jimmy Doyle braced one hand on the wall and forced air into his lungs while he listened for the sound of the barn door opening. Giving Evelyn the space she needed to decide what she wanted was killing him, but he didn't have a choice. He believed in allowing his partners to set the pace, though he had to admit, he'd pushed Evelyn faster than was probably prudent for someone as untutored as she. She made him crazy with need. Thoughts of her invaded his mind nearly every minute of every day. He'd worn out the handkerchief with her scent on it, dragging it out of his pocket often. Once he'd tasted her, he was convinced he could live on nothing more than her pussy. Then he'd made the mistake of fucking her, and Lord help him, he was done for.

He had to have her in his life, and that meant her accepting the part of him he hid from everyone except the select friends whom he trusted to guard his secret along with their own. Bringing Evelyn to the farm was a risk he hadn't taken lightly. Over the past few months, he'd discussed his situation with Grace and Carl on a weekly basis. They knew every move he'd made with Evelyn, and had agreed with his conclusion—she was a good candidate for membership in the club. Inexperienced as she was, her sexual appetites mirrored his in every way.

Sex with her was off the charts, but besides that, he liked her. He liked the way she smiled, and the sound of her laughter. He liked the way she blushed when he said or did something suggestive. Whatever had happened in her marriage, she was a lady, through and through. Though she clearly had issues she'd buried deep concerning that part of her life, she'd gone out and made a new life for herself. That kind of strength indicated she might be strong enough to handle the intense cathartic event it would take to break down the walls she'd built to protect herself from the hurt she'd suffered. If she would let him, he'd demolish those walls and lay waste to whatever demons she kept inside.

If she'd let him.

He knew every creak and moan this old building could make, from the scraping sound of the doors sliding on their railings to the squeak of the third plank in the hayloft. She hadn't left. Perhaps she needed more time to decide, but he was rapidly running out of patience. The orgasm he'd given her in the car might have eased her need, but it had only compounded his. He hadn't been inside her for nearly two weeks, and there were better ways to build arm strength than twice-daily handjobs.

He took a deep breath and let it out, counting to ten as he did so. He'd give her as much time as possible, but if she was still there when he walked out, clothes on or clothes off, he was going to fuck her.

Inhaling again, he pushed away from the wall. Grace had left the hidden cabinet open, correctly assuming he would want something from it. He grabbed a pair of leather cuffs one of the members had made a few years ago as a gift to the farm. Lined with wool, they wouldn't leave marks on Evelyn's delicate skin. He had every intention of marking her today, but not where anyone else would see.

As he exited the tack room, his gaze went first to the spot where he'd ordered her to wait for him, and finding it empty, he inwardly cursed himself for a fool. Then a sound had him jerking his attention to the other side of the room. Evelyn stood there, her neatly folded dress in her hands, the toes of her bare feet curled under. She looked absolutely adorable in her confused state, and sexy as hell wearing nothing but a blush.

"I-I was just—"

"Put the dress on the bench." He closed the distance between them and waited for her to straighten. "Give me your hands." She held her hands out. He fastened a leather band around her left wrist, then her right. She looked on without saying a word, but her chest was rising and falling in a manner that distracted him as well as alerted him to her state of mind.

He held both her hands in his. "Scared?"

"A little," she admitted, looking at her cuffed wrists.

"What's your favorite color?"

"What does that have to do with anything?" God, he loved the spark of annoyance in her eyes. She'd made up her mind and was as impatient as he was to get on with the fucking portion of the program.

"Just tell me."

"Blue."

"If I hurt you more than you can stand, or if you're frightened and want to stop, say *blue*. Don't whisper it; shout it out so there's no mistake, and I'll stop. Can you do that?"

She nodded. "You promise you'll stop?"

"If I don't, you have permission to use that pitchfork over there on me as soon as you're free." He nodded to the far corner where several tools were stored. He almost laughed when she saw the item in question and gasped, though he wouldn't put it past her to spear him with it if he broke his promise. He'd just have to see to it she had no reason to put an end to their playtime. "Ready?"

She inclined her head once. "Ready."

He walked backward, pulling her along with him until his back was to the well-worn wood wall. He spun her around and placed her right where he'd imagined seeing her since the day they'd met. She remained silent as he fastened the cuffs to eyebolts, then stood back to admire her body. "You're the most beautiful creature I've ever seen."

"Creature?"

"Woman, human, creation. You take my breath away." She was perfection. A work of art. And he had to have her. "I'll be right back."

"Wait!" He heard her jerk against the cuffs as he darted to the tack room for one more item he wanted her to wear today. It didn't take him long to find it. Made by the same craftsman who made the cuffs, the collar was designed for a lady. While he was there, he took a long look at the other items displayed for use, slipping one he thought she would enjoy into his pocket.

"Calm down. I'm not going anywhere without you." He held up the length of wool-lined leather. "I want you to wear this today." Her eyes went wide, but she held still and let him fasten the band around her neck, then secure it to a recessed eyebolt behind her.

"There." He took a few steps back. The wide band prevented her from looking anywhere but straight ahead. It was almost as good as a blindfold but gave her enough line of sight to anticipate his next move without being able to do anything about it. "Comfortable?"

"It doesn't hurt, but I wouldn't go so far as to say I'm comfortable."

He smiled at her frank response. He'd never have to worry about going too far with her; she wasn't afraid to tell him what she was thinking. "Good. Now, to add a bit of excitement for you." Before his name passed her lips, he flung the door open, exposing her to anyone who might happen by. No one would; he knew that, but she didn't. Grace and Carl were prepared to steer any new arrivals to rooms inside the house until he gave them the all clear for the barn. Until then, it was just the two of them, and Evelyn was firmly anchored in place.

"Oh, God! What if someone comes out here?"

"What if they do?" He strolled back to stand near her but off to one side so he wasn't blocking the view. "They'll see what I see, a work of art hung on the wall. You sure do dress this place up, sweetheart."

"Jimmy Doyle! Close that door right now!"

"What? You don't want me to let you down? Does that mean you still want me to fuck you, you just don't want an audience?" She was adorable with her legs crossed and her nipples poking out like cherries on top of an ice cream sundae.

"I want you to close the door." She closed her eyes on the admission. She hadn't changed her mind about the sex; it was only the open door making her uneasy. He'd fix that. All he needed to do was give her something else to think about, and she'd forget all about the open door.

"Relax, little one, and spread your legs. I want to taste you."

Her gaze met his for one scorching-hot second. Then with a sigh, she closed her eyes and spread her legs.

"Perfect." He moved closer to her, angling his arm across her torso. He let his fingers glide through her wet folds. "Does this excite you, sweet Evelyn?" He glanced at the open door, then back at her face. Her lips were pressed into a tight line, her eyes closed.

"Open your eyes, Eve."

Her eyes opened, flashing fire. "Don't call me that. My name is Evelyn."

He continued to explore between her legs at a leisurely pace. He inserted a finger and prepared her for him. He flicked his thumb across her clitoris, making her whimper and gyrate her hips.

171

"Why, sweet one? You're as innocent as Eve, and as tempting. I can no more resist your fruit than stop breathing." To add emphasis to his words, he took one nipple in his mouth. With his free hand, he captured her other breast. She whimpered and went up on tiptoe, arching as best she could, offering her delectable tits for his pleasure.

"Mmm, you taste so good." He gave both nipples attention, using his teeth to torment one while he pinched and tugged on the other. Her body responded immediately, writhing in agony, groaning in pleasure, and bathing the hand nestled between her legs with slick moisture. When she tried to close her legs, he released her breasts, and moving fully in front of her, he pressed his body against hers, using his feet to prevent her from moving.

"No, no, no, sweet one. I know you need to come, but I'm not through with you yet." He added another finger to her pussy, shoving in hard enough to jerk her higher against the wall. She cried out, her face scrunching as she absorbed the sudden jolt. "Am I hurting you?" He thrust hard into her again. "Tell me, Eve. Am I hurting you?"

She didn't protest the use of the nickname this time, but he saw it in her eyes. Something about that name set her off. He determined, then and there, he would find out what it was. Maybe not today, but soon.

Her chest heaved, rubbing her magnificent breasts against his shirt-clad chest. He noted the effort it took for her to release the tension lining her face. "No—no, Sir."

"I didn't think so. You like it when I'm rough, don't you?" He repeated the earlier move, fucking her hard with his fingers and adding a flick forward that forced a moan from her lips.

"Yes, Sir."

He knew women who enjoyed rough sex for no other reason that it turned them on, but deep down, he knew there was more to it for Evelyn. Being restrained often made a person feel free to explore what they liked since there was nothing they could do to stop what was happening to them. It was usually nothing more than a mind trick, as it was for Evelyn at this moment. She could stop him with a single word. But she didn't want to stop him. Whatever her reasons for wanting him to continue, he was grateful and more than willing to force pleasure on her. Nothing would please him more.

He brushed his lips over the shell of her ear and whispered, "I'm going to fuck you so hard you won't be able to walk for a week, sweet Eve."

A sob broke from her. Tears streaked from the corners of her eyes. Jimmy Doyle reached for her breast. He closed his thumb and forefinger over the nipple and twisted. She screamed in agony. Her gaze shot to his face. Heat blazing in her eyes dried her tears. He repeated the pinch, watching as she closed her eyes and absorbed the pain without making a sound. His fingers slid easily through the sloppy wetness between her legs.

"Did you use the dildo I sent you, Eve? Did you fuck yourself while I was gone?" It took another hard jolt to her pussy to get an answer.

"Yes, Sir."

"How many times?"

"I don't—"

"Don't lie to me. You know how many times you used it."

"Four. Times. Sir."

"I can see you, lying there in your bed, your pussy filled with a glass cock, your cream coating your hand, filling the air with the smell of sex, and you, choking on your screams. I would have loved to see you that way. You wanted to scream every time, didn't you, Eve?"

Her nostrils flared. She whimpered before answering. "Yes, Sir."

"Guess what?" He reached in his pocket and withdrew the heavy wooden dildo he'd brought from the tack room. "This time, you can be as vocal as you want." He held the smoothly finished phallus up for her to see. Her eyes grew huge, and her lips parted.

"I'm going to fuck you with this, sweet Eve. I'm going to fuck

173

you so hard, and you're going to scream for me. You're going to beg me to let you come."

He had to admit, he'd chosen the carved dick because of its size. Even as wet as she was, he'd have to take it slow getting it inside her. "Want to know what it's going to feel like?" He held the tip to her lips. "Open up, Eve. Suck the big cock."

Oh, his Eve was a naughty one. She obeyed without question. Her lips formed an O, and he slid the head into her mouth. He stroked her cheek with his finger, loving the way her lips stretched to accommodate the girth. "Think you can take it all, Eve?" She hummed what sounded like a yes, then proceeded to do it. He pushed the object deeper until she was forced to swallow.

He stroked her cheek one more time, then gently removed the dildo. "One of these days, I'll have you on your knees, sucking my cock. Would you like that?"

Evelyn licked her lips. "Yes, Sir."

He couldn't help himself. He kissed her, long and hard, sweeping his tongue inside, tasting her. His cock rivaled the wooden one on the hardness scale. He wanted her with a ferocity that seemed unfathomable. He'd never wanted a woman the way he wanted this one, and even though he'd already had her once, he knew he would never get enough of her.

They were both fighting for air when he broke away. Reluctantly, he withdrew his fingers from her tight channel and used them to lubricate the phallus. "I love the way your juices gush from you. There isn't a dick on the planet that wouldn't call your pussy heaven."

CHAPTER SEVENTEEN

Evelyn strained to see what he was doing, but as he dropped lower, the collar prevented her from tilting her chin down. She still had the sense of touch, though. Each hot, openmouthed kiss was an inch lower than the last, until his lips closed over the top of her slit, claiming that part of her. She didn't even try to resist when he lifted her leg and draped her thigh over his shoulder. Somewhere beyond the open door, a tractor drew nearer, mercifully stopping short of the barn. Evelyn didn't have the best of luck with prayer, but she prayed anyway that whoever operated the machinery wouldn't make his way to the barn. Then she held her breath, watching the door, imagining the moment the person would see her. A full-body shiver had her undulating with desire.

"Grace said she'd stop Luther before he came to the barn, but she might have gone in the house. He could still wander this way."

Evelyn groaned and tried to calm her runaway heart. How had he known what she was thinking? She didn't have much time to contemplate her tormentor's mind-reading skills, as he'd begun to probe her folds with his fingers.

"Such a pretty flower, my Eve."

When the rounded head pushed against her opening, she tensed. It had been all she could do to take the thing in her mouth. Nothing that big could fit inside her; she was sure of it.

"Relax, Eve. It will fit, but it will be easier if you don't fight it."

A single word flashed through her brain. All she had to do was shout it out, and he'd stop what he was doing. He leaned back enough she could see his face. The wooden dildo remained snug against her. "Let go, Evelyn. Give your body to me, and I'll make it sing."

The low, confident rumble of his voice caressing her name eased through her, dissolving the tension in her muscles, sweeping away her resistance. The instant her fingers unfurled from the tight fists they'd been curled into, he worked the phallus inside her.

She tensed against the momentary stretch. A kiss to her clitoris, his murmured words, "Beautiful, little one," turned her muscles to soft clay.

Alternating between inching the cock inside and kissing her clitoris until she begged for more, he filled her. Evelyn concentrated on breathing as her body adjusted to the giant intruder. Jimmy Doyle remained on his knees, one hand ensuring the object remained inside her, the other stroking and fondling with a featherlight touch.

"God, you are beautiful." He breathed against her tender tissues. "Tell me if I'm hurting you."

Hurting? God, yes, she hurt, but not like that. The hurt was deep inside, urging her to clamp her legs tight and ride hard and fast.

"Speak to me, Evelyn. Am I hurting you?"

It took three tries, but she got the words out. "No, Sir." She tried to squeeze her legs together, but it was a futile exercise with his wide shoulders holding her open.

"You are hurting, aren't you? I think it's time to do something about that." The instant the phallus slid from her channel, she felt empty. As he eased it back in, she arched her back, thrusting her hips forward and going up on tiptoe on her one foot still on the floor.

"That feels good, doesn't it, sweetheart? You like to have a big cock inside you." She was empty again, then stuffed full a heartbeat later. "Fuck, I love to see you take this into your body."

He set a rhythm then, faster and more forceful than before. When she began to rock her hips up to meet the thrusts, he palmed her ass and helped her. If an entire army had gathered in the doorway to watch, she couldn't have cared less. All that mattered was reaching that point where the tension exploded into ecstasy.

As if sensing her need, he worked the phallus faster and harder. She was close, so close. She closed her eyes, focusing everything she had inward in hopes of ending her torment on her own terms. There. Her mind reached for the switch that would trigger her orgasm. In that same instant when her body hovered on the precipice, one thought, one thrust from coming, the fucking stopped.

She jerked her eyes open. A cry escaped her lips. Her pussy throbbed around the emptiness.

"So fucking beautiful." He stood before her. His hands were busy between them, unbuttoning his trousers and covering his penis with one of those things he'd used before. "I want to be inside you when you come."

"Hurry." She could hardly believe the breathless quality of her voice.

He smiled as his hands slid over her ass, then to her thighs, lifting and opening her to him. "Hurry, what?"

Evelyn's mind went blank. Word games were beyond her. His cock nudged at her entrance. If he didn't fill her soon, she was going to die.

"Ah, sweet Eve. If you're going to order me to fuck you, do it now, and do it right, or I might have to spank you."

Evelyn never thought the threat of punishment would excite her, but the idea of Jimmy Doyle spanking her sent tingles skittering along every nerve ending. She'd have to give that more thought, but right then, the tension lining his face told her that her urgency was his too. Her heart tripped over itself as the impact of his demand took root. He'd give her what she wanted, but not until she acknowledged who was in control.

He leaned in so his warm breath caressed the shell of her ear. "You can do it, Evelyn. Say the words, and I'll take us both there."

Knowing she was crossing a threshold she couldn't uncross, she said the words. "Hurry, Sir!"

He entered her with one hard stroke that drove her higher against the wall, making her almost eye level with him. Already sensitive, her inner walls clenched reflexively around his intrusion. God, he felt good. Her fingertips tingled with the need to touch him, to feel the play of muscle underneath satin-smooth skin. His hard body pressed against hers from chest to groin, reminding her of his superior strength.

As he pounded into her, driving her ever closer to the climax, bound and ravaged, she felt completely helpless. But deep inside, the glow of power burned. She'd seen the look on his face. The stark need etched there. He needed her every bit as much as she needed him.

SHE WAS KILLING him. For an agonizing moment, he'd thought she wasn't going to give him what he wanted.

No. What he *needed*. He needed to possess this woman in a way he'd never needed before. He'd had women submit to him— had them on their knees begging him to get them off—but that had been play.

He wasn't playing with Evelyn. When he was through fucking her today, he wouldn't be walking away looking for his next willing partner. This wasn't an initiation into the life he led—it was more, and she knew it as much as he did.

Those heartbeats between him demanding her submission and her giving it were scars he would carry the rest of his life. Reminders of what he had to lose if he wasn't careful. He'd rushed her, he knew it down to his bones, but he also knew waiting another day to show her the life they could have together had been impossible. Her sexual appetites matched his in every way, down to the need to control.

He almost chuckled when she demanded he hurry up and fuck her. Lord, she didn't know how much fun he was going to have with that dominant streak of hers. He'd allowed it today because they'd both wanted the same thing—to hurry the fuck up. He'd denied himself too long, but that was going to change. Now that she knew about the farm, he'd bring her here more often and take shameless advantage of the power she thought she held over him.

Her tight channel squeezed his dick. *Damn.* She felt so fucking good, like she was made for him. His own climax was a fireball waiting to explode, but he fought it back. Today, her pleasure came first. It was time to push her over the edge. He nibbled her earlobe.

"Beg me, Eve. Beg me to let you come, or I'll stop right now and round up an audience to watch me fuck you with the dildo." Her gasp and the way she jerked her head up to look over his shoulder at the open door told him all he needed to know. The idea of being watched excited the fuck out of her. She wasn't ready to go down that road, but that didn't mean he couldn't use the information to tease her to orgasm. "Beg me, Eve."

He ground his hips against hers, demanding her attention. Her gaze met his. "They'll be here soon to check on us. They're going to see you spread open, being fucked senseless. They might even come closer to see your wet cunt taking my cock inside. It's a beautiful sight, Eve. Maybe I'll let them touch you. Suck your tits, finger your pussy while I ride you. Kiss you."

He nuzzled her ear, slid his lips along her jaw to nibble at her lips. "Beg me."

"Please, Sir."

"Ask for what you want." He was pushing her way past her comfort level, but he couldn't stop himself. She was so much stronger than she thought she was. She could say the words.

Her hesitation lasted less than a breath. Tears spilled from her eyes, leaving wet tracks along both flushed cheeks. "Please, Sir. Let me come."

He thought he was prepared to hear her say the words, but

her sweet voice begging for release twisted him up inside. *Mine.*
Mine.

He fucked her hard and fast until her pussy gripped him tight. A harsh cry tore from her gut, ripped from her throat, and rang through the old barn. Music to his ears.

"Sweet fuckin' heaven." He pounded into her once, twice, a third time as the fireball he'd held at bay rolled through him. He grunted and ground, emptying into her in scalding-hot spurts.

Dropping his forehead to her shoulder, he gasped for air. His heartbeat thundered in his ears so loud, if someone did come in, he wouldn't have been able to hear them. For a few seconds he watched her breasts rise and fall. When they were both breathing more normal, he lifted his head to gaze at her face.

"Are you okay?"

She tried to nod, but the collar prevented her from making anything but a tiny movement. "Yes. I think so."

"That's good." Still hard inside her, he flexed his hips. Her eyes widened, and she let out a startled gasp. "I've got to get us cleaned up." He eased out of her, carefully setting her feet wide apart on the floor. He stripped off the condom and fixed his pants.

God, he liked seeing her that way—all flushed from a good fucking, bound and sated. He'd never get tired of seeing that slumberous expression on her face. He squatted in front of her. He couldn't resist touching her pussy, now stained a beautiful claret from the fucking. "You have no idea what this does to me, Eve. I could fuck you again right now, but you're going to be sore enough as it is."

Rising, he massaged her tender flesh. "Wait here, sweet one. I'll get some water and clean you."

Before she could utter a protest, he went outside to the hand pump to fill a bucket.

❧

Jimmy Doyle dropped her off around the corner from the boardinghouse. She'd gone to great lengths to establish herself as a respectable single woman in a world where women her age were expected to be married and raising a houseful of kids. He respected anyone who lived through adversity and came out on the other side, stronger for the experience. He had no doubt she was one of those people.

She'd trusted him with so much, but he knew there was more. Whatever had happened to her to make her this cautious, he was certain a lesser woman would have given up on life. But not his Evelyn. She was made of strong stuff, and it would take more than opening her up with a huge dildo to get the information out of her.

Driving across town to his apartment, he thought back over the past few hours he'd had with her. She was absolutely magnificent in her submission, so proud and strong facing her fears. The way she'd accepted pleasure shattered him. Yet something dark lurked within her. He saw it in the way she flinched every time he used the shortened version of her name. She didn't like being called Eve, but the moniker fit her well. Some people thought the first Eve embodied the concept of original sin, but he saw it differently. She'd been innocent, yet she held an inner strength few gave her credit for. She'd been smart and able to reason, and faced with the choice to remain ignorant, she'd chosen the path of knowledge. Who wouldn't have been tempted by that? That idiot, Adam, that was who. He'd been weak. Eve had been the one with guts, and Jimmy Doyle admired her for that in the same way he admired his Evelyn.

As soon as he arrived home, he placed a call to the farm. He felt like he'd made headway with Evelyn today, and felt it was time to push her a bit harder. On the drive home, he could almost hear her shoring up her walls. She'd given away a part of her secret with her reaction to the nickname, and she wasn't happy about it.

Grace seemed happy that he'd called, and after insisting he shouldn't let Evelyn get away, she agreed to help him accomplish his goal of breaking down the formidable defenses of one Evelyn Gardner.

❧❦

He arrived at the field early the following day and headed straight for the general manager's office. Contract negotiations would begin with him.

"Hey, Jimmy Doyle." Walter Dobbs greeted him with a handshake. "I guess you heard the good news?"

"That I might be around after the season is over?"

He followed the man into his office and took the seat he indicated. "That's what I'm talking about." The older man rocked back in his desk chair. "Everyone from the top down has been impressed with your stats this season. I have to admit, I was skeptical about a man your age coming back to the game after being out as long as you were, but you've proven us all wrong. You were good when you left, but if it's possible, you've gotten better."

"I'm not as young as I was," Jimmy Doyle said, being honest. "I miss playing shortstop, but first base suits me."

Dobbs nodded. "You're still contributing to the team defensively at first, and offensively? You've got one hell of a bat, Jimmy Doyle."

"Thank you."

"I know you told me when we took you back, but I've forgotten. What did you do to stay in shape all those years out of the game?"

"I worked as a farmhand. Have you seen the new hay balers?" Jimmy Doyle smiled. "Turns out lifting bales of hay builds muscle."

"Maybe we should ask the training staff to add that to the schedule."

He grimaced. "If you don't mind, I'd just as soon never see another bale of hay."

Walter laughed. "Rather play baseball?"

"Anytime."

"I think we can help you with that as long as you continue to keep your nose clean. Hobart Preston is a God-fearing Christian. He doesn't take to any kind of shenanigans going on with his employees."

Jimmy Doyle suppressed the cold shiver running along his spine. He knew all about the team owner's fundamentalist religious views and didn't agree with most of them, but the man had given him a second chance when other team owners refused. He'd be forever grateful for that.

"You've taken a lot of hits this year from players who still aren't convinced you were innocent of the charges leveled against you. Mr. Preston has been impressed with the way you've handled that as well. Turning the other cheek—it speaks well of you."

He'd had little choice other than to brawl with every judgmental idiot in the league, but he kept that thought to himself. Jimmy Doyle had never done an illegal thing in his life, yet he'd lost five years of his career to unfounded allegations. Sometimes he wondered if the accusations and mistrust would ever go away. He thought it was ironic that the one thing in his life Dobbs would most object to was something he'd managed to keep hidden, even when every news reporter in the country was digging into his life. He could only imagine what the team owner would think if he found out about his sexual inclinations. *Scandal* wasn't a big enough word to cover the shit-storm that would be. "I walk the straight and narrow," he assured. "I always have."

"Good. Good." Walter bobbed his head. "You know, the Babe retired last year at forty."

"I understand I've only got a few good years left in me, but I intend to play every one of them."

Dobbs stood, signaling the meeting was over. "Have your agent contact me. I think we can work something out that will benefit both of us." He extended his hand to shake.

After promising his agent would be in touch, Jimmy Doyle headed for the locker room. He had everything he needed in life— baseball and Evelyn. He knew he could live without baseball—had done so for five years—but every minute he was away from Evelyn felt like a lifetime. Now that his career was secured, he was more determined than ever to make her his. And that meant knowing absolutely everything about her.

He could hardly wait to get her back to the farm where he could strip away at her defenses until she had nothing left to hide behind.

CHAPTER EIGHTEEN

"Thank you, Abigail." Evelyn took the earpiece from her fellow boarder, then waited until the girl disappeared up the stairs before facing the telephone and speaking into the mouthpiece. "Hello?"

"Evelyn."

At the sound of Jimmy Doyle's voice, her heart raced. "Yes, it's me." She leaned closer so she could speak softer. The less anyone heard, the better.

"It's good to hear your voice," he said. "Are you okay?" He'd promised he would call to check on her even after she'd told him not to worry. He hadn't hurt her. She'd left the farm the other day feeling a bit sore, but otherwise fine. Still, he'd kept his promise, and that made her feel warm inside.

Physically she was okay, but as soon as she'd returned to her room, a wave of guilt had washed over her. She'd loved everything he'd done to her, and her body ached to do it all again, but that was the problem. Only a sinner would enjoy and crave carnal pleasure the way she did. Nevertheless, she hadn't told him to stop, so it was up to her to put his mind at ease, at least about her physical condition. "I'm fine. Healthy as a horse." As soon as the words left her lips, she regretted saying them. He was sure to make more of the statement than she'd meant.

185

"And a more beautiful horse I've never seen." His chuckle made her blush. "In fact, I'd like to take you back to the farm Saturday afternoon after my game, if you can make it."

"I don't know," she whispered into the mouthpiece.

"I can make you feel good. You know I can."

"That's not it."

"I know it's not. There is no shame in seeking pleasure, Eve."

"Don't call me that," she said. "I don't like it."

"Why is that, Eve? What is it about that name that makes you react so strongly? I'd love to know."

"It's…personal." Evelyn glanced up and down the hallway, making sure no one was eavesdropping on her conversation. Assured she was alone, she continued. "I don't like to talk about it."

"But you need to. I wish you would talk to me, darling. Tell me what has made you so afraid to be a woman."

Evelyn choked back tears. Jimmy Doyle was too perceptive at times. It was one thing to sin in the privacy of one's room, but another to do so in a place where someone might bear witness to your depravity. "I can't."

"You can. I told you before, I want to know everything about you. I know so much already, but I want to know it all. If I don't know what hurts you, how can I make it go away?"

"There's nothing you can do." *Nothing anyone can do.*

"Do you trust me, Evelyn?"

Absurdly, she did. She'd trusted him with her life, more than once, and she'd trusted him with the darkest secret of her lustful cravings. "You know I do."

"Then come with me on Saturday. I'll park around the corner at four o'clock. Wear the same dress as before, with nothing underneath, and tell whoever you need to that you're spending the night with a friend and that you'll be home in time for church."

Spend the night with him? She couldn't. If anyone found out, she'd be more than ruined—she'd be cast out of the boardinghouse without a reference. What would she do then? She had no one she could turn to for help. "I can't."

"Yes, you can. Everything I told you before still applies. The choice is yours to make. I'll be there on Saturday. If you don't come to me by fifteen past the hour, I'll leave. I'll take that to mean you no longer want to continue our relationship, and you won't hear from me again."

"Please."

"What, Eve? Please make the pain go away? Please love you? I can do both, if only you'll trust me. I'll see you on Saturday."

സൗ

Evelyn smoothed her dress with damp palms. No one could tell she was naked beneath, but she was all too aware of the fact. Even though she'd told him she couldn't go with him today, she'd still dressed as he had told her to. "Because you want to go with him," she mumbled to her reflection in the mirror over the bathroom sink. "You want too much, Evelyn."

Hadn't she always? She'd wanted a husband and a family of her own. She'd wanted to be loved and to love. She'd wanted the physical pleasure her body ached for. She'd wanted her husband to share all of it with her. "And look where that got you." She glanced around the small room she called home. Other than her clothes and few items she'd purchased to brighten the place up, nothing belonged to her. It wasn't the life she'd once imagined for herself, but it was the life she had, and she couldn't afford to risk it for one night of passion.

Cupping her breasts in her hands, she massaged the soft mounds until her nipples tingled. The tender flesh between her legs swelled with longing. She squeezed her thighs together, and gripping the edge of the washbasin, she bent over, regretting having stimulated herself when the only relief available was at her own hands. When her breathing evened out, she straightened, placing both hands over her midsection to halt their trembling.

A knock on her door startled her. *Jimmy Doyle!* As quickly as she thought it, she knew better. He'd never get past the front door, much less up to her room.

"Evelyn?" The familiar voice of her friend Ruth called to her. "A messenger boy brought a letter for you."

She took a deep breath, then let it out. In his own fashion, he had found a way to come to her door. "Thanks, Ruth. Can you slip it under the door? I'm not decent." If her friend found that to be odd, she didn't comment. A second later a slim white envelope slid beneath the door.

"Do you see it?"

"Got it!"

"Do you need anything?"

"Thanks for asking, but no. I'm fine. I just wanted to rest for a minute." Evelyn hated to lie to her, but she was afraid her emotions were written all over her face.

She waited until she was sure her friend had left, then darted across the room to retrieve the letter. Using a nail file to slit the top of the envelope, she sat on the edge of the bed to read.

My sweet Evelyn,

I'm waiting for you around the corner as I promised I would. You've convinced yourself that what we have together is wrong, but I must disagree with you. Nothing could be more right.

When I touch you, your soft skin ignites a fire within me, and when I am inside you, I feel as if I have come home.

Giving you pleasure is the greatest pleasure I have ever known, though I have yet to break past the barriers holding you back from experiencing the full extent of pleasure you are capable of achieving.

Come to me, Evelyn. Open your body to me, and I will show you your soul.

Come to me, my darling. Trust me with all that you are.

Come to me, my love, and I will show you what lies on the other side of the wall you have built.

Come to me.

Yours always,

J.D.

Evelyn swiped at the tears streaking down her cheeks. She'd seen her soul and it was as black as the night, but when she was with Jimmy Doyle, she felt as if perhaps it wasn't as stained as she believed. It hadn't always been so dark. As a child she'd been carefree, and everything had seemed possible. Being with Jimmy Doyle made her feel that way again. She'd been without hope for so long, but he made her think it wasn't lost forever.

Each day since her shameful downfall, the walls she'd built became stronger, and never once had she considered knocking them down. Not until now. She'd told no one of her shame, but since she'd met Jimmy Doyle, she had begun to wonder if it wasn't hers to bear as she'd been told. The things he'd done to her…the pleasure he'd given her… None of it had felt wrong.

When he touched her, she felt cherished. When he was inside her, she felt complete.

When he found his pleasure in her body, she felt as if there wasn't anything in the world she couldn't do.

Mind made up, she collected a few things she would need in the morning and put them into a crocheted bag a coworker had given her for her birthday years ago. She knocked softly on Ruth's door. When her neighbor appeared, Evelyn explained that the note had been from one of the women she worked with who was pregnant and didn't want to be alone while her husband was out of town overnight. With the lie fresh on her lips, she forced herself to walk out as if her life wasn't tilting at a dangerous angle.

❦

Her breath caught at the sight of him leaning against the passenger side of his car. He looked utterly fabulous in sand-colored slacks and a white shirt open at the collar. Straightening, he opened the door for her, ushering her inside without a word.

As they drove toward the outskirts of town, the silence between them wore on her nerves. Twisting the handles on her bag into knots, she stared straight ahead and tried not to think of the man sitting beside her and the way he did everything with quiet confidence while she doubted herself at every turn.

"Unbutton your dress. I want to see you."

Evelyn started at the sound of his voice. Open fields surrounded them, not another car or human in sight. Setting her bag beside her feet, she released the buttons and parted the fabric. Her nipples tightened in response to the hot, dusty air from the open window brushing her breasts.

"Drop it off your shoulders, turn toward me, and lay back."

The unwavering tone of his voice made her heart race, but she did as told, exposing her upper body, then reclining on the bench seat. Out of necessity, she bent her knees, then let them fall to the sides. His gaze darted away from the road. "God, I've missed you, sweet Evelyn."

"I've missed you too." More than she could tell him. She shouldn't have come today, but staying away from him was no longer an option. His promises were both frightening and exciting. He'd already shown her more pleasure than she thought possible, enough that her body craved his touch as much as it craved the air she breathed. If he managed to shatter the barriers she'd erected, would she find the heights he promised?

"Let me see how much you've missed me. Spread your pussy open so I can see."

Touching herself was pure torture. Her outer lips were swollen and sensitive, and it was all she could do to keep from rubbing hard to help ease the ache. Embarrassed by her almost constant need of him, she slipped her index fingers into her damp folds to show him the evidence of her arousal.

He glanced at her pussy, then back to the road. A short time later, he braked to a stop. "No. Don't move. There's no one around," he assured when she moved to cover herself. "Spread yourself for me."

With his attention fully on her now, Evelyn focused on the roof of the car and parted herself again.

"I wanted to wait until we were at the farm, but I don't think you can wait, can you, babe?" His fingers played with her inner folds, rimming her opening with a delicate touch.

"I can wait." Her words sounded like the lie they were. With him touching her like he was, she was on the brink of release.

"You should have told me, sweet one. There is no need for you to suffer. If you need to come, you should tell me right away." He coated his fingers in her juices, then slowly filled her, stretching her tight entrance until she groaned with the pleasure of it. "Relax, sweetheart. I'll take care of you."

He withdrew, then plunged back in, rocking her hips up off the seat. "Hold still. Let me do all the work." The palm of his free hand anchored her while he worked his fingers in and out. Wet, sucking sounds filled the inside of the car. Evelyn closed her eyes. As the tension mounted inside her, all thoughts fled except one— how much she loved Jimmy Doyle Walker.

It didn't take long for him to work his magic on her. She came in an explosion of quaking muscles and light bursting behind her closed eyelids. Her whole body trembled from the aftershocks. His wet fingers trailed lower to tease her anus. She froze.

"What's this?" he said, exploring deeper. "Why the tension, Evelyn? What are you hiding from me?"

"Nothing." She tried to squirm away from him, but his hand on her belly held her pinned in place. "Please, don't."

He continued to massage the area, moving back to her pussy for more lubricant. Her body overruled her mind. She shivered with need and pushed against his finger. Shame made her stomach cramp, and once again, she attempted to move out of his grasp. This time, he let her go with an admonition to remain on her back with her legs parted.

She rode the rest of the way to the farm physically open to him, but emotionally hidden behind the walls she'd built to contain her true self. When he paused to identify himself to the guard, he placed his hand on her stomach again, silently telling her not to move. The same titillating shiver she'd experienced being restrained in the open barn skittered over her skin, followed quickly by a rush of shame for wanting another person to witness her depravity.

As if he'd read her mind, he instructed her to sit up and button her dress as they approached the farmhouse. They parked at the end of a row of vehicles that ranged from older models like the one they were in to bright, shiny new ones. Jimmy Doyle helped her from the car, then reached into the backseat. He withdrew a beautiful black box and handed it to her. "Go inside. Grace will help you put this on. When you're ready, come to the barn wearing only what is inside this box. Nothing else."

CHAPTER NINETEEN

Evelyn's stomach muscles quivered under the strain of holding them in while Grace cinched up the back of the corset. She'd never seen anything like it or the panties she'd found in the box too.

"All done." Grace turned Evelyn to face the mirror. "What do you think?"

"Oh!" Evelyn stroked the boned red satin. Her breasts were creamy mounds outlined by black lace. Her waist looked impossibly small—her hips more defined than she'd ever seen them. She'd endured the embarrassment of Grace shaving her mound, but the effect of bare skin beneath the band of lace made it all worthwhile. "It's beautiful."

"You're beautiful." Grace swept Evelyn's hair up, securing it off her neck with a jeweled comb. "Jimmy Doyle is a lucky man, and you're a lucky woman. He'll take good care of you."

The flock of butterflies that had been fluttering around in her stomach ever since she'd spied Jimmy Doyle leaning casually against the side of his older-model car suddenly felt more like angry blackbirds trying to peck their way out. She clenched her hands over her midsection and closed her eyes, blocking out the vision of the sensual woman in the mirror. "What am I doing?"

"Oh, now, honey." Grace slipped her arm around Evelyn's

waist and guided her to a ladder-back chair in the corner. "There's no need to be afraid. Jimmy Doyle is a wonderful man, and a skilled lover. He wouldn't have brought you here if he didn't know you could handle what he has in mind."

"I know." She did know that, but today was different. He'd promised to break past the barriers she'd erected. "It's not that—I mean, it is, and it isn't."

"What you're experiencing is normal for someone who has deep feelings for their partner. Love changes everything. You've given him your body, but that's easy compared to giving your heart and soul."

Evelyn took a shuddering breath. "I'm afraid that when he sees my soul, he won't want me anymore." Her ex-husband had seen only a fraction of the darkness in her soul and had cast her out. "I don't think I could stand it if he hates me afterward."

Grace knelt in front of her, covering Evelyn's clasped hands with hers. "When I said you had nothing to fear when it comes to Jimmy Doyle, I meant it. Trust me, Evelyn. He has a pretty good idea what he's going to find, or he wouldn't force you to see it for yourself. He's a wise man. Trust him to take you where you need to go."

They sat there for several minutes while Evelyn worked up the courage to stand. Facing the mirror, she couldn't believe the image there was really her. How could someone so ugly on the inside be so beautiful on the outside?

"Ready?"

"As I'll ever be." Evelyn faced her new confidant. "Thank you for listening. This is all so new to me."

Grace ushered her toward the door. "It's only the expression of your needs that is new to you. Everything you have been feeling inside has always been there." They stopped in the hallway. "Every one of these rooms is occupied tonight with people just like you. The needs they have aren't the kind polite society speaks about, but they've all come to realize denying their needs is unacceptable. So, they come here, where no one judges them. They're free to express their sexuality in whatever way feels right to them."

As they made their way down the stairs, Grace continued. "You'll eventually get to know many of them. They're all perfectly normal in their day-to-day lives. Our members are politicians, foreign diplomats, lawyers, doctors, housewives, farmers, laborers of all kinds. They might be the chef cooking for you or the clerk at your favorite soda fountain."

At the base of the stairs, Grace halted her. "They are no different than you, and you are no different from them. You'll see some things along the path and inside the barn that may be disturbing, but remember, everything that goes on here is consensual. You have to forget everything you've been taught about what is right and what is wrong between two adults, because at the Farm Club, nothing is wrong if it makes you feel good."

Evelyn followed Grace along the hallway to the back door, where the older woman hugged her before opening the door. Evelyn returned the hug, wishing she'd had someone like her for a mother instead of a woman who looked past her child and saw only the controlling, unforgiving man she'd married. "Thank you. For everything."

"Anytime, Evelyn. Now, go. Let your young man show you who you really are. Oh, and I look forward to hearing all about it whenever you're ready to talk."

Feeling more confident about facing her past, and her future, Evelyn headed down the meandering tree-lined path connecting the house to the barn. The idea that someone might see her walking around in broad daylight wearing practically nothing had her picking up her pace. She'd just hurried past a large oak when a woman's whimper stopped her. Evelyn turned around. A naked woman hung by her wrists from a large branch. Marks all over her body indicated she'd been whipped. Between her spread legs, what looked like the long wooden handle of a rake or shovel had been inserted in her opening. Remembering what Grace had told her, Evelyn turned away, leaving the woman to enjoy her situation.

"She's lovely, isn't she?" A man wearing dark trousers and

bare-chested came from the direction of the barn, carrying a small coil of rope. "Come, take a closer look," he beckoned. Not knowing a polite way to decline such an invitation, Evelyn stepped off the path.

"Deborah was just saying how she wished there was someone to see how beautiful she looks. I went out to the barn for some more rope and to see if I could scare up an audience for her, but everyone out there was busy."

"I was— I'm just—"

"I know," the man said. "Jimmy Doyle said you might be coming by soon. You're Evelyn, right?"

"Yes."

"I'm Orville, and this is Deborah." He slapped the woman's breasts. "Say hello, woman."

"Hello, Evelyn. It's nice to meet you."

Orville tenderly fondled the same breast he'd just struck. "That was very good, baby. Are you feeling okay? Need to rest?"

"No, Sir. I'm okay."

"Ready for me to bind your tits?"

"Yes, Sir. Please, Sir."

"Want to stay and watch?" Orville asked Evelyn.

"No. I mean…I've got to go. Jimmy Doyle is waiting."

"Run along, then. Deborah and I are staying the night too. Maybe we'll see you later on."

She didn't know what to say to that. It hadn't occurred to her that they might socialize with anyone afterward—though she should have considered the possibility. With a polite good-bye, she returned to the path. As she approached the barn, a small cart pulled by a naked man in full harness stopped adjacent to the well pump. A woman with a buggy whip in hand stepped from the cart and led the man to the watering trough, where he was encouraged to drink.

Evelyn hurried on. The whole thing reminded her of a book she'd read when she was a child. Was her personal wizard at the end of this road, or was this all a dream she would wake up from tomorrow?

As she approached the open door, Jimmy Doyle stepped out. He'd removed his shirt but still wore the suspenders that kept his trousers from falling off his slim hips. He was the most beautiful man she'd ever seen, not that she'd seen many, but surely a body as magnificent as his couldn't be common.

"I was beginning to think you had changed your mind." He was only stating a fact, not condemning her for taking so long. The way he looked at her in her skimpy attire, like he wanted to ravage her, made her grateful she hadn't chickened out. Only he had ever looked at her that way, and she couldn't come up with a single reason for that to be wrong.

She shook her head. "No. I almost did, but Grace was so nice. She convinced me that I could do this."

He held out his hand, and she closed the distance between them. "She's been a good friend to me over the years. Sometimes I think she knows me better than I know myself."

Evelyn placed her hand in his. The connection she felt every time they touched went a long way to calming her racing heart. "I felt the same way."

"Everything is ready for you." His gaze softened. "I won't be easy on you today. I'm going to push against every wall you've built until they come crumbling down. As always, you have only to tell me to stop, and I will. Are you ready, Evelyn?"

"Yes. I guess."

"No guessing allowed. You either are or you aren't."

She studied their linked hands. His was so strong compared to hers. He could break her in every possible way, but she knew all the way down to her soul that he would never harm her. What she feared most was losing him. "I don't want you to hate me. I don't think I could bear it if you decide you don't want me."

"There's no chance of that. I love you, Evelyn." He reached for her other hand, clasping both of hers in the warmth of his. "When I look at you, I see a beautiful woman, inside and out. There is nothing you could say to me that would make me see you differently."

"I want to believe you."

"Come, then. Let me show you what I see."

JIMMY DOYLE COULDN'T take his eyes off her. He'd been hard ever since he looked up and saw her walking down the pathway. Pleasuring her in the car tested his control, but seeing her in the corset he'd purchased for her was enough to cause him real pain. He'd have her today. He was going to fuck her every which way, then make love to her all night long. With a little luck, the marathon would ease his constant need of her.

She was like no other woman he'd ever known. Strong and independent, she'd proved she could make her way in the world without anyone's help, but at her core she was submissive. When she finally gave herself completely to a man, she would find the peace of submission she needed.

The way she'd followed his instructions, even when those instructions challenged her to act outside of what most people considered appropriate, triggered an answering need in him. He needed to possess her, to know everything there was to know about her. It ate at him to know she held things back from him when he'd been more open with her than he had been with anyone else. He'd never told anyone other than Grace about what he'd seen in his uncle's barn.

Unlike Evelyn, he'd come to the farm fully understanding what his needs were, needing only a place where he could fulfill them. He'd been miles ahead of where she was at this moment, and still, he'd been afraid.

Yet here she stood, nearly naked and facing her fears head-on. God, he loved her. If she walked away, he'd let her go, but she'd take a part of him with her.

What had Grace told him after that first session when he'd taken hours to systematically break her down? *"You have a gift, Jimmy Doyle, but your brand of dominance isn't for a weak woman. When you find the right one, and she submits to you, her strength will bring you to your knees."*

He was damn near on his knees now—begging.

He'd known today would be difficult for her, but watching her struggle with herself was killing him. She was stronger than she thought she was. Only a person with an iron will could hold so much of herself inside the way she did.

Walking outside wearing nothing but a corset and a few scraps of lace had to have tested her resolve, but she'd managed it— proving again how strong she was, and how much she wanted to believe in his love. But the only way she would ever be completely convinced that he would never abandon her was for her to tell him her deepest, darkest secrets. What was it that sent her to tent revival meetings in search of salvation? What made her think she could possibly be a sinner? He'd never seen a more perfect woman in his life. How in the world she could think he, God, or anyone else could turn from her, he had no idea. But he was going to find out. Today, if possible. Then she would be his, completely and forever.

"Trust me, Evelyn. I won't let you down."

When she looked up at him with troubled blue eyes, it was all he could do to keep from taking her in his arms and telling her to forget it. He'd made a huge mistake bringing her here, expecting her to allow him liberties with her body, much less her mind. Instead, he said, "I hate to see you like this, sweet one. The only way you're going to get rid of the demons making you doubt yourself at every turn is to face them as bravely as you're facing me right now."

She smiled at him—a genuine smile that made him want to dance naked in the meadow it was so radiant. "I'm scared out of my wits, Jimmy Doyle, and you think I'm brave?"

He returned her smile, grateful that she seemed to have relaxed a bit. "You're the bravest person I've ever known."

"I'm a coward, but I'm a tired coward. I'm tired of pretending that I'm okay with a life that isn't living at all. I'm yours. Do what you will with me."

The ground was calling to his knees, but he managed to stay upright even though blood rushing to his groin shifted his center of gravity and made him dizzy. "Don't move." He darted back inside the door, and grabbed the collar and the leather lead he'd prepared earlier. Returning to her, he willed his cock to stand down. This was all about Evelyn and what she needed. His needs could wait.

"You'll wear this." He held up the leather collar. "For as long as we're here." It wouldn't limit her range of motion as much as the one she'd worn the last time he'd brought her here. Mainly, it would serve to remind her who was in charge, and allow him to secure her by attaching leads to the rings spaced every few inches along the length.

If he hadn't been watching closely, he might have missed the flare of excitement in her eyes right before she averted her gaze. Seeing her natural submissive tendencies come to life renewed his conviction that what he was doing was the right thing for both of them. He might just let her have another dose of pleasure before he began disassembling the walls she'd built. A little pleasure would help ease her into a deeper submissive state too.

"On your knees."

There was the faintest hint of hesitation before she sank down in front of him. He'd have to explore that more, but for now, he wanted nothing more than to give her something she had no reason to fear. With her hair up off her neck, buckling the leather band took only a few seconds. Then he lifted her chin, beckoning her to rise. The flicker of surprise in her eyes cemented his plan to explore the kneeling thing further. She'd expected something besides the quick collaring, and he was damn well going to find out what it was. Later.

"Follow me." He led her to the stall he'd reserved for the day. When they were inside, he slid the heavy door shut, affording them some privacy, but having been built to house horses, the upper portion of the door was open except for metal bars designed to let the residents stick their heads out for a bit of attention. He already knew she got off from the possibility of discovery but didn't necessarily want to be watched. Not like Deborah did, anyway. That woman couldn't enjoy an orgasm unless she had an audience. The bigger, the better.

"Go to the far corner. Face-first. Hands on the walls." When she didn't move fast enough, he swatted her ass. She darted forward, taking the position he'd indicated. He stepped in close behind her, but not so close as to make physical contact. She was breathing hard and fast like a racehorse just off the track. "Do you know much about horses, Evelyn? Have you ever tended to one after it's been ridden hard?"

"We had a mare when I was growing up. My father used to ride her—sometimes. When he did, it was my job to tend to her." He couldn't help but wonder what she'd been about to say. Where, exactly, had her father gone on horseback?

"Then you know that sometimes they kick, and that brushing them helps to relax them."

"Yes."

Oh, she wasn't stupid. She'd picked up on where he was going with that line of questioning. "Yes, what?"

"Yes, Sir."

He touched her, tracing his index finger along the underside of her collar. "Horses are unpredictable creatures, so I'm going to hobble you so I can groom you without fear of being kicked or trampled." His statement didn't require an answer, and she didn't give one. Dropping kisses on her shoulder, he reached beneath her arm to remove the lead line, quickly hooking the front of her collar to the short lead attached to the corner. She trembled beneath his lips.

"Relax, sweetheart. I intend to give you nothing but pleasure. Surrender to it."

Without waiting for her to comply, he cuffed her wrists before securing them to hooks in the walls on either side of her head. Taking his time to learn everything he could about her corseted body, he made his way down to her hips. "As lovely as these are, they have to go, for now." He slipped the lace panties off her, then cuffed and secured her ankles. Earlier, he'd caught a glimpse of her bare mound, and he was dying to feel it. He liked a bush as much as the next guy, but he'd once had a thing with a French woman he'd met in New York and come to appreciate the beauty of a smooth pussy. Sometime in the future, perhaps he'd let Evelyn decide for herself which way she wanted to go, but for now, he wouldn't be sorry for having her clean-shaven.

"An important part of grooming a horse is to check to make sure they haven't suffered any injuries since the last time you saw them." He moved upward, sliding his palms over the outsides of her legs. Standing, he pressed his front to her back. God, he loved the feel of her ass against his cock. Fucking her from behind, in either hole, was high on his list. Capturing her waist with one arm, he slid his dick into her cleft. With his free hand, he reached for her mouth. Pinching her cheeks, he forced her lips open. After working his fingers around between her lips and teeth, he forced her tongue down, holding her jaw open until she gagged trying to swallow. "Such a lovely mouth. I can't wait to fuck it, sweetheart."

Her body trembled at the mention of him putting his cock in her mouth. He brushed his fingertip along her lips. "All I have to do is close my eyes and imagine your lips on my shaft, and I get hard. You could drive me crazy with this mouth. Would you like that—to have me at your mercy, begging you to let me come?"

"Yes, Sir."

"That's just one of my fantasies, Eve. I have so many where you are concerned. You understand your body is mine to do with as I please? That I will fuck any part of you I want, anytime I want?"

She shuddered, then swallowed hard. "Yes, Sir."

"Sometimes, I'll want nothing more than to see you come. Like earlier today in the car. Giving you pleasure can be as satisfying as coming myself." He lifted her breasts from the confining corset and plucked at her nipples until she moaned and rocked her hips against him.

"No, no, sweetheart. Keep those hips still, or I'll have to do something about that too." Being pressed up against her was bad enough. Having her rub her ass on his erection was too much. He wouldn't last a minute, let alone long enough to see to her pleasure.

She immediately ceased her movement, allowing him to think again. "Can you stay still while I examine your pussy, sweetheart?"

Her groan brought a smile to his lips. Good to know he was driving her as crazy as he was making himself. "I think so, Sir."

"Not good enough," he growled, nipping at her ear.

"I'll try, Sir."

"Better."

With his lips on her shoulder, he peered down at her breasts spilling over the boned corset. He wondered if she had any idea how sexy she was in the French-made garment. If he had his way, she'd wear it for him on a regular basis—anytime she wasn't naked. Skin like hers should only be touched by him or the finest of fabrics. Just thinking about cheap cloth next to her perfection made him angry.

Working his hand along the deep curve of her waist, he almost lost it when he encountered warm flesh. "Jesus, I can't get enough of touching you." He slipped his middle finger between her bare folds. She was hot and wet, and her skin baby soft.

"Next time, I'm going to watch," he said while his fingers sent images to his brain. "Tell me what you were feeling while Grace shaved you."

"Embarrassed. Scared she might slip and cut me. Aroused." The last came out on a gasp as he found her clitoris and began to play.

"Aroused? What did you want, Evelyn? Did you want to have something in your pussy, or did you want Grace to taste you? Tell me, sweetheart. Tell me what you wanted."

CHAPTER TWENTY

Jimmy Doyle surrounded her in every possible way. With his body wrapped around her from behind, she felt every hard angle pressed against her, felt his heat incinerating her inhibitions. His scent, heightened by the temperature in the barn, was a drug to her senses. She wanted everything he'd promised her, would do anything he asked. But carrying on a conversation while he teased her pussy was near to impossible.

Without hair to act as a barrier, she felt every scrape of his work-roughened hand across her mound. The enhanced sensation chipped away at her sanity and drove her hard and fast toward the pinnacle of pleasure she craved like never before. She was close. So close. Then he stopped. Placing his hand on the wall next to hers, he whispered in her ear. "Tell me what you wanted, Eve."

Tears streamed down her cheeks for the denied orgasm, but the loss of contact allowed sense to return. She let her mind drift back to the farmhouse, to the room, no bigger than a closet, where she had lain naked on a table like the ones in doctors' offices, and let Grace shave her most private parts. So many thoughts had run through her mind, but of those, only a few stood out.

"I was scared, and I wished you were there to hold me. I feel safe when you hold me."

"You can count on me to protect you, always." He tightened

his arm around her waist. "What else?"

"It's so wrong."

"Nothing is wrong here, Eve."

"Please. Don't call me that." Hearing the name her family had called her made her desires feel more wicked. She was going to burn in hell for the things her body wanted.

"Evelyn, then. Tell me what I want to know, and I'll let you come."

His breath against her ear awakened every nerve ending from her head to her toes. Need coiled in her belly. The tender skin between her legs throbbed, just as it had when the razor slid over it, making her want... "I wanted her to kiss me. There."

The admission wrenched a fresh wave of sobs from her. If she could have doubled over, she would have, but her restraints held firm. She was trapped. Trapped in her shame. Trapped in her misery. Trapped in her need.

"Holy merciful God, Evelyn. I love you." He covered her mound with his hand, infusing her with his strength. "But imagining Grace going down on you might be the death of me yet." He laid his cheek against hers—the touch tender yet shattering. He hadn't flinched at her wicked desire. He hadn't turned away from her. He still loved her.

An all-encompassing love for him washed through her. Her heart, so full of emotion, swelled to near bursting. She wanted to give everything to this man, but if she did, she would certainly lose him.

"I promised you an orgasm if you were honest with me. I never go back on my promises."

His fingers slid easily through her wet folds. He pushed them inside her, stretching her, filling her so full it took her breath away. Then he began to move, pumping his thick fingers in and out, fast and hard while his thumb circled her clitoris. In a matter of minutes, she was coming. The hand that had been at her waist now rested against her stomach, holding her backside firm against his erection.

Her insides quaked, the involuntary contractions amplified in the confined space created by the corset. She hurt, but the hurt felt good in a twisted paradox she didn't understand. She only knew this ecstasy was something she couldn't live without. She'd take heaven on earth—even if it meant an eternity in hell.

Drifting in a post orgasmic haze, she was nothing more than a rag doll in Jimmy Doyle's arms when he released her from the restraints and held her close. Just held her. Nothing more, but it was everything she needed. When she finally opened her eyes, the smile on his lips seemed almost sad. She wanted to ask him why, but her head was still spinning with the revelations she'd discovered. Instead, when he placed a tin cup to her lips, she drank greedily. The water helped clear her head. Suddenly, she remembered her shameful confession. Heat bloomed across her chest, creeping upward.

"That's better. I like to see color in your cheeks." He patted her naked bottom. "All of them."

Evelyn ducked her head against his chest. Desire rose like a tidal wave, causing her to squirm in his lap. She'd had an epic orgasm moments before, and here she was craving more. Hadn't she just made the decision to have heaven on earth? She wiggled her butt against his thick erection.

"Ready for more?"

"Yes, please, Sir."

"On your feet, then." He helped her stand, then guided her back to the same corner. This time, he bent her over, attaching the front of her collar to a length of leather anchored to the floor that prevented her from standing upright. One at a time, he fastened the cuffs at her wrists to the walls so her arms were stretched straight out from her shoulders and parallel to the floor. Once again, her legs were spread wide, her ankles secured to the floor. The position was anything but comfortable, but once he stroked her exposed ass, she forgot all about her discomfort.

"I love you, Eve." She closed her eyes at the sound of the hated nickname coming from his lips again. His warm hands glided over her thighs up to her butt, then down again, repeating the process on the insides of her legs. "I want to possess you in every way possible. I want you to be mine. Do you understand?"

"Yes, Sir."

"I don't think you do, or you wouldn't still be holding parts of yourself back from me." He fingered her pussy, aided by the moisture from her orgasm. "Until you trust me with everything, then only parts of you belong to me. I want it all, Eve. Every thought. Every need. Every desire. Every hurt. Every pain. Everything."

She gasped as he pressed one wet finger against her anus. Panicking, she jerked against the restraints like a wild animal caught in a trap. He wrapped both arms around her waist and, bending over her, wrapped her in his strength. "Shh, baby. Relax. You're going to hurt yourself if you keep this up."

"Let me go." The words came out in jerking sobs. "Please. I can't do this."

"You can, Eve. Tell me what happened. Let me take that burden from you."

"I can't. Please, Jimmy Doyle. Don't touch me there."

"I need you to give me everything—including your trust." He shifted. Then she felt his finger there again, gently probing. Desire, hot and wicked, shot through her like a wildfire. "You want me to fuck your ass. I know your body, Eve. You can't hide your desire from me. I felt the change in your breathing when I touched you there. You're scared. Tell me why."

"I can't."

"You can. You will." His harsh words left her as cold as the loss of his body wrapped around hers.

"Please."

"Please, what, Eve? Please fuck your ass, or please let you go?" He knelt beside her. Deep lines were etched into his face, lines of pain she'd put there as surely as if she'd taken a knife and carved them. "If you ask me to let you go, I will, but know that I'll never stop until I have your complete trust. You can tell me now or you can tell me later, but you will tell me. Why do you hold this one part of yourself from me?"

"I can't tell you. You'd hate me."

"Oh, sweet, Eve, I could never hate you. I've told you before." He brushed tears from her cheeks as he spoke the tender words. "Let me show you. Let me claim your ass."

She shook her head as silent sobs racked her body. "Please, don't make me do this."

"Disobedience such as this can't be tolerated, Eve. You'll take your punishment; then we'll see if you have changed your mind."

Evelyn cried out as she jerked against the restraints. "Please. Please don't." She felt the cold wood of the paddle on her ass seconds before it disappeared only to return, laying a band of fire across her buttocks. Over and over again, fire rained down on her ass. Her legs trembled as she strained to remain upright.

Rage, hotter than any desire she'd ever felt, fueled her voice. "Stop! Please! I didn't do anything wrong!" She fought the restraints. "I didn't do anything wrong," she sobbed, weaker this time, but still, the words sounded like they had been pried from her heart with a rusty knife.

Strong arms embraced her, stroked her arms, her breasts, her pussy, kept her from collapsing to her knees. Fingers dipped inside her pussy, then gently worked her slick juices into her tight nether hole. "No, sweetheart, you didn't do anything wrong. Open for me, Eve. Let me inside."

"I didn't do anything wrong," she sobbed as she rocked her hips, offering herself to him.

"Oh, babe, I know you didn't do anything wrong." Hands on her hips, he shoved his cock into her pussy in one swift stroke, in and out. Then the head of his cock pressed against her anus, firm, insistent.

"I need to be inside you, Eve. I need to possess you."

Her head dropped between her shoulders. Defeated, she relaxed her muscles and pushed back against him just as he pressed forward. The head of his cock slipped past the barrier; then slowly, he took possession of her, filling her.

For a long moment, they remained still as statues. Evelyn silently sobbed as emotions warred inside her. She'd given him everything, risked everything for this indescribable pleasure. To belong so fully to someone, to place everything you were in their hands, to trust that when they had taken their pleasure, they wouldn't condemn you for taking yours. That they wouldn't cast you out.

Fear, lust, love. They all combined to heighten the pleasure of his possession. It was done. Whatever happened afterward would happen. She couldn't stop that now. There was only this moment, and the incredible feeling of belonging fully to someone for however long it lasted. A minute? Two? Forever was too much to hope for. She moved her hips in silent encouragement. She wanted more, wanted everything he had to give.

He began to move, sliding almost all the way out, then driving back in. Over and over, he claimed what was his—what would always be his. Working her bottom against his cock, she took as much pleasure as she could. She might have destroyed his love for her by showing him her greatest sin, her greatest shame, but she would love him forever. He held her body, her heart, her soul, in his hands.

"Good God, Eve, you're killing me." He dug his fingernails into the soft pads of flesh on her hips, stilling her movements. "I love your ass. Love your pussy. Love you." As he spoke, he gathered more of her natural lubricant on his fingers, using it to aid his slide in and out. Each time he went down for more, he made a stop at her clit, paying attention to it before returning to his mission. It wasn't long before the now familiar tension began to build low in her belly.

She didn't want it to be over. She knew what came after, the accusations, the condemnation, the shame, the heartache. The loneliness. She'd been down that road before, and now it looked as if she would be heading that way again. Wanting to savor every last minute she had with Jimmy Doyle, she forced thoughts of the future from her mind and focused on the only thing that mattered at that moment, giving herself fully to the man who owned her heart.

FUCK. HER TIGHT ass gripped him all the way down to his soul. Whatever her hang-up was in regards to anal sex, she'd have no reason to keep it from him now. She belonged to him. Every. Last. Fucking. Inch of her. Whatever secrets she had, they were his now. She'd tell him, and he'd deal with it. For her. For them.

Her ass was going to hurt for days, not from the fucking, but from the paddling. He hadn't planned on hitting her as hard as he had, or for as many strokes. Thank God she'd finally broken down and said something. He'd never forget those words or the way they'd come crying out from deep inside her. *"I didn't do anything wrong."*

Who else had she said that to, and what had the bastard done to her in retaliation? He was damn sure going to find out. Tonight. She'd carried the burden alone for too long as it was; he wasn't going to let another day go by while she suffered.

She was close; he could feel the flutter of her stomach muscles every time he flicked at her clitoris. It amazed him how easily he read her body, considering how few times they'd been together. He'd known from the beginning that she had secrets, but even then he'd been willing to take them on because he knew on a visceral level that she would be his.

As he plumbed the depths of her ass, he marveled at her sensuality. Not many women knew the joy of sex or were willing to explore what their bodies were capable of. But that wasn't his Eve. She knew, and though hesitant at first, she'd grown in her knowledge and pleasure. Now that she was his, he would see to her continuing education, giving her as much pleasure as she could accept.

He'd never wanted to do anything more in his life. Not even play baseball, and that was something he'd been born to do. Just like he'd been born to love Eve.

"Come for me, Eve. I want to feel you come around my dick." Supporting her around the waist with one arm, he reached around from the other side to flick at her clitoris with his free hand. After denying himself all day, he wasn't going to last much longer himself. This first time in her ass, he wanted to finish with her. He wanted her to remember the feel of his hot semen spurting into her body and to know she'd wrecked him.

It didn't take long to push her over the edge. Spearing three fingers into her cunt, he let loose, releasing what felt like a massive load of cum up her ass. As he pumped his hips against her soft fanny, hot semen spread along the length of his shaft. God, he wanted to feel that in her pussy. Wanted to shoot his seed straight to her womb. Nothing marked a woman as taken more than a belly swollen with child. His child. Fuck. He was gone. Wrecked. Totally fucked, and he couldn't have been happier.

"Sweet one." Still intimately joined, he freed her from all but the ankle restraints and pulled her up so her back was to his front. "I want to stay like this forever, joined to you, claiming you." He should have been growing soft, but he still felt as hard as minutes ago when he'd first breached her barrier. What better way to hear her story than while he possessed her this way?

"Tell me now, Eve. What happened?"

He held her with both arms wrapped around her waist. Her hands clung to his forearms like she was adrift and he her life raft. Her head lay back on his shoulder, her eyes closed. He could see her throat working as she swallowed hard. He fucking loved that collar on her. And the wrist cuffs. He couldn't wait to suspend her, maybe in the middle of the barn so everyone could witness her pleasure. But first, she had to tell him what had her so uptight about her ass, and the name, Eve, which he preferred over Evelyn.

"Talk to me." He rocked his hips, pushing his cock even deeper inside her.

"Do that again. Please? It makes me feel weak but powerful. Safe."

He rocked into her again. "You are safe, darling one."

"I want to tell you, but not here. Not while you're inside me like this. I don't want anything to taint what we've had together."

"Not had. Have, Eve. Nothing you can say will change the way I feel about you." He loosened his hold on her waist with one hand and, clasping her wrist, guided her hand to her pussy and held it there. "Make yourself come again, babe. I want to feel you come on me again. After that, I'll take you to our room, but only if you promise you'll tell me everything. No holding back. No secrets between us ever again."

"I promise. Oh! Jimmy Doyle, that feels good."

"Right here, babe." He helped her find her clitoris. "Work it while I fill you completely up."

With his fingers in her channel and her fingering her clitoris, her orgasm came fast. Even though he'd spent himself only minutes earlier, his dick twitched and spasmed, giving her what he had left.

When she hung limp in his arms, he called out for help. One of the farmhands quickly responded and helped him by releasing her ankle restraints. He reluctantly slipped from her tight sheath, lifted her into his arms, and headed for the house.

CHAPTER TWENTY-ONE

Evelyn woke to a dark room and the heavy weight of Jimmy Doyle's arm around her waist. She vaguely remembered him carrying her to their room, administering to her sore bottom, and rubbing ointment onto her chaffed wrists and ankles.

"Talk to me, Eve."

She sighed into the darkness. He'd sodomized her, and he was still here, lying naked in bed with her. She took that as a good sign and spoke to the night. "My father is a preacher. The fire-and-brimstone kind. Sinners are going to burn in hell unless they repent. Repent. Repent. There was never enough repentance in our house. Sometimes I thought even breathing might be a sin. Before my marriage, I think I'd spent half my life on my knees asking for forgiveness for one thing or another—wanting a new dress, or shoes that didn't pinch my toes, walking too slow on my way home from school, walking too fast on my way home from school. Nothing I did was right. When my father brought a man home and introduced him as my fiancé, I saw one thing I could do right in his eyes. So a week later, I married Curtis. He was old enough to be my father.

"I tried to be a good wife, but I was seventeen years old and all I knew about being married was that I belonged to my husband, and through copulation, there would be children."

"You knew about copulation?"

She didn't think she'd ever look at that time of her life and laugh, but she did at Jimmy Doyle's question. "A little history here. My father's favorite sermon topics were the sins of the flesh. Adultery, fornication, homosexuality, and sodomy. I didn't know what any of those words meant, but I knew they were bad. Why else would he preach about them so often?

"One day when I was fifteen, I snuck into his office when he was out riding the circuit to visit the parishioners. I read everything I could on the subjects. That was a mistake. Adultery and homosexuality didn't relate to me in any way, but fornication, which I learned was copulation without benefit of marriage, and sodomy? They were all I could think about.

"Maybe it was a combination of my body changing from a girl to a woman and my sudden unholy knowledge of what men and women did together, but I *needed* to experience it. I gave myself my first orgasm, by accident, a few weeks after sneaking into Father's study. I was hooked. I touched myself often—in the bathtub, in bed—and I dreamed of the day I would be someone's wife and could experience those feelings with a man.

"And I wanted children. Lots of them. By then, I understood where babies came from, and I craved sex even more."

"All that is perfectly normal, Eve. Every teenager goes through the same self-discovery. I believe desire is part of God's plan to ensure babies would be born. Think about it. Every animal on earth is driven to mate. Why should humans be any different?"

Evelyn chuckled. "Well, that's what I thought too, but wanting things that wouldn't bring about children was wrong. Or so I found out."

"What happened?"

"First, you have to understand my marriage didn't turn out to be the wedded bliss I had dreamed of. On my wedding night, my husband came to our bed fully dressed. I had on my prettiest gown and nothing else. I was so excited. Finally, I was going to know what it was like to be with a man, and I was going to have babies!"

Evelyn shook her head, remembering the shock of that night.

"He had me sit on the edge of the bed, still in my gown. He unbuttoned his fly, took out his limp penis, and ordered me to prepare him to make me his wife. I didn't have a clue what he wanted me to do. I'd never seen a penis before and I didn't know it wasn't supposed to be soft, so I just sat there, staring at it. He flicked my shoulder with the back of his hand and told me to suck it.

"A few hours earlier, I had vowed to obey him in all things, so I took him into my mouth. After a while, he got hard. Then he shoved me back on the bed, jerked my gown up to my waist, and shoved my legs apart with his knees.

"The whole thing was over in minutes. My gown was covered in sticky goo, and everything between my legs hurt. He buttoned up, told me to clean up the mess, then left. I don't know where he went. I cleaned the blood off my thighs, changed my gown, then went to bed. The next morning I could tell he'd been to bed, but he was gone to work in the fields and I was all alone.

"After that, he came to me about once a month. It was the same thing every time. He never left his seed inside me. By then, I knew there weren't going to be any babies, and that hurt more than him sticking his thing in me."

"I'm so sorry, Eve."

She wasn't sure if he was sorry she wasn't ever going to have children or sorry for the way her ex-husband treated her. Deciding it didn't matter, she continued. "Every Sunday we went to my father's church service. Wait—you have to understand that at this point, I was touching myself almost every day while my husband was out working. I no longer wanted sex just to have children. It was something I thought about all the time. I ached for someone to touch me in the way I had dreamed a husband would. One Sunday we were walking home from the service. Curtis was very quiet, and I was desperate for something to fill the silence I lived with every day. Father had preached another sermon on the evils of sodomy. I don't know why I picked that particular subject, or what

I thought was going to happen.

"I told him I didn't see what all the fuss was about. Why was it wrong? And I told him it sounded like it might be fun. That was the only time in our marriage that he showed any interest in sex. Looking back, I can see I was starved for attention, so much so that I didn't see how angry he was. Not until he'd finished with me and he saw I wasn't frightened by what he'd done."

"God, Eve. I shouldn't have taken you so hard." He tightened his hold on her, and she snuggled closer, loving the feel of him next to her.

"I loved what you did to me." She sighed again. "You don't think I'm depraved?"

"No, sweetheart. I think you're brave, and amazing, and I love you for opening yourself to me so completely."

"You are unique among men, Jimmy Doyle. My ex-husband didn't see it that way. I knew he'd found pleasure in what we'd done, as I had, and for a moment afterward I thought perhaps there might be a new intimacy in our marriage—and perhaps—"

"There would be babies."

"Yes. But I was wrong. I'd never seen him so angry. He practically dragged me out of the house. I remember tripping over my panties when they fell to my ankles. He didn't care—just kept pulling me along. He took me straight to my parents' house, which was a short walk away. I didn't know what I'd done wrong, but as soon as my father saw us, he took us to his office and shut the door.

"Curtis told him I was a whore. A temptress. The devil's mistress. He blamed me for causing him to sin. He begged my father for forgiveness and received it. Then they both turned their wrath on me. My father sent Curtis out in the yard to get branches from the hawthorn tree. They broke them up into strips and put them on the floor. I knelt on those thorns for hours while the two of them condemned me for being all manner of sinner. They didn't even bother to pray for my soul. I was guilty. Beyond redemption. I was given a few minutes to gather what I could in a pillowcase from our house; then they drove me to the bus stop.

"I had blood streaks on my legs from kneeling on the thorns; no underclothes; lard and semen staining the back of my dress; a pillowcase containing a Bible, my everyday dress and some panties, and every cent I'd saved from selling eggs. Two whole dollars."

"Dear God."

"God was no help at all. I bought a ticket on the next bus leaving town. The ticket seller was the father of a friend of mine from grade school. He let me use the restroom at the station to change my dress and clean up, but he never questioned why I was there or if he could help in any other way. I'm sure he'd seen who dropped me off and didn't want to get involved in a family matter. My father had a lot of influence in the community. No one wanted to cross him. I guess seeing the man's daughter left to her own devices, as I clearly had been, was enough warning for Mr. Wilson. He took enough of a chance doing what little he did for me."

"You went to Washington?"

"My ticket was for the end of the line. That turned out to be Washington. I'd never been more than a few miles from home in my life, so any city would do as far as I was concerned. It was summer, so I was able to sleep on a park bench for a few nights until I found a job waitressing. I used the last of my money to rent a room for a week until I got paid. I got lucky finding the boardinghouse. I'd been in town for a year before I got a job with the telephone company. I've made it on my own, and I'm proud of that."

"I knew you were an exceptional woman the moment I saw you, but I had no idea, Eve."

"My parents called me Eve. One of the things my father said to me that day was he never should have named me after a sinner."

"Eve was created without sin."

"But she fell from grace soon enough."

"And you think you have too."

"What else would you call it? I crave the sins of the flesh. I want things I shouldn't want."

"You've done nothing wrong, Eve." He put a finger over her lips, silencing her before she could protest the use of the name. "The name suits you. The first Eve wasn't content with not knowing. She didn't set out to sin. She craved knowledge, and knowledge was sin. Or so the Bible says. Those are stories, Evelyn, made up to explain things ancient people had no explanation for."

Jimmy Doyle rose on one elbow and cupped her face in his hand. "God created you just the way you are, and if you believe that, then you have to believe that nothing about you is wrong. Is it wrong to hunger for food? If so, is it wrong for you to desire ice cream more than green beans? It's not wrong to desire sex. The human race would die out if people quit having sex, just as it would die out if people quit eating.

"Is it wrong for you to desire variations of sex that don't have anything to do with creating babies? It's no more wrong than wanting to eat something that gives you pleasure when you could be eating something that provides nothing more than sustenance.

"There's nothing wrong with you, Eve. Nothing at all. You are one of God's perfect creations."

Tears blurred her vision, but she didn't need to see his face. The tone of his voice told her of his sincerity. Dear lord how she wanted to believe him, but a lifetime of beliefs didn't die easily. "But—"

"No arguments, Eve. Not when we're surrounded by people who are just like us. I believe God created our bodies with the capacity to experience sexual pleasure. What that is for each of us is different, but there's nothing wrong with it, whatever it is."

As he lowered his head, Evelyn closed her eyes and allowed herself to enjoy the feel of his mouth on hers. When his tongue sought entrance, she parted her lips for him. They hadn't kissed much, but she understood the message he was conveying. Her body relaxed under his, softened under his touch. She wanted him to do everything his mouth promised. She let him know, opening her legs in blatant invitation.

"I want you, Eve."

"I want you too."

He reached for a sheath and sat on his knees between her thighs to put it on. "No babies, Eve. Not yet." When he'd rolled the thin barrier on, his gaze met hers. "But soon, sweetheart. I love you so damn much, and I want to give you all the babies you want. Until we're able to do that, I'm going to pleasure you in every way possible."

He entered her with one hard thrust that took her breath away. After his solemn declaration, she expected a quick fucking, but the slow lovemaking she got brought fresh tears to her eyes. He'd committed carnal sins with her, and instead of casting her out, he promised her babies and was making sweet love to her. It was more than she had ever dreamed of. And not enough.

"Please," she begged, rocking her hips up to meet his.

"Tell me what you want, baby."

"Harder."

He braced himself above her on locked elbows. "Wrap your legs around my waist," he ordered. "That's it, baby. Hold on."

Evelyn dug her fingernails into his biceps, holding on as he set a punishing pace that rocked her to her core and set off explosions of pleasure deep inside her. The orgasm took over her entire body, gripping her hard, then flooding her with intense pleasure that was impossible to contain. She screamed his name and implored God at the top of her lungs when Jimmy Doyle emptied himself inside her.

సుప

He'd never wanted to kill another person until he'd heard Evelyn's story. Now there were two people on his list, her father and her ex-husband. God help them both if he ever got within an arm's length of them. He'd murder them both with his bare hands.

How anyone could believe Eve to be a sinner, he had no idea. And to treat her the way they had? Barbaric. All in the name of God. He'd never been more convinced that men like those two were the devil in disguise, working their evil against God's children, destroying one soul at a time. The God he knew in his heart wouldn't condemn an innocent woman for desires of a body created in his image.

It made no sense to him. But he wasn't the one who needed convincing. So, after making love to her in the soft dawn light, Jimmy Doyle took her downstairs to meet more of his friends. She was polite, though he knew her well enough to notice the way her eyes absorbed the shock of meeting a federal judge and a senator who had been longtime lovers—sodomites—freely touching and kissing over the breakfast table.

"I owe my return to baseball to Judge Hallstead," he said, smiling at his friend.

"You don't owe me anything, son. You'd done nothing wrong. All I had to do was make the right people listen. The rest, you're doing on your own."

"I'd been trying for years to get those people to listen. I never could have done it without you."

"Just keep up the good work, and you'll have a solid multiyear contract at the end of this season."

"I'm trying, Judge. I'm trying."

Next, he introduced Evelyn to the woman she'd seen on her way to the barn the day before. "How many kids do you and Orville have now, Deb?" he asked the smiling couple.

"Four, and perhaps another on the way soon."

"Orville owns a print shop. Does a lot of stuff for the government," Jimmy Doyle explained.

"Business is good," the man confirmed.

"It better be if you're going to keep knocking your wife up."

"She wants a brood, and I like putting the little squirts in there," he said with a wiggle of his eyebrows. Evelyn turned red as the kitchen countertop while Deb leaned in to kiss her husband.

"I like that part too. Especially when we can come here. I love it when I can scream all I want. Can't do that at home with all the kids and the neighbors."

Others trickled through, some stopping to eat, others checking out on their way back to the city and their everyday lives.

He could only hope Evelyn saw what he did—normal people who wanted to live their lives without censure.

The last thing he wanted to do was leave, but he had a game that afternoon, and he couldn't be late. And Evelyn needed to get home before someone wondered about her. She was quiet as they gathered their few belongings and got in the car. Taking her hand in his, he thought of what he would lose if she couldn't embrace the truth about herself. Once, he'd thought the loss of his career would be the worst thing that could happen to him, but now he knew losing Evelyn would destroy him.

"What are you thinking?" he asked.

"Do you suppose most people are like the ones I met this morning? Like you and me? Or are we really different?"

He tried not to get too excited about the way she included the two of them into her mental grouping. It was a far cry from actually accepting who she was, but it was a good sign. "I think everyone likes something different. Remember my aunt and uncle? I don't think any less of them for doing what makes them feel good. Everyone expresses their love in different ways. I don't think any way is bad or wrong if the people involved enjoy what they're doing. I think you'd be surprised at what goes on behind closed doors. You know, in some cultures, it's permissible—desired, even—to have many wives. I read about one culture where piercing the genitals, multiple times, is a normal practice."

She was quiet for several minutes. "You don't think I'm a sinner?"

"Do you think the people you met this morning are sinners?"

"No. I don't."

"Neither do I. You aren't any different than they are, Eve. The only difference between those people and others is they've found a place where they can be who they are without people like your father trying to make them feel guilty."

CHAPTER TWENTY-TWO

Before dropping her off at home, Jimmy Doyle made her promise to listen to his game that afternoon on the radio. With thoughts of what she'd experienced over the past eighteen hours fresh in her mind, she really didn't want to spend the afternoon in the sweltering parlor with a bunch of chatty women, but she didn't know anywhere else a respectable woman could go by herself on a Sunday to listen. So, the parlor it would be. Wanting to savor her memories as long as possible, she hurried to her room.

She was surprised at how sore she was in certain places. But it was a good soreness that reminded her of how much she loved Jimmy Doyle, and if the way he'd made love to her this morning was any indication, he loved her just as much. He'd certainly gone out of his way to convince her to let go of the guilt she'd carried for so long.

If she was to be honest with herself, she was still conflicted about the desires of her body, but when it came to the desires of her heart, she knew exactly what she wanted. Jimmy Doyle Walker and all the children he wanted to give her. Just thinking about the heat in his eyes when he'd promised to give her children made her heart sing for joy.

Wearing nothing but the lace panties he'd sent her, she placed a hand over her belly, imagining how she would feel when he planted his seed in her. He wore the barriers to prevent her from becoming pregnant, but he hadn't worn one when he entered her other hole. It had felt so strange and wonderful when he spilled his hot essence inside her. The whole experience had been nothing like the time with Curtis. She'd give anything to forget those few minutes, but she couldn't. And in a way, she didn't want to. After all, if that day had never happened, she would probably still be trapped in a loveless marriage, and she never would have met Jimmy Doyle.

He was the best thing that ever happened to her, and though he hadn't actually asked her to marry him, he'd promised her babies. She imagined him making love to her every night, and maybe even in daylight. He couldn't seem to keep his hands off her.

She giggled, thinking of the way he looked at her all the time—as if he could see right through her clothes. He'd told her he preferred her naked. She blushed at the memory of his hands sliding beneath her skirt in the car on the way home—his fingers sneaking into her intimate places until she came, screaming his name on the wind. She had no shame when it came to him. Being with him felt too right to be wrong. God had made him for her, and her for him. Of that, she was certain.

She'd dawdled too long in her room, and the only seat available in the small room sat in the corner, well away from the open windows and any breeze they might allow in. Evelyn sat, grateful at least that in her cramped corner, no one would be looking at her. She wasn't at all sure her face wouldn't give her feelings away whenever her lover's name was mentioned.

The Diplomats' successful season was all anyone could talk about these days. Evelyn supposed everyone needed something to take their mind off the bothersome heat of a summer that showed no signs of letting up and an economy showing little sign of recovery. The local baseball club was as good a distraction as any. No one commented on her appearance inside, though she often sat in one of the rocking chairs on the porch where she could hear the game announcer through the window. Today, she didn't want to take a chance on missing anything. Jimmy Doyle loved playing the game, and she loved him. Therefore, she was going to learn everything she could about baseball.

The following day, she smiled inwardly as she went through her workday. The announcers for yesterday's game had talked about Jimmy Doyle nonstop, calling him the Pride of the Diplomats. They'd also talked about his contract with the team, which apparently was for this season only. She knew him well enough to know he'd be crushed if his contract wasn't renewed, and she'd be devastated if he moved to another team. But she'd rather see him move than not play at all. He'd given her so much, she could only wish the best for him, and the best was playing the game he loved.

Taking a late lunch break, she headed for the drugstore around the corner where she could find everything she needed—a sandwich from the lunch counter and an update on today's game. Listening intently yesterday, she'd discovered that even if she weren't in love with one of the players, she would listen anyway. Her heart raced at every pitch, every swing of the bat, and sank whenever the Diplomats failed to score. She'd cheered along with everyone else when Jimmy Doyle batted in the winning run.

Taking the last available seat at the lunch counter, she ordered, then tuned in to the game playing on the radio. The home team was locked in a battle for the pennant with the visiting Yankees. A win for the Diplomats would tie the two teams in the standings.

She wanted the win for Jimmy Doyle and for every one of the fans surrounding her. They all needed something positive to cheer about.

As he came up to bat in the fifth inning with a runner on second base, the announcers talked about the record number of hits he'd had this season—better than before his hiatus from the game. Evelyn hung on every word, wanting to learn all she could about the man who knew everything about her. He'd told her many private things, but he wasn't one to call attention to his successes. She was grateful the announcers didn't have a problem doing it for him. He deserved accolades for what he'd done for the team this year, helping lift them from near obscurity to a contender for the pennant.

Evelyn set her sandwich on the plate and crossed her fingers on both hands. A home run would put the Diplomats up by one run, and Jimmy Doyle led the league in home runs this season. The announcer's excitement carried over to the other diners as everyone stopped to listen to the play-by-play.

He stepped into the batter's box, adjusting his cap to shield the blazing sun. As the men described the scene, she imagined him wiping sweat from his forehead with the back of his hand as she'd seen him do, then resettling his cap on his head. She'd never seen him in uniform, but she vowed right then to accept tickets the next time he offered, which he had done many times.

The first pitch to Jimmy Doyle was too low to hit and was called a ball by the official. A grumble of protest rose from her fellow diners. They wanted to see him hit a home run as much as she did.

He clobbered the next pitch. Evelyn held her breath, waiting for the announcer to determine the fate of the ball.

"And it's foul!" The diners groaned as one. The ball had landed in the right-field stands, but out-of-bounds. At least that was what she thought *foul* meant.

Jimmy Doyle, having begun to run the bases, returned to face the pitcher again. Evelyn raised her water glass to her lips and drank. The tension in the room was palpable. She could only imagine what it was like at the ballpark. The crowd, who had gone wild when he hit the last pitch, was silent waiting for the next one. The announcer called the windup, the release of the ball. She heard his words, but they didn't make sense.

Jimmy Doyle had been hit by the ball. The announcer's shocked voice pierced the thick fog of fear isolating her from the world. Jimmy Doyle had crumpled to the ground.

Everything seemed muted, the crowd at the stadium, the announcers. Even the normal sounds of the diner fell away as everyone waited to hear something—anything—about the player downed on the field by a wild pitch.

Evelyn carefully placed her glass on the counter before it slipped from her shaking hands. She felt numb, suspended in time, the reporter's words registering somewhere deep inside her. "He isn't moving, folks."

God, please. Please. Please. Get up, Jimmy Doyle. Please, God, let him get up.

Through the rising outrage of the people surrounding her, she strained to hear every word from the announcers. "We can't see what's going on down there. The entire Diplomats squad surrounds their fallen hero. We can only hope and pray that the Pride of the Diplomats will recover."

Her vision blurred with unshed tears. A few words made their way to the place she'd gone within herself where she tried to shelter herself from the pain of possibly losing the man she loved with all her heart. *Deliberate. Unsportsmanlike. Stretcher. St. Mary's.*

She didn't remember making the decision to move. Her body simply refused to remain where it was—not when Jimmy Doyle needed her. Or maybe it was her who needed him, but she placed a dime on the counter, gathered her purse, and left the diner. Some inner force directed her to the hospital.

"I'm here to see Jimmy Doyle Walker," she told the dragon sitting behind the front desk.

"Are you related?"

"I'm his fiancée." Where the lie came from, she didn't know. She prayed it was enough to get her past the gatekeeper to the one place she needed to be. The dragon's face changed from forbidding to wary, but she directed Evelyn to a set of chairs along the wall.

"Wait there. I'll be right back."

Evelyn sat for what felt like an eternity before the dragon lady returned with a nurse in tow. "What did you say your name was?"

"Evelyn Gardner. Jimmy Doyle calls me Eve. Sometimes."

She wasn't sure how she'd managed it, but both women's faces softened. "Come with me," the new arrival said. "I'll take you to him."

She saw nothing of where she was. Nothing mattered except getting to the man she loved. At last, her guide stopped and flattened her hand on a wooden door. "He's going to be fine."

Relief flooded through her. "He is?"

"See for yourself." The nurse smiled, then pushed the door open.

Evelyn stepped inside. The relief she'd felt a moment ago had been minor compared to the rush of feeling that swamped her when the man in the bed opened his eyes and smiled at her. Only then did she allow herself to believe what she had prayed for. He was alive. She hadn't lost him.

"I thought I was hallucinating when a dragon came in and asked me if I had a fiancée." His voice was weak but steady.

"What did you tell her?" She stepped closer to the bed, the audacity of her claim just now hitting her.

"That her name was Eve, Eve Gardner, and that she was the most beautiful woman in the world."

"You are hallucinating," she teased as heat crept into her cheeks.

"Come closer. Let me see for myself."

Evelyn approached the bed. Automatically, she lifted her hand to the bruise on his left temple, stopping herself before she touched. "I was listening on the radio." Unable to not touch him, she brushed a stray lock of hair off his forehead.

"I was right. You are the most beautiful woman in the world. And apparently, you're all mine."

She stepped back, appalled at the lie she'd told. "I'm sorry. I needed to see you. I shouldn't have lied."

He held his hand out, silently asking for her to come back to him. Heart pounding, she stepped back to his bedside and placed her hand in his. The warmth of his touch reassured her as nothing else could have. "I'm glad you did. I needed to see you too."

"You did?"

He nodded, wincing at the pain of doing so. "The first thing I thought about when I opened my eyes was you. I was afraid you'd find out about this before I had a chance to tell you. And I was right to worry. I'm sorry for scaring you."

"You're going to be all right? The nurse said you would."

"So they tell me. I have a concussion, but nothing is broken. The doc said they want to keep me overnight, but that I can go home tomorrow. I'll have to miss a few games, but I'll be as good as new in a few days."

She squeezed his hand. "That's wonderful."

He shrugged. "Could have been worse, so I'm not complaining." He tugged her closer. "Sit with me?"

Evelyn sat on the edge of the bed so her hip grazed his. It was the place for a wife or a mother, but he wanted her there, and there was no place she would rather be.

"It seems we've jumped the proposal and gone straight to the engagement." She smiled at the humor in his voice.

"My fault."

"No. My fault. I wanted to do this right, to make it special for you, but I'm sure the dragon has already told someone else about you. It's only a matter of time before everyone hears the news. So…Evelyn Gardner, will you marry me?"

"Jimmy Doyle. You don't need to do this."

"Oh, but I do. I want you to be my wife. I knew you were mine the first day I met you. Now that you've declared yourself"— he laughed softly—"I think it's high time we make it official."

If her heart didn't slow down, she was going to need medical attention too. Her cheeks felt like they were on fire, and she wasn't sure she was breathing. Hope and love tangled up with shame and embarrassment. She hadn't thought about the consequences of her statement, but now they couldn't be avoided. He was a public figure—a hero to the Diplomats fans. His engagement would be big news. "I didn't mean to trap you—"

"You didn't trap me, Eve. I bought a ring for you weeks ago.

It's in a drawer at my apartment."

They both looked up at the sound of the door opening. Evelyn recognized the man entering as the friend who had driven them back to town the day they met. She scooted off the bed, mortified at having been caught in such a compromising position. How many mistakes could a person make in one day?

"Hey, man. Good to see you," the new arrival said. He spared Evelyn a glance before coming to stand at the foot of the bed. He held a hat in front of him, twisting the brim with nervous hands. "You gave us quite a scare, old man."

"Doc says I'm going to be fine. Head's too hard, I guess."

"The whole goddamn team is in the waiting room." He looked at Evelyn. "Beg pardon, ma'am," he said, turning back to Jimmy Doyle. "They sent me in to see if you were dead or not. Glad to see you ain't dead."

Jimmy Doyle's laugh turned into a groan. "My head hurts like the devil, but I'm fine." He paused. "Harvey, you remember Evelyn, don't you? From the revival meeting you dragged me to?"

"And it's a good thing I did. You have a real propensity for getting hurt. Never hurts to be on the big guy's good list, ya know?" Harvey turned to Evelyn. "Nice to see you again, ma'am."

"Evelyn, this idiot is Harvey Timmons. He plays—"

"Second base. It's nice to see you again, Mr. Timmons. It's good of you to come check on Jimmy Doyle."

Harvey smiled at her.

"Don't even think it, Harv. She's mine. In fact, she has just agreed to be my wife."

"No shit! I mean, no kidding, ma'am." His grin was anything but apologetic. "Congratulations to both of you. Wait until the rest of the guys hear about this!" he said to Jimmy Doyle.

Evelyn blushed and ducked her head. If she'd thought before she'd opened her mouth…

"Harv, can you do me a favor?"

"Sure, man. You need me to take care of your woman for you?" Harvey failed miserably at appearing serious.

"No! Keep your hands off my woman," Jimmy Doyle said. "I do need you to take her to my place, then bring her back here. I need some clothes to wear out of here tomorrow, and there's something else I need out of my desk."

"I can't—"

"Sure thing." Evelyn and Harvey spoke at once.

"Key's under the mat," Jimmy Doyle said to Evelyn. "My brown suit, maybe? A shirt. All the usual stuff. I keep my shaving kit packed for out-of-town games. It's in the bathroom. And look in the center drawer of my desk. You'll know it when you see it." He turned to Harvey. "Go tell them I'm alive and I'll be back on the field before the next series. Get rid of them, then come back for Eve."

She spent the first few minutes after Harvey left trying to convince her new fiancé that she hadn't been expecting a proposal, but he cut off her argument by pulling her to the bed and wrapping his hand around her nape, guiding her lips to his. At the sound of Harvey's return, they jerked apart. Jimmy Doyle held her gaze until Harvey cleared his throat.

"All gone. Everyone, including that asshole, Snodgrass, said to take it easy. Coach said he'd be by to see you later." He dipped his head toward Evelyn. "Pardon my language, ma'am."

Evelyn hid a laugh behind her fingers. If anyone needed to attend church, it was Harvey Timmons. "Apology accepted."

"You ready to go? A couple of reporters are camped out in the lobby. We can go out the back way and catch a taxicab on the next block. I'll have you back here in no time."

"Take care of her, Harvey," Jimmy Doyle said. "I'll hold you personally responsible if anything happens to her."

CHAPTER TWENTY-THREE

She found the ring easily enough and couldn't resist taking a peek while Harvey gathered clothes for the patient. She'd never had an engagement ring, just a simple gold band she'd received when she said her vows. The ring was beautiful in its simplicity. A single blue stone was surrounded by small diamonds in a practical yet lovely setting. It couldn't have been more perfect. Harvey cursed loudly in the other room, something about handling underwear. Evelyn closed the tiny box and slipped it into her purse, turning around just as her companion came back carrying a small satchel in one hand. A suit dangled from the other.

"If he needs anything else, tough shit. He'll have to get it himself."

Being around someone who cursed so freely was a new experience. Harvey's outbursts, instead of offending, helped relieve the stress of the day. "I'm sure he'll be fine with whatever you have there," she said.

"Did you find what you were looking for?"

"Yes," she said, thinking she'd found so much more than what she'd been looking for. For the first time since her father had introduced her to her future husband, she felt as if she had everything she could want in life.

☙❧

He sat on the edge of the bed, dressed and more than ready to go home. Harvey would be arriving any minute with Evelyn. He hated that he had to ask his friend to escort his fiancée around, but the sharks were trolling for a story and he didn't want her to be alone in the water when they caught up to her. At least she had his ring on her finger. Knowing she had proof to back the statement she'd made the day before eased his mind.

Today, they'd walk out of here together and face the reporters. He'd love to keep Evelyn all to himself, but that was never going to happen. Not as long as he played baseball. He'd won a lot of his fans back this season, and they were hungry for news about his life.

Up until he met Eve, there hadn't been much to tell. He'd been wrongly accused of betting on games. After years of legal maneuvering, he'd cleared his name and been allowed a second chance at the game he loved. His friend, Bartholomew Fine, who was also his lawyer and agent, had come by earlier to make sure he was still alive, and Jimmy Doyle told him what Walter Dobbs had said. They'd talked about the kind of money he expected to be offered and other terms he wanted in his next contract before the man left, promising to report his good health and engagement to Grace and Carl.

With a new love in his life, every reporter in the region smelled a story. They were going to get one, a very brief one, and hopefully, that would be the end of it. If there was one thing he'd learned from his years before the scandal, it was boring doesn't sell. He and Evelyn were going to be boring.

The second she walked into his room, he knew his life was going to be anything but boring as long as she was in it. She took his breath away. Dressed in her Sunday best, something he'd insisted upon, she was absolutely radiant. Her skin was luminous, her eyes bright with love and trepidation. The sparkling sapphire he'd given her couldn't compete with her. The reporters were going to eat her up.

"Come here," he said after sending Harvey to bring his car around to the front door rather than the back where he had brought Evelyn in. "I need to hold you for a few minutes."

She came willingly to him. Her arms slid around his waist, and she looked up at him. "Checking out my head?" he asked.

"Yes, and you're going to let me." She grimaced at the sight of the nasty bruise blooming on the side of his face. "I hate seeing you hurt."

"I've been hurt before, and I'll be hurt again."

"The papers are saying it was deliberate."

"Maybe it was. Maybe the ball just got away from him. It happens."

"Harvey says it was on purpose. He says things like this have been happening a lot since you came back."

"Harvey talks too much." He'd thought the players on the other teams had gotten over punishing him for what had happened years ago. His name had been cleared by the courts, but many in the league still believed he'd been involved in the gambling ring. A few of them felt entitled to their pound of flesh. "It's more likely he was just trying to put me on base. With two outs, the pitcher would have had a better chance facing Cochran. He had to know that."

"I still don't like it."

"Me either, baby. Now kiss me, and make me forget all about how much my head hurts."

She ducked her head to capture his lips with hers. He'd been away from her too long. He took the kiss deeper while he slid his hands beneath her skirt until he encountered lace. He groaned, breaking the kiss but nipping at her lips to keep her close.

"What color?"

"Pink," she said, her face turning the same shade, which was the reason he'd chosen that color to begin with. She felt so good in his arms that he didn't want to let her go, but Harvey would be back any minute. Reluctantly, he removed his hands, making sure her dress fell back in place. She wasn't ready for that level of display.

"I love you, Eve."

"I love you too."

The sooner they got the inquisition over with, the sooner they could get on with their lives. With both his heads now aching like a son of a bitch, he pushed her away and stood. He reached for the bag containing the uniform he'd had on when he'd been admitted. He needed a few minutes to get his body under control before facing the reporters in the lobby. They wouldn't print it, but they would notice if he was sporting a hard-on when he walked out. "Did you have any trouble at work?" She'd mentioned that she might since she hadn't returned from lunch the previous day.

"Some. I thought about telling them I'd been sick and needed to take today off too. But then I figured someone might see my name in the newspaper after today, and they'd know I'd lied."

"What *did* you tell them?"

"The truth, sort of. I told them my boyfriend surprised me with a proposal over lunch, and that I needed to take today off."

"Good girl." He loved that she hadn't outright lied to her boss. Which was why he couldn't be anything but honest with her. "They aren't going to leave us alone, baby. The Diplomats are on a roll, and I'm having a great season. If me ending up in the hospital overnight wasn't news enough, having my fiancée show up and ask to see me is a story they won't walk away from."

"I know. I want to be with you, and though I like my privacy, I'll do whatever you need me to do. I don't ever want to be a burden for you."

"I have more reason to protect my privacy than most," he said. "If they ever found out about the Farm Club, a whole lot of folks would suffer, and my career would be over. The Diplomats gave me a one-year contract with a promise of a multiyear contract if I kept my nose clean and contributed significantly to the team this season. So far, I've been able to do both."

"I would never say anything about the farm." Her cheeks reddened. "What we do there is none of anyone's business but ours."

"God, I love you, Evelyn Gardner. If I hadn't already asked you to marry me, I'd do it again, right now."

→

Jimmy Doyle was glad to be back with the team, even if the bruise covering the left side of his face made it appear he'd been in a brawl with his hands tied behind his back. The only thing he regretted was that he was rejoining them for a series of out-of-town games. That meant nine days away from Evelyn. Days he knew were going to be pure torture. He'd come to depend on seeing her, touching her. Even the thrill of hitting a grand-slam home run couldn't compare to giving her an orgasm. She made him feel like a god when she screamed his name in the throes of ecstasy.

Upon his release from the hospital, news of their engagement spread like wildfire. In the days he'd been confined to home, he'd received dozens of telegrams from fans and players. It seemed there were more people out there who had accepted his return to the game than he'd originally thought. According to Harvey Timmons, even the most vocal holdout on the Diplomats, Ray Snodgrass, had changed the tune he'd been singing all season long.

As if Jimmy Doyle had conjured the man with his thoughts, Ray took the facing seat in their private train car.

"You look awful, Jimmy D."

"Thanks. The ladies love it, though. You should try it. Might help you get laid."

Ray had more than his share of women clamoring for his attention, so the insult rolled off his shoulders as the friendly banter it was. He smirked. "I hear it worked for you, old man."

"Unlike some people I know, I don't kiss and tell." Jimmy Doyle was used to this kind of joking around with many of his teammates, but acting friendly with Ray—or rather, Ray acting friendly with him—was a new occurrence.

"I'm offended," the left fielder said, covering his heart as if he'd been wounded. "I only said the girl had a mouth like a tornado. That could have meant anything."

"We all know what it meant, asshole." The conversation was getting uncomfortable. "Change of subject."

Ray stared out the window for a moment, then turned his attention back to Jimmy Doyle. "Look, man. I just wanted to say I'm sorry. I've given you a hard time this season, and you've been nothing but up-front with all of us. You've taken more than your share of hits for the team, but the one the other day"—he shook his head—"that was different. He didn't go after you for something that happened years ago. He went after you because he was chicken to face you like a man. That asshole knew you were going to hit one out of the park, and he took the easy way out, knowing it would look like more of the same—retaliation. Only, everyone knew it wasn't."

Jimmy Doyle was stunned into silence. He'd never heard the man string together that many words at one time. Ray moved to the edge of his seat, preparing to stand. "Congratulations on your engagement. I saw her picture in the paper. She could certainly do better than you!" He slapped Jimmy Doyle on the knee, then stood. "Friends?"

Jimmy Doyle extended his right hand. "Friends." They shook hands.

"Don't suppose you'd want to join a card game already in progress, would ya?"

"No, but thanks. For everything." He meant it. He'd worked hard to build back friendships that had crumbled when he had been expelled from the league. It felt good to know that others had thought this latest incident had been bullshit.

"No problem. Glad you're gonna be okay. We need your bat."

He chuckled as Ray wove his way along the aisle to the group of players engaged in a game of cards. It had taken months of hard work, but it seemed he had finally jumped the biggest hurdle— earning the respect of his teammates. Ray's opinion mattered to a lot of people who would follow his cues.

He hoped Bart would have good news for him soon in

regards to a new contract. He'd proved his worth on the field, which meant he had options if the Diplomats didn't want to keep him, but he didn't look forward to starting all over again with a new team. He wanted to stay right where he was. Uprooting his life meant uprooting Evelyn's too, and he didn't want to do that if he didn't have to. They'd have to leave the Farm Club behind as well, and he wanted to explore everything the club offered with the woman he loved. To that end, he'd meet with management when he returned home. Get the ball rolling. The sooner he had a signed contract in hand, the better.

Evelyn folded the newspaper in half, hiding the photograph of her standing next to Jimmy Doyle in the hospital lobby. The flash had taken her by surprise, causing her to jump. That was all the excuse her new fiancé had needed to end the question-and-answer period with the reporters, but the damage was done. Her face was all over Washington and possibly the state of Virginia. The Diplomats were big news. And now she was too.

She carefully placed the paper in the bottom of the drawer where she kept everything related to Jimmy Doyle. Her life in no way resembled the life she'd led a week ago, before their relationship had gone public. Once hardly noticed by her fellow boarders, she had become a sort of celebrity, sought out for information. They wanted to know every detail, from how she met the star baseball player, to when the wedding would take place. She and Jimmy Doyle had no time to discuss plans before he had left with the team, and truthfully, she was still trying to absorb the fact that she was engaged—to anyone, let alone a famous baseball player. Her future was a blank canvas, and she couldn't imagine what the finished painting was going to look like.

Where would they live? Would he expect her to quit her job? Did he expect her to travel with him? What would she do on her own if she didn't go with him?

Overwhelmed with questions she had no answers for, she

dressed for work. Her coworkers treated her differently since the news broke. Some were like the women at the boardinghouse, wanting to know every little detail, while others looked at her as if she'd grown two heads overnight. She had no idea what that was about.

Later that day, as she left work, she stepped out to the sidewalk and came face-to-face with her father. Icy tendrils of fear froze her feet to the pavement before reason intervened. They were in the middle of Washington, DC. There was nothing he could do to her here. And in truth, he'd forfeited any claim on her when he'd left her at the bus station.

She hadn't seen him since he'd turned his back on her. He hadn't changed one iota. For a moment, she simply stared at his face, wondering how he'd found her, and more importantly, why. Someone bumped her shoulder, forcing her gaze away from him. She wasn't his daughter anymore. He'd made that painfully clear. She'd survived on her own, no thanks to him, and she was engaged to a man who loved everything about her, including the very things her own father condemned her for. She owed him nothing. Not even a hello.

She turned on her heel and headed to the trolley stop, arriving just as the car left, loaded with weary workers heading home. Another would be along soon, but not soon enough for her. She didn't know if her father had followed her, but finding him outside her place of employment hadn't been coincidence. He'd come looking for her. Getting on a trolley wouldn't stop him from saying whatever it was he'd come to say. She turned. He wore the same expression she'd grown accustomed to as a child—the one that said she'd been caught doing something forbidden. Since nearly everything had been forbidden, she'd seen the look often. Faced with his disapproval, it was hard to remember that she was a grown woman now and that he couldn't hurt her.

"Eve." His voice held the disdain she knew too well. He wasn't happy to see her.

"Why did you come?"

He glanced around at the commuters waiting for their ride home. "Do you want to have this conversation here?"

She didn't want to have a conversation at all, but he'd never been one to hold his tongue when he had something to say. She thought about letting him spew his venom there on the street, but then she remembered her fiancé and cringed at the thought of how an ugly encounter with her father would reflect on him and his career if a reporter were to get wind of it. "No." She searched her limited knowledge of the area for a place to talk that afforded some privacy, but where she could still call for help if she needed to.

"Follow me." She led the way to a church a few blocks down. The opposite side of the street was lined with town houses. They could sit on the steps of the church and be in plain sight of the residents coming and going. It wasn't ideal, but it would have to do.

Taking a seat on the top step, she waited for him to sit too. When he chose to stand, she did the same. No way was she going to let him tower over her. She wasn't the meek little girl she'd been when he dumped her out in the world without a care for her well-being. "What do you want?"

"Is that any way to talk to your father?"

She wanted very badly to respond to that question, but in the interest of ending the conversation sooner rather than later, she chose to ignore it. "What do you want?" she repeated instead.

For a second she thought he might hit her for her insolence, but he took a breath to calm himself and spoke. "I read about this man you want to marry. Does he know the kind of woman you are?"

Evelyn felt the trembling begin deep inside and clenched her arms around her middle, hoping to contain it before it engulfed her entire body. "He loves me." A sickening tendril of doubt began to twist around her stomach.

"He doesn't know you the way I do, Eve. He doesn't know you ran out on your husband, left him without a word."

"That's not what happened!" Dear God, had he rewritten

history to suit himself? And to what purpose?

"Your husband has been looking for you. He wants you to come home. He says he'll forgive you if you swear you won't run away again."

"I didn't run away!" Panic gripped her bowels. This couldn't be happening. Not now, when she was on the verge of having more than she'd ever dreamed of. A real marriage, a man who loved her, and a family. "You cast me out." Her voice sounded weak, defeated.

"I acted hastily. Your husband had second thoughts."

"He's not my husband."

"Did you divorce him?"

She was no longer able to contain the tremors rocking her body. Her skin crawled with the cold seeping from her insides. "No."

"If you marry this baseball player, you'll be committing adultery and bigamy. Come home, Eve, before you ruin another man's life."

Evelyn sank to the stone steps and began to rock. *No. No. No. No.* This couldn't be happening. She couldn't still be married to Curtis. The last thing he'd said to her was that he was going to have the marriage annulled. As if she hadn't given him her body countless miserable times. She knew now he'd never really wanted her the way a man should. In leaving, she'd done them both a favor. He could find someone he truly desired and loved, as she had.

Jimmy Doyle. Oh, God.

"Are you sure? He told me he was going to annul the marriage."

"He applied. The petition was denied."

She was going to be sick. Her life was crumbling before her eyes, and there wasn't a thing she could do about it. She was married to Curtis, and he had every right to demand his wife return home. She couldn't marry Jimmy Doyle.

"I can't just leave. I have a job. My things." *Jimmy Doyle.* She had to see him, to try to explain that which had no explanation.

"I'm catching the next train out of this den of sinners. If you aren't home in two days, I'll tell the world you're an adulterer and a slut. Do you think your fancy baseball player will want you then? The press loves him now, but they won't when they find out about the kind of woman he thought he was going to marry."

She listened to the sound of his heels clicking on the stone steps, hearing their echo in her soul long after he was gone. People strolled by on the sidewalk, but none stopped to see if the woman sobbing on the steps was in need of help. As she had been when she first arrived in the city, she was grateful for the insulation of strangers. She couldn't explain to anyone what was wrong for fear they would tell the wrong person, and there would be no way she could stop the scandal before it touched the man she loved.

He'd worked so hard to repair his reputation. Something like this could derail everything he'd accomplished this season and ruin his chances of renewing his contract for a longer period of time. She loved him way too much to let that happen. She had no choice but to return to her husband, but she couldn't leave without telling Jimmy Doyle why. He deserved that much.

CHAPTER TWENTY-FOUR

Jimmy Doyle closed the lid on the box containing his latest gift for his bride-to-be—a soft pink silk nightgown that would look ravishing on her. She would have no need of such things once they were married, because he planned to keep her naked, especially in bed. But until she became his wife, he wanted to think of her sleeping in something he'd bought for her. Something that would caress her lovely skin with as much reverence as she deserved.

Having just returned from a successful trip, the team had tomorrow off. He planned to spend as much of it as possible with his fiancée. He'd called the boardinghouse earlier, asking for her, but she hadn't returned from work. After placing a second call only to be told the same thing, he began to worry. Because of who he was, her life had been dragged out into the public eye too. What if someone still harboring a grudge for what they believed he'd done years ago took it upon themself to approach Evelyn? He'd never forgive himself if she was hurt because of him.

He was pacing, trying to decide if he should go looking for her or call the police, when someone knocked on his door. He threw the door open. Relief flooded him. She had come to him! It took only a second for relief to turn to concern. Her eyes were red, her face swollen and blotchy from crying. He drew her inside and folded her into his arms. "What's the matter, sweetheart?"

She looked as if she'd been crying for hours, but a fresh wave of tears poured from her along with a story. All he knew for sure was she said she couldn't marry him. The rest was a mess of tears, hiccups, and wails he couldn't decipher.

He'd eased her to the sofa and cradled her in his lap, her presence there making him instantly hard for her. He couldn't imagine a time when he wouldn't have the same reaction to her. She was all he wanted, and he wanted her all the time. Even when she sobbed as if the world were coming to an end.

When she had finally cried herself out, he tilted her face to his, intending to kiss her until she stopped talking nonsense. Of course she could marry him. She would marry him. Before his lips could touch hers, she turned so his mouth brushed her cheek. She'd never turned away from his kiss. Whatever had happened had truly upset her. "Tell me, Eve."

She clung to his shirt like she was afraid he was going to disappear on her. "I'm not going anywhere," he said, trying to ease her mind.

She drew in a couple of shuddering breaths, then gazed up at him. "I can't marry you."

"Sure, you can. We stand at the front of the church, say some nice things to each other; then it's done." His poking fun at the situation only made her begin to cry again. The unease he'd felt when she hadn't returned home at her usual time flared back to life.

"What happened this afternoon?" He'd fuck the information out of her if he had to, but he was going to know what had upset her to this degree. And then he was going to fix it.

"My father came to see me," she sniffled. "He said if I didn't...didn't come home to my husband, he would tell everyone that I'm an adulterer and a slut."

He held himself perfectly still, afraid if he moved, he'd destroy something. Not Evelyn. Someone—her father, apparently—had already done that. No, he wanted to throw something. To smash something to bits. Then he wanted to get his hands on her father and strangle his sorry neck until he breathed his last breath.

Instead, Jimmy Doyle tried to focus on the important parts of what she'd said. "What husband?"

"He said I'm still married to Curtis!" The sound that came from her tore at his heart. He was going to kill someone. He'd start with her father; then he'd murder the bastard claiming to be her husband. His career be damned. The only thing that mattered to him was Evelyn.

"Tell me everything he said, babe. Don't leave anything out."

⁂

It was going on midnight when he drove her to the boardinghouse. She'd declined to stay the night with him, the insidious venom already poisoning her thinking. A few words from her father and she was a child again, taking his word as gospel, buying into his brand of control. He'd told her not to give in to the blackmail for his sake, but on the other hand, he'd do whatever it took to keep her name out of the mud. There had to be a way.

Stopping in front of the boardinghouse, he took her hand in his, refusing to let it go when she tried to pull away. "Don't go, Evelyn. Promise me you won't go anywhere until I have a chance to figure this out. There has to be a record of the annulment or the divorce. I have connections. Give me a chance to find out the truth. Then we'll face whatever it is together."

"It's no use. If he hasn't divorced me by now, he's never going to. I don't have a choice."

"Please. All I'm asking is one day. Twenty-four hours." He didn't add that he didn't trust her father as far as he could throw the man. He didn't know why the man was lying, or what he could gain by bringing her home to a life she hated, but he was going to find out.

"I've got to tell my boss. And pack my things."

"Pack slow." Though it pained him to think of her leaving, if it came to it, he'd let her go before he'd let her father publicly disgrace her. "If I can't find a way to stop him, I'll take you to the train station tomorrow morning. I promise, if you promise to wait for me."

"I don't deserve you, Jimmy Doyle Walker, but yes, I'll wait for you."

He kissed her then, long and hard, and he didn't give a damn who might see them. She was going to be his wife, and fuck anyone who didn't like it. "I love you," he whispered against her lips.

She scooted out of the car without another word. He prayed to God she wasn't scooting out of his life. *Please. Let her be here when I get back.*

⋘⋙

The guard met him with a shotgun. He'd expected nothing less in the middle of the night. After identifying himself, he was allowed to continue to the house, where he was grateful to see a faint light in the kitchen. Carl sometimes had trouble sleeping and would come downstairs for a glass of milk and one of the tea cakes Grace made like no one else.

No doubt concerned at the sight of the approaching car, the older man met him at the door, rifle in hand.

"Just me, Carl," he called out before approaching. Even without overnight guests, the house held too many secrets for the inhabitants to let down their guard. As he stepped into the kitchen, he wasn't at all surprised to see Grace, eyes bright with concern, standing behind her husband. She gave a final tug to the sash on her robe.

"Jimmy Doyle. What brings you here at this hour of the night?"

"Trouble." He held up his hand to stall the instant wariness in their gaze. "Not for the farm. It's Evelyn. She's going to leave me if I can't find a way to stop her."

"Sit down. Tell us everything." Grace indicated a chair at the kitchen table. He sat, cradling the top of his head in his hands while Grace stoked the old woodstove and put a pot of coffee on to boil.

She placed a glass of milk in front of him, then sat next to her husband. "Coffee's on. Talk."

Jimmy Doyle talked. And talked. They consumed the coffee, and he paced as Carl placed discreet but urgent calls to key members who might be able to help, requesting they come immediately. Within an hour, the kitchen overflowed with club members. He repeated the story for a federal judge, a senator, his lawyer and agent, and a clergyman.

"We need to shut him up. I can't allow him to drag her good name through the mud. Why would a father do such a thing to his own daughter anyway? What kind of monster does something like that?"

"What did you say his name was?" Reverend Thomas Truebridge had been silent throughout. Jimmy Doyle snapped his gaze to the man wearing a white cleric's collar.

"Gardner. Frank Gardner. He's a circuit preacher of some sort. Preaches fire and brimstone. According to Evelyn, his favorite topics are sodomy, adultery, and fornication."

"Things he knows a lot about," Thomas said. "I think I know how you can keep him quiet."

Everyone turned questioning eyes on the preacher. "I know the guy. Well, I know of him. He has quite the reputation in the hills of central Virginia. He has a pretty big circuit of mostly isolated enclaves—not really towns, just groups of people, families, living in close proximity. Every homosexual male in the region knows who he is. He's had sex with most of them. A few years ago, he quit making the rounds, and word through the grapevine was he had something permanent going on."

"How long ago was this?" Jimmy Doyle asked.

"Five, six years?"

"About the time he forced his daughter to marry a man old enough to be her father."

"What better way to keep your lover close and not raise suspicion than to have the man marry your daughter?"

"Dear God." He put his elbows on the table and rested his head in his upturned hands. "What a bastard. Preaching about the evils of adultery and sodomy when, by his own standards, he's the biggest sinner around."

"It's usually the ones who protest the loudest that you have to worry about. They hate themselves for what they are, so they rant and rave to appease their guilt," Thomas said. "I see it all the time in my line of work. Guilt's a bitch. Pardon my French."

"Pardon granted," Grace said.

"You don't happen to know the husband's name, do you?" Thomas asked.

"Curtis something. He's a farmer. She never said more, and I didn't ask."

"Curtis Wells." Everyone turned to Senator Williams. "Age and occupation fit. He's from those parts. Family never amounted to much. Poor as church mice and too lazy to do anything about it. Most of the men in the family favor other men, so the family is dying out."

"Sounds like you know them pretty well," Grace said.

The senator shrugged. "I grew up in that area. You get to know like-minded folks, if you know what I mean? Doesn't surprise me at all that one of that clan latched on to a way to appear respectable. Wonder what her father promised him to get him to marry the girl?"

"What do you mean?" Carl asked.

"Gardner must have promised Curtis something—money, I'd guess—for him to marry the girl. Or maybe Curtis thought Gardner really loved him. I've seen men do some stupid shit to be with a man they loved."

"From what Evelyn has said, they didn't have much. A little land, and most of that came from her mother's family."

"That's probably it, then. I'd bet her father promised to turn over some of the land, and all Curtis had to do was marry the daughter, act like the perfect husband in public, and screw Preacher Gardner on the sly."

"Her father wouldn't want that cozy arrangement to become public knowledge, would he?" Jimmy Doyle saw a glimmer of hope on the horizon. Still married or not, he had ammunition to use against her father.

"I suspect he'd do anything to keep this quiet. After all, the man has a wife and a congregation to think about."

"How could his wife not know?" Jimmy Doyle asked.

"Who knows?" the reverend said. "Maybe she does, but I've seen men go to great lengths to hide things from their families" He sipped his coffee, then set the mug back on the table. "Maybe she's always known. Maybe she has no idea. I could see it working either way, depending on the situation."

Judge Hallstead stood. "I've got enough to go on. I'll find out if divorce or annulment papers were filed in Virginia." He gestured to the hallway where the telephone hung. "If I can use your phone, Grace, I'll have my team start searching as soon as the courthouse doors are open."

"Please," Grace said.

The judge went to telephone his staff, sending them off to the county courthouse where the papers most likely would have been filed.

"If the papers aren't there, I'll file for a divorce immediately. Obtaining a restraining order against her father and husband shouldn't be a problem. And with Hallstead's influence, we can rush the divorce through if it comes to that." Bartholomew had been quiet while they sorted things out. His law firm had handled Jimmy Doyle's defense since he'd first been accused of betting on games and had never asked for a cent in payment, as several of the firm's top lawyers were members of the club. When Jimmy Doyle was reinstated in the league, he'd asked Bart to handle contract negotiations with the Diplomats for him—effectively making Bart his agent too. Over the years, they'd become friends, sharing a love of submissive women and baseball. He was more than grateful to have the man's support as he tried to make sense of what was happening.

"How long, Bart?"

"A month. Two."

There'd be no way to keep something like that out of the newspapers. The fact that he was engaged to a married woman, soon to be divorced, wouldn't help his career any, but that was the least of his worries. All he could think about was Evelyn, and what her father's threats, if carried out, would mean for her. If there was any way he could shield her from the humiliation, he would. After what the men in her life had done to her, she deserved better.

"I know this is lousy timing, but I have good news regarding your contract."

Jimmy Doyle huffed out a chuckle and sat back in his chair. "Lay it on me, brother. I need some good news."

Bart went over the basic terms—eight years at a salary of thirty-five thousand dollars a year. And they'd agreed not to trade him without his approval. "They gave you everything you asked for, including a private room for out-of-town games."

Pain speared him in the heart remembering why he'd asked for the private room. He didn't know how he was going to continue if he didn't have Evelyn by his side. "Thanks, Bart. You can tell Mr. Preston that I accept."

CHAPTER TWENTY-FIVE

Quitting her job had been easier than she thought. Her boss told her he had been expecting her to quit ever since he'd heard about her engagement to the famous baseball player. A man in Jimmy Doyle Walker's position wouldn't want his wife working, he'd said. It was easier to let the man think that than to explain the real reason she was leaving. Besides, the broken engagement would be news soon enough without her telling anyone.

She had packed everything that mattered, her clothes and the gifts from Jimmy Doyle, hours ago. All that was left to do was tell Mrs. Rubenstein she was leaving. But she couldn't make herself do it, not yet anyway. Jimmy Doyle had promised he would find a way to get them out of the mess she'd gotten them into, and though her brain told her there was no way, a spark of hope lived in her heart.

As the endless hours ticked by with no word from him, she lay on the bed reading the letters he'd sent her over the few months she'd known him. If he couldn't find a way to stop her father, if she was indeed still married, the letters and the beautiful things he'd given her would be all she had to remember him by. Because no matter what, she wasn't going to leave them behind. She might legally belong to another man, but her heart would always belong to Jimmy Doyle.

She woke sometime later to the sound of girlish chatter and

rapid footsteps on the stairs outside her room. The knock on her door brought her fully awake.

"Evelyn! Are you in there? Your fiancé is here to see you!"

Instantly on her feet, Evelyn went to the window and parted the curtains. On the street below, Jimmy Doyle leaned against the side of his car, his legs crossed at the ankles, peering up at her room. A weak smile kept him from looking too gorgeous to bear. Her gaze met his, and she saw weariness and love in his eyes.

Heart thudding in her ears, she called to him. "I'll be right there."

A gaggle of excited girls waited outside her door. She didn't want to be rude, but she felt her time with Jimmy Doyle ticking away, and she didn't want to waste a second of it. She pushed past them without a word and sailed down the stairs as if she had wings on her feet.

When she came down the steps, he opened his arms to her, and she flew into his embrace, not caring who saw them.

"God, I've missed you," he said, tilting her face up to his for a kiss that warmed all the places inside her that had been ice since her father had dropped his bomb on her.

When they came up for air, she looked closely at him. His skin was sallow, and dark circles had formed under his eyes. "Did you sleep?"

"Not a bit. How about you?"

"I fell asleep a little bit ago, reading your letters."

His fingers traced the lines of her face while he gazed at her as if he was trying to memorize every detail. "I'm sorry you were worried." He kissed her again, sweeter this time, but no less stirring. How would she ever live without the way he made her feel? "Can you come with me? I have something to tell you."

"Sure." He opened the car door for her, and she got in. He drove around the block to the park. Holding her hand, he guided her to the same park bench where she'd given him the handkerchief soiled with her juices. That day seemed a lifetime ago. They'd come so far yet were right back at the beginning.

After they'd sat, he continued to hold her hand. "Your husband was Curtis Wells?"

"Yes."

"Your father was right about one thing—Wells never divorced you. As for the denied annulment, that was a lie. Curtis never filed for one. However, you are no longer married to him."

"What? How is that possible?"

"He died several years ago. A farm accident, according to the death certificate."

"Oh, God." Suddenly, she wondered how much of what her father said had been true. Had Curtis regretted the way they'd treated her? Had he looked for her?

"I'm sorry," Jimmy Doyle said. "I couldn't think of another way to tell you."

"No." She shook her head. "I never loved him the way a wife should love a husband—like I love you—but I didn't wish him dead."

"I know you didn't. You have too kind a heart for that."

"How did you find out?"

"A friend of mine has a lot of efficient people on his staff. He set them to searching records, and that's what they came up with."

"This won't stop my father." He probably had another unsuitable man picked out for her to marry. Why else would he demand she come home?

"No, but I have information that will."

When Jimmy Doyle was through, she sat staring into space. He'd told her what he'd learned from his friends, concluding with the plan he'd devised to free both of them from her father's clutches.

"I thought about going to see him by myself, but I thought you might want to come along. That way, you'll know for sure that he won't be bothering either of us, ever again."

"Yes. I want to go along. When?"

"Now. I don't have to be at the field until tomorrow afternoon. We can take the train, take care of our business; then if you aren't too tired when we return, I'd like to take you out to the farm."

She wanted nothing more than to spend tonight, and every night for the rest of her life, in Jimmy Doyle's arms. "I like your plan."

He borrowed a car from the station manager, who smiled when he recognized Evelyn. Like everyone else, it seemed, he'd read of her engagement to the Diplomats' first baseman and was happy to assist the couple in any way he could.

After promising to return the car in a few hours, they headed to the farm where Evelyn had grown up. Lost in her thoughts and the storm of feelings the imminent confrontation churned up, she almost missed telling Jimmy Doyle where to turn.

"You don't have to say a word, if you don't want to," he said.

"I don't know what to say. I can hardly believe what you said is true, but somehow, I know it is."

"He's going to deny it."

"Yes, he is. But he's hidden it so well, for so many years, he won't want us to tell anyone."

When the house came into view, Jimmy Doyle stopped the car and turned to her. "I want you to know that nothing is more important to me than you. Not my career, or my reputation. Not anything. So, no matter what he threatens, the only thing that matters here is getting you free of his reach. I can live with anything but losing you."

"You've worked so hard—"

"And if the only thing I get out of it is having met you, then that's enough for me. You're everything to me, Eve. Everything."

"Don't make me cry," she sniffled, wiping at the tears streaming down her cheeks. "I love you so much, Jimmy Doyle Walker. I'd do anything for you, even go back to Curtis if he were still alive."

"I don't want to speak ill of the dead, but thank God that isn't an option. Come here." He reached for her, and she went willingly into his arms. "I wanted to surprise you, but I think now would be a good time to tell you."

"Tell me what?"

"When we get back to the farm tonight? Reverend Truebridge is waiting there to marry us. Grace said she'd stand up for you if you want her to. Judge Hallstead said he'd take care of getting a license and making sure it gets filed in the morning. That is, if you still want to marry me."

"Oh, goodness, Jimmy Doyle! Yes! Yes, I want to marry you!" Fresh tears filled her eyes. "You are the sweetest man!"

"Hey." He held her and rubbed her back. "It was all Grace's idea. She was afraid I'd do something stupid and let you get away."

"You're stuck with me, mister. I mean, Sir." Peace washed over her as she used the title he preferred when he dominated her.

"Our wedding night might be short, but I promise to consummate the marriage, good and proper. Several times." She could feel him smiling against her hair and knew, no matter what transpired at her parents' house, she would be leaving with the man of her dreams. And come morning, she would be his wife.

"Let's get this over with, then, shall we?"

HER FATHER'S SMUG expression dissolved the moment Jimmy Doyle stepped from the car. If the man thought his day was bad now, he couldn't wait to make it worse. If any person on the planet deserved to be miserable, it was Frank Gardner. And Jimmy Doyle Walker was just the man for the job.

"Mr. Gardner. Might I have a word with you?"

"Coveting another man's wife, Mr. Walker?"

"No, sir. Widows are free to marry whom they choose. Evelyn has chosen me." He'd rot in hell for the joy he felt at seeing that look on her father's face. The man clearly had underestimated Jimmy Doyle's determination to make Evelyn his wife.

"She's bad news. A slut. Drove her sainted husband to sin and loved every second of it." Evelyn tensed beside him, but he tightened his hold on her waist, letting her know he was there and she had nothing to fear from the beast standing on the porch.

The screen door opened behind him, and a slim, tired-looking woman wiping her hands on a dish towel appeared at Frank Gardner's side. "What's going on here?" She squinted into the sunshine. "Eve?"

"It's me, Mama. Go back in the house. We aren't staying long."

"Nonsense," the woman said. "I've got coffee on. Come in and sit a spell."

"Really, we can't."

"I think that sounds like a fine idea," Jimmy Doyle said, drowning out her protest. "We appreciate the hospitality, don't we, sweetheart?"

HE TURNED HIS gaze to her, imploring with his eyes for her to go along with him. The last time Evelyn had entered this house, her husband had been bent on destroying her. She knew part of the why now, but not all of it. Which was one of the reasons she'd agreed to come with him instead of letting him come alone. She wanted to know what had made her father act the way he had that day, and why he wanted her back now. Jimmy Doyle's fingers curved into her waist hard enough to get her attention, but not hard enough to bruise. Reason returned. When she entered the house this time, the man at her side would be there for her. Not anyone else.

"Yes, we'd like a cup of coffee, Mama, if it's not too much trouble."

"Heavens, no, girl." Miriam opened the screen door. "You and your young man come right in. I read about your engagement in the newspaper. I'm so happy for you."

Jimmy Doyle's confused expression mirrored Evelyn's feelings as they scooted past her father into the house. Her mother was either a skilled actress, or she knew nothing about what her husband had done to her daughter or even what he'd done this week to get her back.

"What's going on?" Jimmy Doyle whispered in her ear as they

255

followed Mrs. Gardner to the kitchen in the back of the house. Evelyn shrugged her answer. Could her mother be that clueless? Hadn't she wondered where Evelyn had gone five years ago?

When they were all gathered around the kitchen table with cups of coffee, like civilized people, Jimmy Doyle glanced at her. She nodded, ready to get the uncomfortable conversation over with so they could return to Washington and get married. Just thinking about pledging herself to this man for the rest of her life made her warm inside.

"Mrs. Gardner, your husband came to Washington yesterday and threatened your daughter. He told her that her husband wanted her back, and if she didn't come home, he was going to publicly humiliate her."

"But Curtis is dead." The woman set her coffee cup down hard. She looked first at Evelyn, then at her husband. It was easy to see she was taken aback.

"That's a lie!" her father protested. "I went to see some folks on the other side of the ridge!"

Jimmy Doyle ignored the man's outburst. "Did you know about the romantic relationship between your husband and Curtis Wells?"

Evelyn almost felt sorry for her mother. Her face had gone chalk white, and she was visibly shaking.

"Mama," Evelyn interjected. "Father used my marriage to Curtis as a way to keep his lover conveniently close and above suspicion."

"I did no such thing!" Frank brought his hand down on the table, causing the cups to jump.

Finding strength in Jimmy Doyle's arm around her waist, she continued. "I was never anything but a good, dutiful wife to Curtis, but the entire time we were married, he was having a sexual relationship with my father. Your husband."

"This is an outrage!" Frank stood. "You are a slut and a whore. Curtis told me what you did, tempting him to sin—to commit sodomy. No righteous woman would do that, much less enjoy it." He leered at Evelyn. "I saw your desire with my own eyes, girl. I said it then, and I say it now. Get thee out of my sight! And take this weak excuse for a man with you."

Jimmy Doyle stood. Evelyn rose to stand beside him. "We're going, Mr. Gardner, and if you so much as have a negative thought about your daughter again, we're prepared to tell the world about the affair you carried on with Curtis Wells, and before him, Raymond Sellers. How long do you think your congregation would continue to support you once they found out their oh-so-holy leader is the biggest sinner among them?"

They scooted around their chairs toward the door. Evelyn was shaking on the inside, but her heart felt free and light.

"Wait!" They'd just gained the front door when Mrs. Gardner spoke. Her face was as white as her husband's was red. She took a step away from Mr. Gardner. "I'm so sorry, Eve." Tears rolled down her cheeks.

"Everything you said is true, Mr. Walker. I knew about Frank and Curtis." She looked down at her hands, clasped tightly together at her waist. "And I knew about the others. I've known all along, but I was afraid to say anything."

"Out of my house, woman!" Frank bellowed at his wife and pointed a shaking finger at the door. "I will not have a lying bitch in my house a minute longer!"

"Come, Mama." Evelyn stretched her hand out to her mother. The older woman glanced once back at her husband, then walked past them all and out to the yard. As much as it hurt Evelyn to hear that her mother had known all along and hadn't said anything, the woman had raised her, and she couldn't find it in herself to be cruel to her.

"Is the old house still there?" The house she'd lived in with Curtis had once belonged to her mother's grandparents.

"Yes. Frank wanted to rent it out, but I wouldn't hear of it. I hoped you'd come back."

Not knowing what else to do with her mother, Evelyn gave Jimmy Doyle directions. The outside of the place was overgrown but otherwise looked the same as the last day she'd seen it. Evelyn stood in the front parlor. The house looked as if she had never left. "How long has Curtis been dead?"

"The accident happened a few months after you left." Miriam Gardner took the dish towel out of her apron pocket and swiped at a speck of dust. "I come every week to clean."

Jimmy Doyle raised an eyebrow at her. Evelyn shrugged. She had no idea what was going on in her mother's head. "Where did you think I'd gone?"

"I saw them drag you out of the house. I was so scared. I didn't know what to do. Frank never said a word, and neither did Curtis, and I was afraid to ask since they didn't know I'd seen them take you away. Honestly? For a few days, I thought they might have murdered you, but then I saw Mr. Wilson in town. He was so kind, asking if you were okay. He said he'd seen you get on the bus, but he'd been worried about you."

Her mother dropped into a chair that looked like it could fall apart at any moment. "At least I knew you were alive. I prayed you would come back once you heard about Curtis's death."

Evelyn shook her head. "I'm not coming back, Mama. Not as long as he's alive." They both knew she meant her father.

"I'm so sorry I let you down, Eve. I knew your father had lovers over the years, but I never dreamed he would bring one home and use you as a way to cover up his sins. I didn't know he and Curtis— I didn't know until it was too late."

"Will you be all right here?" She hated to leave her mother alone in a house that probably should have been knocked down decades earlier, but as bad as she felt for what the woman had lived with, she had her own future waiting for her.

"I'll be fine. I have some money saved." Miriam glanced at the old urn sitting on the mantel. "I'll get by."

"We've got to go. Jimmy Doyle has a game tomorrow." *And we have a wedding to get to.*

"I'm happy for you, Eve. All I've ever wanted was for you to be happy."

"I'm happy, Mama. I'm really, really happy."

EPILOGUE

Their wedding had been simple, vows spoken quietly before a small gathering of Jimmy Doyle's friends. Her friends now too. Grace had outdone herself, using her precious stores of sugar and flour to make a cake for the occasion, which she'd served with finger sandwiches and lemonade.

Evelyn's dress had been the one she'd worn to confront her father, but when she'd gone to their room for the night, she'd found the most beautiful rose-pink negligee waiting for her on the bed. She'd never seen anything as beautiful as the lace bodice. The sheer silk skirt swirled around her ankles, leaving nothing to the imagination. When she'd seen her reflection in the cheval mirror, she could hardly believe the seductress before her was really her. And the moment her husband walked in and saw her, she felt like a goddess.

"It's more beautiful on you than I imagined, and believe me, I gave it a lot of thought." He reached for her hands, pulling her against him and pinning her hands behind her back. "My wife should wear silk all the time."

"I like the sound of that."

One corner of his lips lifted. "A silk wardrobe?"

"No. *Wife.*"

"Mrs. Jimmy Doyle Walker. My wife." Holding her wrists with

one hand, he brushed her hair back from her temple, then placed a gentle kiss there. "I love you, Eve. More than you can ever know."

"I love you too." His strength and warmth surrounded her. For the first time since the day of her family's betrayal, she felt truly safe. "Thank you."

"For what?" Silk shifted as his free hand roamed her body, blazing a trail straight to the heart of her.

"For not giving up on me. For years, I've been…suspended, I guess. I couldn't go back, and I couldn't go forward. I thought there was something wrong with me."

He framed her jaw in his hand, tilting her face up to his. His gaze searched hers. "You are perfect in every way. Don't ever think otherwise."

"I'm not perfect by any means." She smiled at him. "But I have to think I'm not beyond redemption since God led you to me."

"I'm not sure God had anything to do with it, but I owe Harvey Timmons for taking me to that revival meeting. I'm sure he had no idea the favor he was doing me."

"And me."

He lowered his mouth to hers. When his tongue traced the seam of her lips, she parted them, allowing him access. He tightened the arm banding her, bringing her flush against his rock-hard body. She squirmed, trying to get even closer, causing the lace on her bodice to chafe her nipples to tight nubs. The only sane thought in her head was that there were too many clothes between them.

Still imprisoning her wrists behind her back with one hand, he dug the fingers of his other hand into her hip, halting her movement. "Hold still, wife." He nipped her lower lip. "Or I'll have to punish you."

His words caused a rush of heat to wash through her. Once, the thought of punishment struck fear in her heart, but now that she was Jimmy Doyle's wife, the word made her giddy with desire. She welcomed his brand of punishment. She ground her hips against his erection.

"You're being naughty, wife." She almost smiled at the hint of amusement behind his stern warning.

"I'm sorry, Sir." She wasn't all that sorry, not if her actions achieved the result she wanted. But if there was one thing she'd learned in his arms, it was how much he valued the truth. "It's just that I need you so much," she added.

"Do you think I won't see to your needs?"

"No, Sir."

"Then you are trying to rush me." He inched her toward the bed, stopping when the backs of her thighs hit the footboard. "This is our wedding night, wife. I intend to take my time. Do you have a problem with that?"

He was already securing her left wrist to a leather strap dangling from the corner post while he pinned her in place with his body. "No, Sir."

In short order, she was bound at wrists and ankles, with nothing but sheer silk to shield her from his hungry gaze. He looked sexy, standing there in his rumpled shirt, the sleeves turned back to reveal muscled forearms, his suspenders draped below his hips. As much as she loved his thoughtful wedding gift, she wished it and his clothes gone so there would be nothing between them.

"The bindings aren't too tight?"

"No, Sir." She tested their strength, finding she had very little leeway. Folding her left hand into a fist, she felt for the wedding band on her third finger. Touching it reassured her. He'd taken vows to love, honor, and cherish her. If *cherish* and *ravish* were the same thing, his expression as he took in her splayed state indicated he was bent on cherishing the heck out of her tonight.

So slowly she wanted to scream, he removed his clothes so he stood before her, all rippling muscles and the evidence of his manhood standing erect and proud—like a warrior's sword. She hated the fading bruises on his ribs and face. He'd paid for something he hadn't done with years of his life and continued to pay every time he faced a new opponent on the field. She remembered the pride in his voice on the way home as he told her about the new contract awaiting his signature. Eight more years with the Diplomats; then he would retire. Maybe coach or manage a team if she didn't mind him playing at games for a few more years.

He stepped forward, taking her breasts in his hands, kneading and thumbing her nipples until she groaned and had to bite her lip to keep from begging him to do more. The tip of his penis brushed against her stomach. The flesh between her legs throbbed with need. He could do anything he wanted with his career as far as she was concerned. She loved him, not the job he held.

He tugged her nipples through the lace. "Relax, Eve. I'm going to play with your body. I've much to learn about what turns you on, and what doesn't." He released her and crossed the room to the chest of drawers. Seeing his tight backside, she balled her hands into fists and cried out in frustration.

"Patience, my love." He opened a drawer, reached in for something, then closed the drawer. When he turned, whatever he had fit in one palm, hiding it from her view. He strolled back to her, dropping his loot on the bed behind her. Once again, his hands closed over her breasts. "So lovely," he said, driving her wild with nothing but his touch.

He pinched her nipples hard, startling a gasp from her lips. Heat pooled between her legs. "You like a bite of pain here, don't you, babe?"

She nodded, adding weakly, "Yes, Sir."

"I love the way the lace looks stretched over your breasts, but it can't stay there. I have to touch you, sweet Eve. Do you mind?"

She shook her head, wanting his touch more than anything.

Careful not to rip the fabric, he lifted her mounds free. He took her right one in both hands, squeezing the bulk of it with one hand while the other tortured the nipple. She closed her eyes, reveling in his rough handling. Her whole body craved his touch in a way she no longer saw as sinful, but an expression of their love.

When he bent and took her nipple in his mouth, drawing hard

on it, she writhed, wanting to grasp his head and hold him to her. Pleasure shot like a dagger to the pulsing flesh between her legs. She let her head drop back between her shoulders, enjoying his attentions. An audible *pop* sounded, followed by cool air brushing her wet skin. His hands were on her, and then something clamped down on her nipple. Searing pain blinded her, steeling her breath. She struggled against the leather bindings, desperate to free her hands and rid her body of whatever had ahold of her. Jimmy Doyle grabbed her head in his hands, forcing her to look up.

"Breathe, sweetheart," he said. "Breathe through the pain." She could feel his breath on her face.

Forcing her eyes open, she made out his face through the tears distorting her vision. Her breast felt like it was on fire. She filled her lungs, letting the air out along with a whimper across her trembling lower lip.

"You're going to be okay, sweetheart." He stroked her cheek, his eyes imploring her to believe him.

"Hurts," she managed to push past her lips.

"Yes. Give it a few seconds more, darling. Keep breathing." He held her jaw with one hand while he massaged her breast with the other. Tears flowed unchecked down her face as she continued to draw in shaky breaths.

"Better?" he asked after what seemed an eternity.

Mentally assessing her physical state, she realized the pain had waned to a dull ache. "Yes, Sir." She knew he would never harm her, but she had no idea what he'd done to her. "What?"

"Look," he said, easing back from her so she could tilt her chin down.

At the sight of the clothespin dangling from her nipple, she gasped. With a finger beneath, he pushed it upward, sending another sharp spike of pain in a straight line to the pulse point between her legs. She groaned at both the pain and the eroticism of seeing the wooden clamp fastened to her breast. She sniffed back a sob. "Oh, God."

She was still staring at the object attached to her body when she realized Jimmy Doyle was slowly raising the hem of her gown. When he had it above her hips, he gathered the bulk of it behind her, fastening it there.

"Handy things, clothespins. Don't you think?"

Evelyn looked past her pinned nipple to her exposed mound. A downy fuzz had grown back since the day Grace had shaved her. Bound, clamped, and exposed, she appeared every bit as wanton as she felt.

"Yes," she croaked out, not daring to glance at her husband for fear he'd know how desperately she liked what she saw.

"Ready for the other one?" he said, breaking into her thoughts. She gazed into his eyes, saw the determination there. He wasn't through with her.

"Yes."

This time, she kept her eyes open, watching him ready her nipple, sucking and tugging on it until it stood out stiff and proud. She forced herself not to look away as he plumped the nipple one last time, then pinched the clamp in place.

She hissed in a breath, fighting to keep a scream at bay. Watery stars danced before her eyes as the pain radiated through her breast. Knowing it was coming did nothing to lessen the shock.

"Breathe." She focused on his voice, on his hand stroking her abused flesh. Slowly, she became aware of his other hand, moving in warm circles over her belly.

The momentary pain quickly became something more that followed the same path as the pleasure had before. She rocked her hips forward, needing him to ease the ache growing there.

"I wish you could see yourself," he said, his gaze raking her body in carnal appreciation. Her gaze darted to the cheval and back to her husband as she recalled how she'd admired her new gown in the mirror. Not much got past his notice. He, too, looked away for a second. He turned his dazzling smile on her. "Your wicked ways please me, wife."

She fought for every breath as he moved the mirror into place where she could see herself on display. At first, she tried to avert her gaze, but he was standing to her side, stroking her body, murmuring words of praise and love. "See how beautiful you are, my wife? You are so brave, so perfect in your submission."

He flicked the pins on both nipples, sending bolts of lightning to her core. Almost against her will, she looked at her reflection. The expression she saw on her husband's face made her weak. He gazed at her body with such pride—and love. His erection was enormous, and she judged him to be in as much pain as she was. She watched helplessly as his hands moved over her, worshipping with his touch while stirring her need.

Seeing herself as her husband saw her, she was overcome with emotion. She loved him beyond reason, and that he could look upon her in such a wicked state and still love her filled her heart.

"Do you see how beautiful you are?" He clasped her nape; his fingers speared through her hair. His penis lay against her hip. "When you remember our wedding night, remember this, sweet Eve. I am a slave to your pleasure." With his free hand, he stroked his cock. "I will always want you, no matter what. Your pleasure is my pleasure. Together, we'll explore the limits of your beautiful body, finding all the things that make your pussy weep with desire and indulging in them to our hearts' content."

Her body vibrated with her need for him. "Please," she begged, her gaze fixed on the reflection of his penis.

"I'm going to have you, darling, many times over tonight, but first, I must tend to my bride."

She moaned as he dropped to his knees and pressed his face to her aching flesh. She felt the flat of his tongue scrape across her clitoris. Then he parted her folds with his thumbs. He feasted on her, switching constantly between tenderness and gluttony—keeping her on edge. All the time, she watched him in the mirror. The play of muscles in his shoulders and back fascinated her. Never in her wildest dreams had she envisioned a man such as him at her feet, but now that she had him, she couldn't imagine life without him—without feeling the way he made her feel.

She teetered on the brink of orgasm. One more lick, one more nip to her clit. One anything, and she'd go over into the bliss she'd only known with this man. The muscles in her thighs tensed; a tingling deep inside signaled her impending release. She closed her eyes, focusing inward to that spot where pain became indescribable pleasure.

Then he was gone. It took her a second to recover her senses, to realize his mouth was no longer on her. Then her ankles were free, and he was hoisting her up. Her bottom came down on the crossbar of the footboard. His hands slid along her thighs to her calves, guiding her legs around his waist. The head of his cock nudged at her entrance, spreading her inner lips to take him in.

He froze. Cupping her face in both hands, he compelled her to look at him. "Are you ready, wife? I'm going to take the clamps off. Scream all you want."

Drugged with her need to have him fully inside her, she nodded.

"God, I love you, Eve. You are everything to me."

He didn't give her time to respond. He pinched the ends of the clips, freeing her nipples. In the next instant, he grasped her hips and shoved into her. The rush of blood to her tortured nubs, coupled with his cock filling her, was more than she could bear. She screamed, tears of pain and joy running down her cheeks. Jimmy Doyle thrust hard into her, making her breasts bounce, adding to the sensations overwhelming her.

"I've got you, wife. You're safe. Let it out."

She screamed. She cried. And when he tensed, pounding into her with short, hard thrusts, and poured his seed inside her, she laughed with joy.

HE THOUGHT HIS heart was going to break a rib the way it was knocking against his chest. Without letting go of his wife, he released her wrists and walked them around to the side of the bed. He sat her on the edge but, with hands on her ankles, urged her to stay put while he pulled the gown he'd bought for her over her head.

He lifted her again and managed to get them both in bed without breaking the intimate contact he had craved since the day he met her. Lying atop her, he was more content than he'd ever been in his life. He'd just poured his seed into a woman for the first time without protection, and the idea of Evelyn round with his child ignited a new flame in him.

When he'd been kicked out of the league, he'd thought his life was over, but now he could see that everything that happened had led him to this moment. Regret for those lost years evaporated like so much sweat, leaving him feeling like he'd been born again. And he owed it all to Evelyn.

He'd accomplished everything he'd intended to this season. He'd set personal, team, and league records. He'd reestablished himself as a key player on the field, and he'd regained the respect of his teammates. There was a substantial contract awaiting his signature.

But he'd been prepared to give it all up rather than lose Evelyn.

Braced on his forearms, he swept silky strands from her face. "I wasn't too rough?"

"No. Not at all."

"Your wrists. Your ankles? Your beautiful tits?"

"All fine. I think my breasts are going to be sore for a while, though."

He'd take care of them soon. There was a jar of Grace's homemade ointment on the chest of drawers. At the moment, he had other things on his mind. "What are we going to name the first one?" Just in case she didn't know what he was saying, he nudged his still-hard cock deeper inside her. He loved the way her eyes widened, then lit with heat. God, she was perfect. He was one lucky bastard.

"James Doyle Walker Jr.," she said without hesitation.

"You've been thinking about this, haven't you?"

"Maybe." The blush coloring her cheeks amused him. She couldn't possibly have been thinking about him more than he'd been thinking of her.

"What if it's a girl?"

"Grace Evelyn Walker."

He raised an eyebrow in question. "After our Grace?"

"I've always loved the name, and she's special, you know?"

"Not as special as you." He moved inside her again, setting a smooth rhythm that would ensure neither of them came too fast. "I love you, wife."

"I love you too, husband."

Jimmy Doyle buried his face in the crook of her neck, inhaling her scent and silently thanking God for his Eve.

ABOUT THE AUTHOR

USA Today Bestselling Author, Roz Lee is a displaced Texan who lives in New Jersey with her husband of almost four decades, and Bud, an overly large rescue dog who demands regular romps in the woods no matter how busy his parents are.

The mom of two daughters, Roz collects Depression glass, and teacups with rose patterns. Her favorite food is Tex-Mex, and she's never met a piece of chocolate she didn't like.

When Roz isn't writing, she's reading, or traipsing around the country on one adventure or another. Warning—she brakes for antique stores!

Learn more at www.RozLee.ne

AUTHOR'S NOTE

I hope you enjoyed reading Jimmy Doyle and Evelyn's story as much as I enjoyed writing it. This book was truly a labor of love. If you are so inclined, check out my contemporary series in which Jimmy Doyle's grandson, Doyle Walker is the manager of the Texas Mustangs.

As always, reviews are welcome. Please consider leaving one.

I love to hear from readers.

Email me at RozLee@RozLee.net

Made in the USA
Middletown, DE
24 November 2019